ENSLAVEMENT

One Bright Future: Enslavement
Copyright (c) 2014 by Melinda Friesen
All rights reserved.

Published by Rebelight Publishing Inc.

Rebelight Publishing Inc.
23-845 Dakota St., Suite 314
Winnipeg, Manitoba, Canada
R2M 5M3

www.rebelight.com

Library and Archives Canada Cataloguing in Publication
Friesen, Melinda
One Bright Future: Enslavement / Melinda Friesen.

This book is a work of fiction. Names, characters, places and incidents are products of the author's imagination or are used fictitiously. Any resemblance to actual events or locales or persons, living or dead, is entirely coincidental.

Cover art and design by Melanie Matheson, Blue Claw Studio, Winnipeg, MB

Issued in print and electronic formats

ISBN: 978-0-9939390-0-6 (pbk)
ISBN: 978-0-9939390-1-3 (epub)

1.   Word one – Young Adult fiction I. Title.

Printed and bound in Canada
10 9 8 7 6 5 4 3 2 1

ONE BRIGHT FUTURE

BOOK ONE

ENSLAVEMENT

BY MELINDA FRIESEN

2014 rebel!ght PUBLISHING INC.

To my grandmother, Lela, who I lost before I could share this book with her.
Thank you for teaching me to stick to my convictions, no matter how much it hurts.

To my grandmother, Lela, who I lost before I could share this book with her.
Thank you for teaching me to stick to my convictions, no matter how much it hurts.

CHAPTER ONE

The End of Everything

DOZENS OF BANK SECURITY OFFICERS in black uniforms and dirty boots shout orders and tramp through our house.

Crouching beside the sofa, I clutch my two-year-old sister, Alyssa, to my chest and shield her eyes. I stroke her back and tell her lies. "Shhh. Everything is going to be okay."

Officers swarm up the stairs. Others search the living room and kitchen. Drawers are dumped. Spoons, forks, spatulas clatter onto the tile. My grandmother's china is flung to the floor. It pops and shatters and crunches under their feet. A crystal vase tumbles from the top shelf. I jolt as it explodes into a thousand glittering shards.

From the bedrooms, thuds and crashes rake my ears, splintering wood and clanking metal hangers. We've made their search easy. Dad already traded away most of our belongings. A few family treasures, now in pieces on the floor, were all we kept. But they would've gone soon too. Hunger trumps sentimentality.

My fifteen-year-old brother, Silas, sits on the sofa and stares at the floor. He jams his white-knuckled fists against his ears.

Mom kneels beside Dad, sprawled unconscious on the living room floor. She brushes her quaking hand over the gash on his head where they clubbed him for trying to protect us. A thread of blood winds around his ear and soaks into the ivory carpet.

An officer grinds his knee into Dad's back, fixes a plastic zip-tie around his wrists. He grabs Dad by one arm and drags his limp body through the front door. Mom's glassy gaze follows him, her hand hovering over the blood-stained carpet. She looks down at her red fingers, her face shiny with tears.

Another officer digs his fingers into Mom's shoulder and hauls her upright. He pins her arms behind her back and snaps a plastic cuff around her wrists too.

Mom in handcuffs—why? My parents are not criminals.

"Please." Sobs convulse Mom's shoulders. "Please—please let me say goodbye."

Alyssa wrestles away from me. "Mommy!" She reaches her arms out to Mom, clenching and unclenching her tiny fists.

"I love you so much." Mom's voice trembles.

The officer lifts his chin and indifference flattens his features. He clutches her elbow, mumbles "filthy Resistor," then pushes her toward the door.

My throat aches. Don't take her. Please.

Alyssa wails and lunges after Mom. She kicks and writhes against my grip, but I hold her tight. She turns and buries her face in my neck. Her tears soak into my collar.

I stare at the pool of Dad's blood on the carpet. My hands and feet turn numb. "Mommy and Daddy will be okay."

The lies aren't just for Alyssa.

A middle-aged man in a suit and trench coat marches through the door. When he sees me, his small dark eyes narrow. He slows and his movements become smooth and strategic. I'm a rabbit thrown into a terrarium. The man in the trench—a thick boa constrictor—slinks toward me. He'll squeeze me until I suffocate. He'll digest me to make himself stronger.

I tug Alyssa closer and my arms form a protective cage around her.

An officer approaches the trench coat man from behind. "We're searching the house. Juvenile Division is on their way."

Trenchcoat peers down at me and tilts his head. "Well, then, we don't have much time, do we?"

He pulls a holo from his coat pocket. The mercury-coloured device morphs like molten metal to the shape of his hand. He swipes his thumb over the screen and a silvery-blue glow appears. The glow separates from the screen and expands into a holographic image of the OneEarth Bank symbol. It hovers above the device—two silver rings spin around a blue cylinder resembling a tree, branches stretching upward and roots extending downward.

"Rielle James, do you know the whereabouts of Rick and Charlotte Ericsson or their children Kara and Grace Ericsson?" Trenchcoat asks.

Brow furrowed, I search his face. My world is collapsing and he's asking me where he can find another girl's family. Why would I know where the Ericssons are and why would it matter?

Her family is one of the only others in the neighbourhood like mine who resisted the chip insertion, and most people avoid us like we're a contagion. Not that it drew us together. We're both juniors at the same high school, and our parents see the commerce chip as a first class ticket to hell. That's about all we have in common. For all I know, Trenchcoat has done the same thing to Kara's family that he's doing to mine.

I shake my head in response to his question.

Trenchcoat's face hardens. He seizes Alyssa's arm.

Panic surges through me and I steel my grip around her chest. "No! No, I don't know where they are!" Alyssa's fists curl around wads of my shirt.

He releases Alyssa. "When was the last time you saw the Ericssons?"

"I don't know. Kara hasn't been at school for days."

He squares his shoulders and stares down his nose at me. "How about your aunt, Angelique James? When was the last time you saw her?"

"We visited her last summer."

"You haven't seen her recently—say in the last couple weeks?"

I shake my head. "No."

An officer walks up to Trenchcoat, Dad's ancient laptop computer balanced on his hands. "This is all we've found. It's been wiped."

Trenchcoat taps his fingers on the plastic shell. "That has to be considered an antique by now. You didn't find a holo?"

The officer's shoulders tense. "No, sir."

Trenchcoat's pale lips pull tight over his teeth. "Well, keep looking." He returns his attention to me. "Where are your father's and mother's holos?"

"They don't have any."

"I find that hard to believe," he says.

I bite my cheek. Dad refused to buy a holo, even back when we had money. Holos don't have their own memory. They use Unified Intelligence, a centralized virtual server that stores everyone's information. Dad calls it "the Brain." He's always been paranoid. He said he didn't want his data floating around out there where everyone could access it, so he stuck with the old laptop he'd bought before he and Mom got married. There's a computer graveyard in the basement, shells harvested of components that kept his unit working.

Trenchcoat motions to the Bank Security officer behind him who holds a metallic cone. The officer sets the cone on the floor and presses a button on top. The contraption swells and crackles, then transforms into liquid silver that flows down the cone's base. The reflective liquid pools on the carpet around a now empty framework, then separates into hundreds of droplets. Spider-silk-thin metallic legs sprout from each one, curl down and lift the droplets off the floor. Some drops stretch into long tubes. Some flatten foil-thin, while others remain spherical. Their mechanical legs beef up until they resemble spiders and scorpions, each with one red eye.

The officer retrieves his holo from his belt pouch. With a swipe of his thumb, a glowing image rises from the screen. He touches it and the robotic bugs march and slither away from the cone in every direction, like ripples from a stone tossed in the water.

Trenchcoat glowers at me. "You know they'll find whatever you're hiding. It will go better for you if you just tell me. In fact, if you tell me where your aunt is, I could let you go."

My heart leaps at his offer. Let us go? I glance from Alyssa to Silas. I could keep at least part of my family together. "She lives in Ontario on a lake."

Silas springs to his feet. "Rielle, no!"

I meet Silas's gaze, questioning his reaction to the information I shared. I wasn't supposed to tell anyone where she lived, even to keep us together?

"Quiet!" Trenchcoat shouts.

One of the bugs climbs onto my knee. I flick it away. "Lake of the Woods I think it's called."

Trenchcoat lets out an exasperated sigh. "I'm afraid that's not the information I'm looking for." His mouth twists into a sneer. "Too bad for you."

"I told you what I know. Please let us go. Please!"

A bug skitters around Silas's feet. Its red beam colours Silas's shoe. He crushes the thing underfoot.

Trenchcoat turns away from me. In three long steps he's at Silas's side. "You seem to know more than your sister. Perhaps I can give you your freedom."

Silas stares at Dad's blood on the carpet. He raises his eyes to meet Trenchcoat's gaze, his cheeks flaming. "Go to hell!"

Trenchcoat swings his hand and snaps Silas's head to the side with a loud pop.

"No!" I shout.

A stream of blood dribbles over Silas's lip, but he doesn't loosen his stare on Trenchcoat. Silas's hands contract into fists and he straightens his back until he's taller than the creep who hit him.

Trenchcoat scowls. "They'll fix that attitude at reform school." He tucks his holo in his pocket and turns to one of the officers. "They don't know anything."

Silas settles back onto the sofa as silver bugs dig into every crevice of our home. They climb up the piano—my piano—their metallic legs tapping against the wood. They flatten, paper thin, and squeeze into the narrow space between the keys. Strings ping high and low as they pick over the inner workings.

Rage and despair, like dull rusty knives, twist in my gut. I gather Alyssa closer. Bank Security officers are bad, but worse is coming.

Tears burn my eyes. I suck them back, swallow, but they choke me. I have only minutes left with Alyssa before we're separated. I hug her, kiss her wispy golden hair and skim my hand over her arm. I savour her soft skin and her sweet smell—graham crackers and strawberry shampoo. I need to remember everything.

"I love you. You're my precious baby girl. Remember that, Alyssa. Please, please, remember that."

Her breathing hitches with each trembling sob. She winds her fingers into my hair.

I look to Silas, with his jaw tensed and the tendons lining his forearms pulled tight and swallow the lump in my throat. "I love you Si, don't forget me, okay?"

He lifts his gaze to mine long enough for me to see the tears glistening on his lower lashes. "I won't. Love you, too."

A middle-aged woman with short cropped salt and pepper hair walks through the door and leaves it gaping open behind her. An icy wind gusts through the house, and Alyssa curls into my chest so closely I can feel her heart flutter. I snuggle her tight and rub her arms to warm her.

"Viola Hess. Caseworker from juvenile division," the woman says. "Silas James, come with me."

Silas flinches, but he doesn't join her.

Hess bristles and purses her lips. Coral lipstick has bled into the wrinkles around her mouth. "It will be easier for you if you come under your own power."

I bite my lip. "Please don't take him away."

The caseworker turns her emotionless stare to me. "Don't worry. We have a place for all of you."

I force my voice louder, bolder, "We'll do whatever you want. We'll take the chip. I can look after Silas and Alyssa. We'll be fine. We'll obey."

Hess cocks her head and peers down at me. "How can I believe anything a child of Resistors says? You're all liars and thieves. Silas James, come with me now or I'll get one of the officers to help me."

My brother steps toward her. I take a mental picture of him, a younger image of Dad with chestnut hair and steel grey eyes, tall and gangly, but strong. An officer ushers him toward the door. Silas stops, squares his shoulders and looks back at me, his gaze intense. "Rielle, never give in."

"Move!" the officer barks and pushes him through the door.

Hess grabs Alyssa's right shoulder. "Time to go."

Alyssa screams. I wrap my arms around her tighter, tighter. "No! Don't take her."

The woman plants her other hand on Alyssa's left shoulder and rips her from my arms. Alyssa kicks and arches her back. She stretches her arms toward me, strands of my hair still caught between her fingers. Her keening cuts into my ears—and my heart. I lunge for her, but a Bank Security officer throws his arm across my chest and drags me back. I wrestle against him. He shoves me against the wall and locks a zip-tie around my wrists.

The caseworker carries Alyssa out the front door. Her cries echo off the neighbouring houses and rip the strength from my legs. I fall into a heap, sobbing. This can't be happening. This can't be real.

When they take me, I'm too numb to make a fuss. An officer loads me into the back of a cruiser. I take one last look at my home. The windows are dark, the house an empty shell. The front door stands open, yawning in the cold air. Nothing holds me to this place anymore. Everyone I love is gone. With my hands secured behind my back, I can't wipe away my tears. They drop from my chin, mixing with Alyssa's on my soaked collar.

The officer starts his car and drives away from the curb. My home and then my street disappear behind me.

CHAPTER TWO

Useless Skills

THE CRUISER STOPS IN FRONT OF THE OneEarth Bank Security facility, a soaring A-frame with a limestone facade. The jagged remains of a crucifix scars its smooth surface.

The officer yanks me from the car by my arm. He marches me to the door and swipes his hand in front of a black box with a small red light. A reader scans the chip beneath his skin. The light turns green and the door clicks open.

A series of cubicles fill the Bank Security foyer. Fluorescent lights throw a green sheen over the former church's now bleak institutional interior. A sheep pen without sheep. They've found a new use for it.

I spent countless hours in a place like this as a child. Before Bank Security confiscated it, the church would have had red carpet, not the generic white industrial tiles now covering the floor. The church smell still lingers—varnished wood and stale coffee, aged paper and leather.

Women in skirts with toddlers clinging to their pantyhosed legs used to visit here. Old men in suits traded hard candies for smiles from children. Men in crisp collared shirts used to clutch paper cups full of steaming coffee, fingers pressed against brown stir sticks to keep them from jumping out. Black leather bound Bibles with silver edged pages were tucked under arms. Black ribbons split the books, dangling like limp serpents' tongues, lost in the middle of so many pages.

I release a ragged breath. I'm in the middle too. Lost. Lost from family. Lost from home.

The officer guides me inside a cubicle and removes my restraints. He pushes me down onto a folding metal chair in front of a wide desk with chrome legs and fake wood grain top. I rub the deep red impressions the zip-tie left in my wrists and wiggle my fingers to get the blood moving again.

Two women busy themselves behind the desk. One brushes her fingers over her holo and the other rifles through a stack of bulging envelopes.

"You're here late, Deb," the officer says.

The woman at the desk, Deb, pushes her black-rimmed glasses up her nose. "Hey, Bernie. Yeah, Lisa called in sick. Just filling in. I'm missing my kid's hockey game."

"They make it to play-offs?" Bernie asks.

"If they win tonight's game they will." She spreads her fingers over the holo image to enlarge it. The tree-like OneEarth Bank image hovers in front of her. "Alright, who do we have here?"

Bernie fiddles with his holo, and a text image leaps above the device. He reads from it. "Rielle James, age seventeen. Resistor. Potential thief."

For refusing the commerce chip, we've been called Resistors and thieves. Some people have even called us terrorists. Deb strokes a virtual page. Her eyes roam over the information, then she raises her eyebrows and peers over her glasses at the officer. "Rielle James?"

Bernie's mouth curls up at the corner. He nods.

My name is familiar to them. Why?

Deb reads off my particulars to a frizzy-haired woman who taps hot pink nails over a virtual keyboard glowing on the desk.

"Do you have any *useful* skills?" asks Frizzy-hair. Her eyes narrow, appraising me.

I swallow to wet my throat. "I can play piano." I inspect the lines on my hands. Do they consider that a useful skill?

"No one needs a musical Contract," Deb snaps, looking at me for the first time.

A Contract? That's what they're doing to me? They're placing me into a community service Contract. My punishment for my parents' resistance to their laws. They tell everyone that Contracts are a way to rehabilitate kids from Resistor families, but it's just a politically correct way of saying "slave".

Deb rolls her eyes before continuing. "Are you able to fix anything? Can you cook? Do you have experience caring for children?"

"No." The only child I want to care for is my sister.

The two women lean their heads together and Deb whispers, "She's too slight to be good for any hard labour. Weak."

The longer I sit here, the smaller I shrink. I want to shrink until I disappear. These women are right. I'm not strong. I was too weak to help my brother or my sister.

Powerless.

I hang my head.

Frizzy-hair casts her critical gaze at me. "We'll put her down as housekeeping. We won't get much for her."

Worthless.

Deb rolls backward in her office chair and retrieves a manila envelope from an organizer attached to the wall. She squeezes it open and holds it out in front of me. "Remove your necklace."

I throw my hand over the oval pendant. My mother's necklace and my grandmother's before hers. "Please, can I keep it?"

"No. We will keep it for you until your Contract is up."

I close my fist around the warm gold locket. "And when will that be?"

Bernie kicks my chair. Clanging metal echoes through the room. "Quiet!"

I flinch and fold my shoulders inward.

Pathetic.

Deb sets her lips in a hard line and waits. With trembling hands, I unclasp Mom's necklace and drop it into the envelope. She peels off the white strip from the self-adhesive flap and seals the envelope. She slips my envelope into the middle of a wire basket filled with other envelopes.

I swallow the lump in my throat and blink back tears. She didn't bother writing my name on it. My necklace is lost. Lost. Like me.

Bernie leads me by the arm through a series of stations. At the first my fingerprints are scanned, and at the second my photograph is taken. At the third station I'm issued a set of faded green scrubs stamped PROPERTY OF MN STATE BANK and a pair of flimsy canvas shoes that are two sizes too big.

Bernie leads me down a flight of stairs into the basement and toward another room. As we step inside, the sharp smell of rubbing alcohol burns my nose. Overhead, a bare fluorescent tube flickers and buzzes. A single chair waits at the center of the room, its yellow foam padding erupting from the cracked vinyl seat. A man wearing blue latex gloves works over a metal tray on wheels.

My knees lock, but Bernie puts his hand on my shoulder and pushes me forward, then down onto the chair. The gloved man rolls the tray to my side. A disinfectant swab protrudes from a wrapper on the tray beside a plastic gun-like object with a long syringe jutting from the barrel.

Gloves holds out his hand. "Left hand."

"What is that?" I look at the syringe gun.

"An insertion gun."

I study the contraption, my hand held close to my side. Maybe I misunderstood everything that happened upstairs. Maybe they're just giving me a chip and letting me go. My heart leaps at the idea. I won't have my parents, but I'll be able to live a normal life. I can go back to school. And get a job. No Community Service Contract. No more trading work for food. No more being stuck at home because I can't go anywhere without a chip. I offer him my hand.

Gloves scrubs the disinfectant swab over the soft flesh between my thumb and index finger. It chills my skin.

"I'm getting a commerce chip?"

"Of course not. This is a tracker chip. In case you try to escape."

A tracker chip? No! A commerce chip means freedom. A tracker chip means enslavement. I yank my hand from his rubbery fingers and hug it to my chest. He grabs it back and locks it in a cold steely grip, his fingers digging into my flesh. "Hold her," he says to Bernie.

Bernie grips my upper arms and slams me against the back of the chair

"No. No! I don't need this. I haven't done anything wrong!" I kick Gloves in the thigh. He stumbles backward.

Something cold touches the back of my neck. My teeth hammer together so hard I think they might shatter. My heart explodes in my chest. A convulsion tightens, seizes, twists every muscle. I can't breathe! I fall, smacking my head on the icy concrete.

Bernie pulls the cold object away from my neck—a rectangular black plastic box with a metal plate at one end—and tucks it into a holster on his belt.

My muscles stop twitching. I suck in a lungful of air, finally able to breathe again.

Gloves drops to his haunches and takes my hand again. I command my arm to pull back, but my muscles won't respond. He pushes the point of the syringe gun into my skin. The needle sinks deeper and deeper into my flesh—so deep I wonder if he's going for my elbow. Pain and pressure roil up my arm. I clamp my teeth together to stifle a scream. Gloves depresses the trigger to insert the chip.

A tear creeps down my cheek. The thing—the tracker—is inside me now. Though the chip should be too tiny for me to feel, it burns like poison.

Gloves scans his holo over my hand. An electronic female voice announces, "JAMES, RIELLE. CONTRACT NUMBER 08645."

Bernie half carries, half drags me down a dank corridor and abandons me in a room full of cots with at least fifty others like me dressed in the same green scrubs. I slink along the wall for support to an empty cot in the far corner. The girl in the next bed says something to me, but the words jumble somewhere between her lips and my ears. I ignore her.

I unfold a thin cotton blanket from the foot of the mattress, pull it around my shoulders and lay down facing the wall. I allow tears to fall. There are no words to my thoughts. Just faces. Mom. Dad. Silas. Alyssa. They flash like strobe lights in my head. I've lost them all. I've lost everything.

The mattress is soaked with tears before the life raft of sleep drifts toward me, but when it does, I climb aboard and leave the horror behind.

The next morning alarm bells startle me from a restless sleep. I open my eyes to bright, cold fluorescent lights and squint against them. I move my hand. Pain. The chip insertion. Bank Security. My family.

My heart pounds frenetically. Yesterday should've been a nightmare—a dark world I could wake from—but I'm still here. This is really happening. Yesterday morning I was free. I got ready for school and had an argument with Silas over who got to take the last cookie for lunch. I called him a jerk and told him I wished I didn't have a brother, then walked to school.

Today, I'm a prisoner and my brother is gone. My whole family is gone.

I sit up and place my feet on the concrete floor, sweeping my gaze over the room to get my bearings.

The girl next to me pushes herself upright, her cot creaking under her shifting weight. She tries to make eye contact, but I look past her. I don't want to make friends I'll lose within the day.

A young guard in the standard black Bank Security uniform shouts, "Line up!"

The crowd of new Contracts, all about my age, shuffle heads down across our musty sleeping quarters to form a line, the tall boys ducking to avoid low hanging pipes. The guard commands us to follow a yellow stripe running down the middle of the hallway. I walk the yellow line like it's a balance beam, down the hall and up a flight of stairs to a heavy steel door.

Four officers work their way down the line, barking at us to hold still, locking us in leg restraints and handcuffs. They tighten mine until the metal pinches my skin. After chaining us together, they pry open the heavy door and a blast of cold air raises goose bumps on my arms. They march us outside onto the snow dusted parking lot.

CHAPTER THREE

One Bright Future

I WAIT IN THE FREEZING WIND BEHIND a dozen others for my turn to be loaded onto a bus. Snowflakes swirl around me. The restraints around my ankles and wrists conduct the cold to my skin, like icy knives digging into my flesh. Chains clank as Contracts pivot away from the whipping north wind.

Security officers holding rifles diagonally across their chests are stationed around the edge of the parking lot. Snow partially obscures an officer crouched on the roof of the facility with his gun trained on us. I scan the surrounding buildings. More gunmen. Seems like overkill for a group of bound and terrified teens.

The chain of Contracts tugs me toward the solar bus. Its magnetic skis rest on parallel steel ribbons, sunk into cracked asphalt. The door folds open and the line begins to file in, one kid at a time, until an officer scans the chip of the boy in front of me. "GRAFTON, ADAM. CONTRACT NUMBER 08629." The boy climbs aboard and another officer removes his chains. Then he walks down the aisle to choose a seat.

My turn. The guard scans my chip. "JAMES, RIELLE. CONTRACT NUMBER 08645," the device chants. The officer's eyes widen. "James," he says, as though it's a curse. The guard unlocking the chains snaps his head in my direction.

What's going on? Why would my name bring that reaction last night and again now? It's as though it's familiar to them—and not in a good way.

Perplexed, I climb the bus stairs and hold out my wrists, eager to be free of the frigid metal. The officer pauses and a scowl sours his face. He jerks my hands and jams the key into the lock on the cuffs. He leans in and his hot breath singes my ear. "You people are finally getting what you deserve."

I crank my neck to get a good look at him. A mix of victory and gross pleasure plays on his features. You people? Does he mean Contracts? He didn't say this to anyone else. Does he mean me? Why?

I head down the aisle toward an empty seat at the back. An acidic odour spoils the air.

"Stop! You! Contract James. Sit here." He points to the front seat. With a sigh, I back up, plop down on the worn front seat and slide over to the grimy window. Water pools on the floor at my feet as though they just hosed out the entire bus.

I clench my jaw to stifle my tears. Why do I have to sit up front? I don't know why I bother trying to make sense of any of this. Bank Security has been trying to control my life for a long time. This is just more of the same. I shiver and rub my arms to keep warm while the remaining Contracts take their seats. Are they shivering from the cold or from the trauma? Or both?

Two large boys drop onto the seat beside me. The boy in the middle nudges me over, pressing me into the side of the bus. I fold my shoulders forward to make room.

One officer positions himself at the back of the bus, while another stands at the front, his rifle slung over his shoulder. He looks as if he belongs in the military with his buzz cut and squared posture. He peers directly at me, then out the window at the parking lot, his face tight, tendons stretched taut at his temple. The engine starts with a pulsating hum and the bus lifts off the magnetic tracks and lurches forward, throwing a few Contracts out of their seats. The driver makes a right turn off the parking lot, then takes an exit ramp onto the freeway.

I rest my forehead against the frosty window so no one can see me cry. Tears stream over my cheeks as Minneapolis falls away behind me. Will I ever see home again?

They've never set any Contracts free. More tears spill over my cheeks.

The bus glides south on the I-35, its windshield wipers slapping away heavy snow. A sky full of oppressive clouds and mounds of dirty snow caked on the roadside make the entire world appear grey.

The officer with the buzz cut spends most of his time staring down the length of the bus, but when I shift, he shifts. His trigger finger twitches and his eyes flinch toward my side of the bus.

Between overcast skies strangling the beams of solar energy and snow collecting on the rooftop solar panels, we have to stop to recharge and clean snow off the bus roof twice within the first couple of hours.

The sky clears after we pass Rochester, but my anxiety condenses. I feel like there's a rubber band between me and Minneapolis, and the miles stretch it—stretch it so far it's about to snap. Air thickens around me. I try to expand my ribs to pull in more oxygen, but there's no room to breathe with the boys crowding me. I clamp my teeth to stifle a claustrophobic scream—a scream might just send the jumpy officer over the edge. He watches me squirm.

I need to focus on something. To think of anything but being dragged further and further from home against my will. When we were kids, Mom used to play the alphabet game with Silas and me to distract us on long road trips.

I search out the window. *A.* Avenue. I meter my breathing. In. Out. In again.

B. Exit B.

C. Corolla.

My heart slows as I search roadside signs and license plates for the next letter. In the distance, a sun-washed billboard peels at the corners like floppy dog ears. Little girls in flowing white sundresses skip through a field of ripened grain, golden and bent by a breeze. As the bus speeds toward the advertisement, the lettering, faded blue like a worn pair of jeans, gives me a *D,* an *E* and an *F.* And three familiar *O*'s that send a shiver down my back.

The OneEarth Bank motto: *One World. One Currency. One Bright Future.*

One bright future—except for people like me.

Hatred boils up in my gut. That slogan lit the spark that ignited all my problems. I didn't understand what was happening back then. Fourth graders don't tend to be interested in the economy. The adult world had worries I didn't understand.

One day the teachers crowded us onto our gym bleachers for a special assembly. History in the making, they said. Hundreds of students fell silent as lights dimmed and a huge deep screen flickered to life. A three dimensional, life-sized image of the President appeared. He smiled and waved. We waved back as though he were really with us. He gave an impassioned speech.

"The OneEarth Bank promises a bright hope for the future," he said. "A glorious tomorrow for our nation." The broadcast ended with a scene of people from every nation holding hands and smiling. A woman's soothing voice announced, "One world. One currency. One bright future."

I believed every word. I truly thought something amazing was happening. When I arrived home from school that day bouncing with excitement, I gave my parents an animated synopsis of the broadcast. But they seemed uneasy. Concern crinkled the skin between their brows.

At first, commerce chips were optional, but the media pumped their advantages. Just walk into a store, take what you want and leave. Chip detectors at the door would instantly record your entire transaction.

My parents resisted the commerce chips.

I still remember Dad perched in front of our antiquated flat screen TV, worry adding decades to his appearance as he watched a report about thieves who refused the chip so they could steal merchandise undetected. That report launched growing suspicion over anyone who resisted chip insertion. Laws were passed, forcing us to conform. Only those with evil intent wouldn't want a chip, they said.

My parents still resisted. They said the Bible forbade it, that my soul was at stake.

If we had known what was coming, we could've run away. Lived off the grid with my eccentric aunt, Angelique.

The bus makes its first stop at a Bank Security facility in Des Moines. Everyone sits stock still as the guard checks a list on his holo. He calls out names and two girls shuffle to the front of the bus, their eyes cast down. They descend the stairs into oblivion. I refuse to think about them again. I turn my head the other way as the bus drifts back onto the interstate. The further south we drive, the warmer the weather turns and the stuffier the bus gets. Someone near the back of the bus gags and wretches.

Night falls. I long for sleep to rescue me from anxious thoughts, but between the boys squishing me against the bus wall and their chainsaw snores, I can't sleep. Instead, I listen to the hushed sobs of a Contract behind me and worry about Alyssa. Is she scared? Does she think we abandoned her?

Morning breaks and though I'm relieved that the long, miserable night is over, an oppressive ache settles into my chest. More tears tumble from my eyes—will they ever run dry? Grief flows into panic the more I think about Silas and Alyssa. Where are they? What's happening to them? What if they need me?

The bus stops in Kansas City, then Topeka. At each stop, I hold my breath as the officer calls names. I didn't want to get on this bus in the first place, but now I don't want to get off.

Everyone needs a shower in the worst way, including me. More people lose their recharge station cheeseburgers. Vomit sloshes under my seat. The reek of ripe armpits and acidic bile hangs so thick in the air that I can taste it. I keep my nose pointed toward the window, open a crack.

As the bus rolls down an endless stretch of asphalt, the boy beside me lets out a single gust of humourless laughter. "Got the runs."

These are the only words he's spoken the entire trip. I want to see what he's talking about, as though he's chosen his words carefully and they somehow hold wisdom, so I look up. He's staring out the window, his acne riddled face lacquered with oil and sweat. I stroke oily grime from the window to get a better look. A red semi-truck travels beside us. "Livestock Transfer," read the arching letters on the door. The truck tows an oxidized metal trailer punched full of air holes, like tiny portholes. Bristly pink flesh and corkscrew tails protrude the holes. A spray of gritty brown greases the side of the trailer, blown backward by the wind—as if the poor creatures stuck their backsides out the windows and gave a squeeze.

I chuckle. I don't know why—exhaustion, hysteria? Silas was a master of bathroom humour. I can still see Mom's pursed lips and her stifled smile. She didn't want to encourage him. I wanted to be more mature than fart bubbles and diarrhea squirts, but I always laughed. My chest constricts as sadness rolls over me. I'll never laugh with him again.

Brake lights flash in front of us; the bus slows in response. The vomit on the floor slides forward like a viscous serpent. I lift my feet to let it pass. We have something in common with those pigs. We're taking our last ride. At the end of their ride—slaughter. What awaits me at the end of mine?

We get another bathroom break in Oklahoma City, an oasis amidst the brown and desolate prairie. I can't help but notice I'm the only Contract who gets an armed escort to the bathroom by the officer with the fidgety trigger finger.

With too much time to think about my parents, hot stinging anger replaces the ache and longing in my chest. I always thought they put their children first. I was wrong. Their ideologies were first, they chose their religion over Alyssa, Silas and me. They damned me to this. At seventeen, my life is over.

My life. I can't even call it mine anymore. Someone bought it. Not even the clothes on my back belong to me. They belong to my owner. My life stretches hopelessly before me, a chasm so deep that I can't see the bottom.

I cry myself to sleep.

The next morning, blinding sun wakes me from another troubled sleep. Every joint in my body aches and a constant diet of recharge station cheeseburgers is taking its toll. I wipe vapour from the windows as we pass a colossal casino and the Texas state line marker. Only a handful of Contracts remain. We stop in Fort Worth where a billboard reading "Prosperity for all!" hovers over the parking lot. The giant face of a grinning politician with an epic comb-over stares down at me from the sign.

Liar.

Another name is called. Another kid gets off the bus and we move on. They'll call my name soon.

Razor sharp anxiety stabs my chest. Where will I go? What will they make me do? How will they treat me? Will I be taken care of or used up and discarded? Will they hurt me?

I'm in danger of being lost, swallowed whole by hopelessness, of becoming a nameless, faceless slave. And what does that mean? Slave. A shock of indignation rolls over me. I am not a slave. That's not who I am. I planned to go to college to study music, maybe get married someday and have my own children. Are all those dreams dead now?

Reality kicks me in the chest, stealing my air, making my heart constrict in painful gushes.

I have to find something to hold onto—something to remind me that I used to be free until freedom is mine again. Like a child hunting for her security blanket, I search for something to cling to. Is there anything they can't take?

I stare down at my damp, sweaty scrubs. What's left? My home? My family? My clothes? They're all gone. I have nothing. Despair crashes over me like a tsunami. I grind my teeth to force back the tears. I can't allow this to destroy me. I have to survive if I'm ever going to see Si or Alyssa again.

I want to scream, "I don't belong to you!" But I swallow the words. And then it hits me—something I can hold on to. I do have one thing. I haven't spoken a single word since I left the Bank Security facility a couple days ago. There's something comforting about silence—my thoughts being mine and mine alone. It's one thing they can't control. They can't force me to talk. Silence will be my one freedom.

With only two Contracts left aboard, the bus idles onto a large blacktop parking lot at a mall in San Antonio. The Bank Security officer activates his holo and looks at me. "Rielle James."

CHAPTER FOUR

Arriving in Comfort

I SWALLOW HARD, STAND ON STIFF LEGS and step into the aisle. The officer spins me around and handcuffs my wrists. Me. The girl who never even skipped school.

The officer leads me off the bus, where a man in a dark suit waits. "I'm here to collect Rielle James on behalf of Arthur Hayes."

"ID please," the officer says.

Dark Suit holds out his hand. The officer waves the holo over the man's wrist. A beep, and Dark Suit's face and name appear above the metallic surface. "She's all yours," the officer says.

Dark Suit brushes his jacket back, revealing a holstered pistol under his arm. He retrieves his holo from his pocket and waves it over my hand. The device proclaims JAMES, RIELLE. CONTRACT NUMBER 08645. He's chosen a sultry voice for his interface.

He takes my arm and guides me to a white solar mini-van with tinted windows and *Alamo Courier* emblazoned on the door. He slides it open revealing two officers in the back row wearing military camouflage. Both cling to rifles.

So many officers. So many guns. Are they afraid I'll escape? I've never heard of Contracts escaping, but why else would so many officers need to guard one small girl?

I settle into a captain's seat in the middle row, which is like sitting on a cloud compared to the rigid bus seats. Dark Suit climbs into the driver's seat. The smooth ride and gentle sway of the vehicle adds weight to my eyelids, but I resist the temptation to sleep. I want to see where he's taking me. He drives north for almost an hour, down a six lane freeway before taking an east off ramp. "Welcome to Comfort," the roadside sign states.

Comfort. Yeah, right.

The van speeds through the arid Texas countryside over parallel magnetic steel ribbons cut into the asphalt. Limestone gravel, dry grasses and scrubby trees with brilliant green foliage flank the roadway. I hold onto my seat as we skirt rolling hills and plunge into narrow valleys, my stomach lifting and falling. If I wasn't so anxious about what awaits me I might think the landscape beautiful.

We fly across narrow concrete bridges with towering signs that resemble giant thermometers, marking the height of predicted floodwaters. Despite the tinted windows, bright sunlight makes me squint as I peer down at the meandering creek. How could such an insignificant trickle of water possibly swell enough to reach meters above the bridge?

We pass driveway after driveway guarded by iron gates. Which gate will enclose my prison? The turn signal clicks and the van slows. We pull up to a wrought iron gate embellished with gaudy flourishes and the initials, *A.H.*

My heart doubles its pace and I gulp. This is it.

Dark Suit rolls down his window and presses a button on the black speaker box. Static crackles from the speaker. "Yes?"

"Alamo Courier with a delivery for Arthur Hayes."

The gate jerks and slowly rolls open.

The van idles down a winding flagstone driveway, past towering oak trees draped with mistletoe. It stops in front of a magnificent house—old world Spanish, like pictures of missions I've seen in history books, but with over-sized windows and iron accents that give it a modern edge.

Dark Suit slides my door open, pulls me from the car and unlocks my handcuffs. He leads me down the shaded walk, keeping a firm hold on my upper arm. The warm air, heavy with humidity, clings to my skin. A buzzing and clicking sound vibrates from the shrubs. Some sort of bug maybe? Soaring columns guard the veranda like massive jail bars. Dark Suit and I climb the expansive front steps to the door of my prison. He presses the doorbell and my stomach churns.

Hold it together.

I draw deep focused breaths, but I still tremble.

A young woman wearing a grey house dress opens the door, her gaze lowered. "Please come in." She must be a Contract too.

Dark Suit directs me inside. The sharp scent of bleach tightens my throat. I step onto a Persian rug, an island of colour in a sea of shining white marble that reflects double staircases wrapping either side of the circular entryway. Sunlight streams through floor-to-ceiling windows at the rear of the house, bouncing off every surface. It makes me squint.

A short round man lumbers toward us.

"Arthur Hayes?" Dark Suit asks.

"Yes."

Dark Suit extends his holo to the round man—Hayes. "I just need verification."

Hayes swipes his hand over Dark Suit's device. His name and pudgy face hovers above Dark Suit's holo. Dark Suit moves his finger over the holo image to find another page, scans the chip in my hand and a new image appears. He touches an icon and Hayes' pocket beeps. Hayes' pulls the beeping holo from his pocket. My face and name glow above it.

Dark Suit strides out the door without another word. My pulse hammers in my ears. I want to run after him. Please don't leave me here! Take me home! I meter my breathing, trying to keep it even, but it only makes me feel like I'm suffocating.

The girl closes the door.

Hayes skims his fingers over my holographic image and reads for a few moments while the girl waits beside me. She peeks at me from the corner of her eye and presses her lips into a sympathetic smile.

"Lydia, call all the Contracts together," Hayes says.

Lydia bows her head, then scurries down the hall.

Hayes raises his chin. "I'm the owner of this home, which means I'm burdened with the task of your rehabilitation." His gaze moves over me from top to bottom. "I feed you. I house you. That means you will listen to my instructions and follow them to the letter. I've brought you here for housekeeping and I expect perfection. I do not tolerate disobedience, laziness or disrespect."

Hayes turns on his heel and marches down a wide hall to the left. Am I supposed to follow? After a moment's hesitation I dash after him, hoping I'm doing the right thing. The hall ends at a swinging door. Hayes shoves it open to reveal a large kitchen professionally outfitted with gleaming stainless steel and honey coloured granite. Other young people about my age scamper into a line before us.

"This is Rielle. She will assist Lydia with housekeeping," Hayes begins. "You are all responsible for ensuring she understands the rules. If she messes up, I'll hold all of you responsible. Lydia, after you show Rielle her sleeping quarters she will join you in completing your duties."

My heart sinks. No rest after my long journey. I may drop from exhaustion, but he doesn't care. I don't like this guy—my *owner*. I fidget with the seam of my pants as anger flows hot beneath my skin.

He barks orders at the others. They stand stone-faced, like soldiers in front of a drill sergeant. A short, fat drill sergeant. I scrutinize Hayes, watching his three chins vibrate with every abrupt word. How does he get his shirt buttoned around that thick neck?

At the end of his oration he turns toward the door and shouts, "Get back to work!" He waves his hand as if to sweep us away, like bread crumbs off a table. As Hayes marches through the swinging door, the Contracts begin to scatter, one to the sink, another toward a sliding glass door at the rear of the kitchen.

The moment Hayes is gone, everyone stops and steps back toward me. Lydia turns to me with a smile. "Hi Rielle, I'm Lydia. It's nice to meet you. This is—" She starts rattling off names, "Jasmine, Jonah..." And three other names that get tangled somewhere between my ears and my sleep-deprived brain. A red-haired girl rolls her eyes; a tall, imposing boy clenches his jaw. The other new faces flash weak smiles and nod. I try to smile in return, but it feels like nothing more than lips stretched over teeth.

"I'm sure you won't remember all that," Lydia says. "Don't worry. I can reintroduce them at dinner. Come with me, I'll show you around."

Lydia stands a few inches taller than me and wears her shiny brunette hair gathered into a tight bun, not a hair out of place. Her heart-shaped face holds bright and friendly brown eyes that sparkle when she smiles. Her smile feels like an oasis in the desert.

She leads me up a narrow wooden staircase off the kitchen, the steps creaking as we climb. From two stairs above me, she glances over her shoulder. "I know you must be scared, but it's going to be okay. As long as we do what we're told, we get treated pretty well."

When we reach the second floor she begins the tour. "This is the women's quarters. Men aren't allowed in here and we aren't allowed in their rooms."

The upstairs hall branches off in opposite directions. Lydia points to the left.

"Roberta and Jasmine's room is down there, beside the girls' bathroom. That's the only bathroom female Contracts are allowed to use. If you use the bathrooms in the main house, you'll get in trouble."

I nod, glad Lydia is doing all the talking. But I know it's coming—the moment she'll want a verbal response—the moment I'll have to stick to the vow of silence I made on the bus and refuse to speak.

She pivots to the right and leads me into a small room with a slanted ceiling and two single beds. It's basic and sparse but clean, with white walls and wood floors. Sun spills through a small square window between the white metal frame beds and throws a warm glow on the yellow sheets and blankets.

"We're sharing a room." She grins as though thrilled by the idea. Pointing to the bed closest to the door, she says, "This is my bed and the other is yours."

Lydia crosses the room and lays her hand on a chest of drawers. "The top three drawers are yours, the bottom three are mine." She pulls out the drawer second from the top. "Your uniforms are in here. The Banker prefers we wear dresses when we're doing indoor work, but we get to wear pants if we're working outside."

The Banker? That must be what she calls Hayes.

You'll have to wear your hair in a bun. The Banker says anything else is sloppy. You'll miss meals if you don't look neat and tidy."

Miss meals? Lydia's idea of getting treated "pretty good" and mine are different.

She taps her index finger on her chin. "Let's see, what do you need to know? Where should I begin?" She brightens. "Are you from the North?"

I nod.

"Okay, then, you probably don't know about scorpions."

My eyes widen. Scorpions?

"Make sure you shake your shoes out before you put them on, and don't go to bed with your hair wet. They like cool, moist places. And trust me. The stings hurt. It's best not to reach your hand into dark places. There are a few poisonous spiders too."

I shudder and scratch a sudden itch on my head. What kind of place is this?

"I know this is hard, but it's going to be okay," Lydia says. "If you ever need anything, just ask. I'll leave you to change into your uniform and fix your hair. When you're ready, come downstairs and I'll show you around the house. Then we can get to work."

She offers one more smile before she leaves the room and closes the door. I feel like I should unpack something, but I have nothing. I shuffle across the room and sit on the bed, run my fingers over the bedding. After my nights spent on the bus, even the stiff mattress and coarse blanket seem inviting.

Tears blur my vision. This place is so far from home. All I want to do is lie down, put the pillow over my head and fall apart. I blink my tears away. My body longs for sleep, but that doesn't matter. I'm someone's housekeeping tool now, like a mop or a vacuum cleaner.

I strip off my disgusting travelling clothes. The pant cuffs are stiff with dried vomit from the bus floor and my shirt reeks of armpit. I want to burn the clothes, but I drop them in the laundry basket instead. The grey fabric of my new uniform is crisp and rough but smells clean, like detergent and bleach. I pull the one-size-fits-all dress over my head. Too big. It hangs like a bed sheet on my slight frame. At least it doesn't say 'PROPERTY OF' anywhere on it. I tie the drawstrings tight to give the dress some shape and shuffle off to the bathroom to style my hair into the required bun.

The pale girl in the mirror is a stranger to me. I find a washcloth under the sink, run cold water over it and press it to my swollen, blood-shot blue eyes. The water soothes them, but doesn't reduce the swelling. I look like I haven't slept in a month.

I descend the stairs to the kitchen where Lydia waits for me, her brown eyes wide and eager at my approach. "Are you okay?"

I nod, though I don't feel okay. I want to run screaming from this place. I take a deep breath to steady myself.

"It's okay if you don't feel like talking. I know this is a lot to take in. All of us have been where you are now. Come with me and I'll show you around."

CHAPTER FIVE

Pasta Dreams

LYDIA MOTIONS TOWARD THE SLIDING glass door in the kitchen. Beyond the glass a lake of manicured grass stretches toward a stuccoed fence that rises from a row of shrubs.

"That fence is our boundary. It has sensors that will activate your tracker chip and set off alarms."

I touch the tender spot on my hand where Bank Security inserted the chip.

Lydia turns away from the window and leads me through a door off the back of the kitchen. "This is the laundry and utility room. All the cleaning supplies are in here." She swings open a few cabinets to reveal plastic bottles full of chemicals and a stockpile of bleach. Another cabinet holds scrub brushes, washrags and a small tub full of toothbrushes with splayed, worn bristles.

She guides me out of the kitchen, down a marble tiled hallway and around the spacious main floor. It's about the size of ten of my houses put together but well laid out, so I'm not worried about finding my way around.

I follow her upstairs and over a wide landing into a hall. She halts in front of a set of double doors. "This is the master bedroom and the hall to the right is where Lily and Caleb, the Banker's children, have their playroom and bedrooms." She raises her palms, as though to stop me. "We are not to go near the Banker's children or his wife. If you need to clean a room and they're in it, you'll just have to wait until they leave. You'll also see Inez around. She's the nanny. She's not a Contract. Don't speak to her either, unless she speaks to you first."

Lydia turns to the left and keeps walking. "The first door in this hallway is the Banker's office. It's off limits to Contracts. The rest of the rooms in this hall are guest rooms. They never get used, at least not since I've been here. But we still have to clean them every week. Vacuum, dust, clean the bathrooms, wash the bedding, that sort of thing."

She looks at me apologetically. "Now that I've totally overloaded you with information, do you have any questions?"

Yeah, when can I leave? I shake my head.

"Okay, so today we're cleaning window blinds. I'm about halfway done, so we'll probably be finished by dinner."

I follow her to the living room where we wipe dust from white wooden blinds that shade the soaring windows. As we work, she informs me of more rules. "We're forbidden from using holos and watching deep screens. It's not exactly a temptation. If we're anywhere near the deep screen when the Banker is watching, he'll shut it off or tell us to work elsewhere.

"The Banker wants everything perfect. He comes around and inspects our work at the end of the day and if it's not quite right we have to do it over. Sometimes we get punished. And be careful with the Banker's things."

Lydia looks down, pressing her lips together, then looks back up at me. "He gets really, really angry if you break something. So if anything is too heavy for you to lift or move, it's better to ask for help than to risk damaging it. Nathan is really good about helping us out if we need it. Morris works with the horses so he's usually not available. I guess you could ask Jonah, but…well," she considers her words, "if it's really heavy it's just better to ask Nathan."

Nathan? Morris? Probably two of the names I missed earlier. Hopefully Lydia will keep her word and reintroduce everyone at dinner so I know who to ask for help.

"Jasmine is really sweet, but she's gone most of the time. She goes to work with the Banker. She's his—," she seems to be searching for words again, "his assistant. And Roberta is, well…Roberta probably has a good heart, it's just that this is a tough situation and it doesn't always bring out the best in people."

I understand now. Lydia is searching for kind words and I can see it's difficult for her to find kind words about this Roberta. Maybe she's the red-haired girl who rolled her eyes. Not exactly a welcoming response to a newcomer.

Lydia continues. "The best thing you can do is just ignore her when she's being difficult."

Difficult? What does that mean?

Lydia pauses. "So, where are you from?"

I sigh and look down.

She seems to get the message that I don't want to talk, so she fills the silence on her own while she wipes down another slat. "Um, I'm from Utah. I've been here just over a year. I have two sisters. One older and one younger. The younger one, Lucy, is at a reform school. My older sister, Allison, is a Contract too. I don't know where she ended up." She stops, her hand mid-swipe, and glances down, her eyes dewy.

A reform school. That's where Trenchcoat said Silas was headed. And Alyssa, what about her? A painful lump grows in my throat. Is Alyssa scared? Is she wondering why we abandoned her? I bite my cheek to get my mind off one pain and onto another.

By the time evening rolls around Lydia has revealed more information than I can possibly remember. If only I had a holo to record it all. The Banker doesn't seem like the type to extend much grace to newcomers. Especially since the words "spotless," "perfect" and "punishment" come up so often when Lydia speaks of him.

When we pass through the kitchen to put away our cleaning supplies, the smell of garlic, basil and fresh bread fills the air. With the nausea leftover from the bus ride finally gone, my appetite is back. The delicious aroma makes my mouth water and my stomach growl.

More than anxious to get a heaping plateful of lasagna, I fall into line behind a couple of other Contracts to get my food. My heart sinks. The lasagna is not for us. Our dinner consists of a large, dry biscuit and a bowl of split pea soup. My disappointing meal in hand, I follow Lydia into the backyard where all the Contracts are gathered in a circle to eat their meals under the shade of a sprawling tree.

I sit at Lydia's side and peer up at the tree, an ancient giant with dozens of thick arms stretching, bent and contorted, in every direction. A tree climber's dream.

"It's a live oak. Pretty, isn't it?" Lydia says.

I nod and nibble at my biscuit. Lydia pulls off a piece of hers, dips it in her soup and tosses it in her mouth. After swallowing she says, "Why don't you reintroduce yourselves? I don't think Rielle caught everyone's name earlier."

The boy on the other side of me with strawberry-blond hair and a crowd of freckles over his nose, extends his hand. "I'm Jonah."

I shake his hand, thin but firm, and manage a half smile.

Lydia leans toward me. "Jonah does a little bit of everything here. Sometimes he helps Roberta in the kitchen, sometimes he helps with the cleaning and sometimes he helps the guys with grounds keeping."

Jonah grins. "Yep, that's me. Jack of all trades, master of none."

"And I'm Jasmine," says the beautiful olive-skinned girl beside him.

There's a gap in the circle between Jasmine and the red-haired girl, who leans against the tree instead of sitting with the rest of the group. All eyes turn to her and, after a moment of awkward silence, Lydia speaks up. "That's Roberta."

Ahh, Roberta. The difficult girl. I guessed right.

The next boy, his skin deeply tanned and the tips of his dark hair sun bleached, dips his head in greeting. "I'm Morris." The one that Lydia said works with the horses. I imagine that if Morris weren't wearing canvas work clothes he'd be wearing blue jeans, a plaid shirt and a pair of cowboy boots.

The tall, broad-shouldered boy between Morris and Lydia smiles, his hazel eyes curving into half-moons under his sandy blond hair. "I'm Nathan—it's nice to meet you." He also extends his hand and gives me a firm handshake. He's the one who looked tense when I first arrived.

"So, Rielle, where are you from?" Jonah asks.

I press my lips together and drop my gaze. Guilt tugs at me for not answering, for appearing rude, but I promised myself. I'm not going to talk to anyone. I look to Lydia. She and Nathan exchange concerned glances.

"That's okay," Lydia says. "She doesn't really feel like talking, but I think she's from the North somewhere." She screws up her nose. "Somewhere where they don't have scorpions or tarantulas."

I listen to their pleasant banter while I eat my dinner. Jonah seems to be the clown of the group, always trying to make the others laugh with his corny jokes. Morris tells a story about a horse named Goliath that kicked the farrier, whatever that is. Jasmine keeps quiet, only cracking a smile when Jonah nudges her to respond to one of his jokes. Jonah's eyes move to Nathan every time he says something, as if he's looking for approval. Nathan must be the leader of the group.

My stomach aches for more food even after I wipe my bowl clean of every last molecule of soup with my biscuit. But more is not an option. Jonah, last in line, scraped the last dregs of the green slurry out of the pot.

Exhaustion weighs me down, so I pull my legs to my chest, lay my head on my knees and listen as Jonah imposes new words on a song that was popular a couple of years ago. Everyone chuckles. It might be funny, but I'm too tired to laugh.

The warm breeze tousles a few stray tendrils of hair that escape my bun. I close my eyes and remember eating dinner with my family.

We always ate dinner at the round table in the kitchen. The more tense things got at home, the further away Silas and I sat from our parents.

The past few months, Dad had been gone a lot. I don't know where he went. It wasn't like he had a job to go to. He was always vague when we asked him—meeting with people at a place—that's all we ever got out of him.

One particular night Dad hurried in after we'd already prayed for the meal. He kissed Alyssa on the head and plopped down in his seat beside Mom. Mom chopped spaghetti with a fork on a small plastic plate and scraped it onto Alyssa's highchair tray. Just noodles. No sauce. The pantry was empty. My own plate held spaghetti with butter and garlic powder and a slice of homemade bread.

Dad cleared his throat. "The school called today, Silas."

Silas stared at his plate and twirled his fork in the spaghetti. "Oh, yeah?"

"Do you know why they called?" Dad asked.

"I have a pretty good idea."

Dad put down his fork. "Where were you?"

Silas shrugged. "Walking around. Hanging out."

"You skipped school just to walk around?"

"Yeah."

Dad lowered his voice. "You're grounded."

A flush spread over Silas' cheeks. "Why?"

"What do *you* think, Silas? Because you skipped school."

Silas dropped his fork on his stoneware plate with a clang. "Why do I need to go to school? I mean, what's the point? It's not like I can go to college or even get a job!"

"Your education is still important," Mom said, her tone soothing, like a breeze on a hot day.

Silas chuckled sarcastically, sat back in his chair and crossed his arms. "Excellent. What are you grounding me from? Breathing? I can't go anywhere or do anything anyway."

Anger tinted Dad's cheeks. "You'll be spending Saturday with me. A guy I used to work with needs his fence repaired and painted. He's going to pay our electric bill and give us some groceries in exchange."

Silas rolled his eyes.

"I'll need your help for that matter too, Rielle," Dad said.

My mouth dropped open. "What? I didn't do anything wrong."

"The more hands we have the faster it will get done."

"I have plans. I'm going to Megan's house."

Dad's face went from red to purple. "If we don't pay this bill the electricity gets shut off. How would you like going into winter without heat?"

I twisted my napkin. I usually didn't talk back to my parents, but months of frustration bubbled to the surface. "If you hadn't lost your job we wouldn't have that problem," I mumbled under my breath.

Dad placed his palms on the table and leaned forward. "Aubrielle Angelique James. What did you say?"

He used my real name. Not good. I sucked in a breath, wishing I could draw the words back in just as easily. He waited. I searched for a gentle way to repeat what I said. "I just wish you hadn't lost your job."

I looked down at my lap. No, that wasn't it. I peered directly into Dad's eyes. "Why can't you just take the chip? Then everything could go back to normal."

"You know why, Rielle. I don't like this anymore than you do."

"I'm sure God could forgive you. If God forgives serial killers, I'm sure you'll be forgiven for having a small piece of metal in your hand. I've seen pictures of them. They don't have sixes anywhere on them."

"It's symbolic! The Bible says clearly—"

"Yeah, yeah, the mark of the beast, I know." I shook my head.

"Our souls are eternal. We can't trade them for temporary comforts."

A tear rolled down my cheek. I wiped it away with my fist, then pushed away from the table, stomped to my room and slammed the door.

"Rielle. Rielle, are you all done?" Lydia's voice pulls me from my memories. I lift my head from my knees. I'm done. I'm so done.

Lydia rises to her feet and brushes off her dress. "I think Rielle needs some rest. Good night all."

I struggle to my feet and follow Lydia up the squeaky stairs. It takes all the strength I have left to lift my feet high enough to clear each tread. I stumble twice. I'm torn between sleep and the need to wash three days of grime from my body. My own stench might wake me in the night.

I climb into the shower and shiver as the warm water pours over me, loosening oil and salty deposits of dried sweat and soothing my aching hips. The air is permeated by a steamy soup of deodorant, sweat and the perfume I dabbed on the morning before Bank Security came for me. I can't find any shampoo, so I use a bar of soap to wash my hair.

The scent of my favourite perfume swirls down the drain, like the last remnant of my freedom—the last remnant of home. What's left of me disappears into the sewer. All that's left is a soapy smell. Generic. Nondescript.

The water feels so good that I don't want to get out and face the alien world I've been thrust into. As if the shower curtain can protect me from all of it. I close my eyes, pretend I'm at home and finally begin to relax.

Someone pounds on the door. I jump. A second later another round of banging, this time so fierce it sounds like the door might rock off its hinges from the blows. "Time's up!" A shrill voice pierces the steamy air.

I turn off the water, towel dry my hair and wrap the towel around me to the sound of more knocking. I swipe my hand across the steam-coated mirror, run a comb through my hair and open the door.

Roberta's scowl greets me on the other side. "What do you think this is? A spa?"

I shake my head.

She plunks her hands on her hips. "We all have to share the shower. You get five minutes. That's it!" Her top lip curls, exposing her teeth.

I press myself against the wall to edge past Roberta.

"That's my fault, Roberta, I forgot to tell her the time limit." Lydia's sweet voice calls from behind Roberta.

"Gee, thanks Lydia, that makes me feel *so* much better about my cold shower." Roberta darts into the bathroom, slamming the door behind her.

Lydia and I return to our room. I search drawers for underwear and something to wear to bed. Thinking about Roberta's anger sets me off again. I swallow back more tears. Their salty bitterness curdles my stomach.

"Don't worry about it, Rielle. Roberta is just cranky sometimes. I'm sorry for not telling you."

I don't respond. It's all I can do to pull on a nightgown before I collapse into bed.

CHAPTER SIX

Hunger

AN ALARM PENETRATES THE FOG OF SLEEP. I ignore it and it goes away.

"Rielle." Someone nudges my arm. Why is Mom waking me so early? I've only slept a couple minutes. I roll over and pull the blanket around my shoulders. The blanket feels strange—too thin and too rough. And the smell—bleach.

"Rielle." Not Mom's voice. Where am I? I peel open my eyelids and look up at a new but familiar face. Lydia. As I struggle to get my bearings, dismal reality sinks in.

I want to shoo Lydia away like I used to shoo Silas when he'd wake me on Saturday mornings. He thought he was so funny, waking me up and then going back to bed and sleeping until noon. My irritating little brother. A dull ache, a gaping emptiness settles in my chest. He could wake me every Saturday morning. I'd never complain again.

"Hurry, Rielle. You'll get in trouble if you're late."

I wash, dress and stagger down the stairs. I shove the last spoonful of plain oatmeal into my mouth just as the Banker waddles into the kitchen wearing a three-piece suit and black patent leather shoes. We scramble into line. He clears mucus from his throat and issues orders in a mild Texas accent. He starts with the boys and ends with Lydia and me. "Rielle, did Lydia go over the house rules with you?"

I regard the expectation in his eyes as he waits for my answer. It's one thing to maintain my silence with the other Contracts, completely another with him. But my silence is especially for him. I nod.

He knits his brows together, lifts his chins. "You will answer me when I speak to you. Did Lydia go over the rules?"

I clamp my tongue between my teeth. Defiance is hard for me. Crimson flushes the Banker's cheeks and he glowers, shaking my resolve. I've always been the good kid, never crossed my teachers or my parents. An angry glance or a raised voice was all it took to make me fall in line. I look down at my shoes and nod again.

"Stop wagging your head like a dog's tail! I told you, I do not tolerate disrespect. There will be no food for you until you can give a proper answer. Do you hear that, Roberta?"

I glance sideways at Roberta. She smirks. "Yes, sir."

The Banker marches from the room.

I glance at Lydia. The area between her brows sports two deep creases. "I know this is hard, Rielle, but it will be easier if you do what he asks."

My shoulders slump. I don't think anything can make this easier—only varying degrees of terrible.

Lydia leads the way as we collect laundry. She shows me how the Banker insists everything be folded. She tries to teach me to iron. We even have to iron bed sheets. My personal favourite, though, is starching and ironing the Banker's gigantic boxer shorts. Apparently, he likes stiff underwear. Weird.

Keeping up with Lydia and her instructions is difficult on an empty stomach. My muscles burn with fatigue, as if I'm swimming through paste.

At lunch I follow Lydia into the kitchen. The smell of peanut butter in the air makes my stomach ache. Eager to get out of the kitchen and away from the food, I march past the lined-up Contracts toward the door.

"Wait, Rielle!"

I stop, peer over my shoulder.

Roberta holds a sandwich out to me. "Aren't you going to have some lunch?"

I stare at her, my mouth gaping. Is she seriously going against the Bankers orders and giving me lunch? Maybe she's not so bad after all. I step toward her.

She yanks the sandwich back and plumps out her lip in a drama queen pout. "Oh wait, I forgot. You can't." Her eyes glint with pleasure.

I spin around and dart out the door. Sure, she forgot. I'm starting to think when Lydia called Roberta "difficult" she was being overly kind.

Watching all the other Contracts eat has my mouth watering. I lean against the live oak and fold my arms around my middle to muffle my stomach's complaints. Everyone but Roberta seems uneasy eating in front of me. She makes a show of taking slow bites and moans with pleasure after each one.

When the long, miserable day finally ends, I collapse into bed. I'm too troubled by hunger pangs and nightmares to sleep well. Alyssa's cries dominate my dreams. I chase her. I almost reach her. A red-eyed giant metallic scorpion locks its pincer around her. "No! Don't touch her!" I scream. Then it yanks her away from me.

The alarm clock rings after I manage to get a couple hours of sleep. Sitting up, I rub my eyes and swallow hard. My throat feels raw, as though I really spent my night screaming at that robotic bug.

I don't know if I'm happy for the morning or irritated by it. I can do without the nightmares, but the day isn't exactly something to look forward to. I wait until I'm sure the others are finished breakfast before I go downstairs. I've never been so hungry in my life.

We line up and the Banker asks the same question. I refuse to answer. His face turns red and tight like an over-filled water balloon. In two long strides he's in my face.

"Answer me!"

I hold my breath as his warm, stale coffee breath oozes over my face. I shift backward, biting my lip in refusal. He turns to leave without issuing any edicts about food. I let out my breath. Maybe it's over, maybe—

He steps back and shifts his weight to the side. He whips his arm. A gold ring flashes and sharp pain rips at my right cheek. My head snaps back. I fall sideways and hit the floor with a bone-rattling thud. My pulse throbs in my cheek. I throw my hand over my cheek then draw it away. Crimson stains my fingers. The tang of blood fills my mouth.

Lydia gasps and lurches toward me.

"Do you have a problem, Lydia? Leave her, else you'll get the same!"

Lydia stops short. "I—I'm sorry, sir."

Nathan's boots shuffle beside me.

"Nathan, you'll back off too, if you know what's good for you!" The Banker's voice is strained. "No food!" He marches out of the kitchen.

Tears obscure my vision and sting my broken skin. My stomach churns and heaves, but I swallow back the bile. I try to get up, but my legs don't exist. They lay beside me in a heap, as likely to support my weight as a rubber band.

Two large hands encircle my upper arms and pull me upright. "Lydia, can you fix her up?" Nathan asks.

Roberta folds her arms across her chest. "Oh, geez, suck it up."

Lydia moves to my side. "Roberta, she's not used to this."

This is something I'll get used to? The air is too thin. I gasp, trying to draw in more air than my lungs can hold. I want to hide. The way they're talking about me—the humiliation is almost as painful as the Banker's backhand. I understand my actions more than they know. I knew there'd be consequences.

Lydia clasps my face between her hands. "Rielle, look at me. It's going to be okay. I'm going to take you upstairs. You'll be as good as new."

She takes my trembling hand. Although my legs are still shaking, I manage to follow her upstairs to the bathroom. She orders me to sit down on the edge of the bathtub. After retrieving a small white box from the cupboard under the sink, she flips open the lid and goes to work.

"His ring caught your cheek, but don't worry—it's just a little cut." I wince as she dabs the wound with a cloth. She squeezes the cut closed and presses some adhesive strips over the gash, then rips open a paper package, removes a square of gauze, covers the wound and tapes the bandage in place. Finally, she wets a rag with warm water and washes the blood off my cheek and hands.

I breathe. In. Out. In. Out.

Get a grip, Rielle. You chose this when you chose to keep silent.

Lydia speaks in a soft voice, "I'm kind of the unofficial nurse for all the Contracts. It's nice not having to go to the Banker for minor injuries."

Especially when he inflicts them.

She rinses and wrings the cloth. "My mom is a nurse...was a nurse. I mean when she was still allowed to work. Even when she couldn't work at the hospital anymore, she helped other Resistors who needed medical attention. She always made sure we knew first aid."

Lydia must have inherited her compassionate nature from her mother. It's hard to believe that anyone could think someone like Lydia would be a threat to national security. Though I don't know her mother, a stab of indignation roils through me on her behalf.

A weak smile touches her lips. "You'll probably have a bruise tomorrow. The cut should be fine. You might end up with a little scar. Hardly noticeable."

I peer into her eyes. I need the kindness I find there like I need my next breath.

"I know you're not feeling well, but we need to get to work before the Banker notices we're gone. He's already upset. Do you think you're up to it?"

I nod. Even though she phrased it in the form of a question, saying "no" is not an option. I descend the stairs on jelly legs, hoping no one will be in the kitchen to see me. More tears escape despite my attempt to "suck it up." Roberta sneers when I pass her in the kitchen, but everyone else has scattered. I wipe my tears on my sleeve and follow Lydia to our next task.

Every heartbeat hammers against my skull. My hands continue to quake— hunger, shock, fear—and, as the day wears on, the trembling intensifies in my legs. I don't want Lydia to suffer for my stubbornness, so I push myself to keep up with her. As we work she begs, "Please, Rielle. If you're able, just tell him what he wants to hear and this will all be over. You don't have to say much."

I ignore her and scrub harder.

She touches my shoulder. "Are you *able* to speak?"

I peer into her concerned eyes. Am I able? Technically, yes. I don't want to lie to her. And yet, my silence is my only freedom. I can't give that up.

I shake my head. No. I can't speak.

She presses her lips into a sympathetic frown and pats my shoulder.

At mealtime, I sit outside the circle and try to keep my eyes off the other Contracts as they eat, but the salty aroma and the sound of chewing draws my attention. I find myself staring, wishing. No! It would be better to starve to death than to give in to the Banker.

I open my eyes to another morning. It takes every ounce of energy I possess to pry myself out of bed. I drag my feet to the bathroom, throwing my hands against the hallway walls for support.

I splash cold water on my face. The mirror reflects a sunken cheeked, dull-eyed stranger. I touch my face to confirm it's my image staring back at me. Only a sliver of blue iris peeks through my swollen eyelid. A flood of purple, green and putrid yellow spreads over my cheekbone. I hold my breath against the pain as I rip off the bandage and replace it with a fresh one.

Lydia meets me in the hall when it's time to go downstairs, her forehead wrinkled with worry. "I'll try to tell the Banker you can't speak so he won't keep punishing you." She twists her hands together.

I shake my head. I don't want her involved in this. Brushing past her, I descend the stairs, weak in the knees and terrified of what he'll do to me today, but resolved.

When the Banker arrives with the same question, I press my lips into a hard line and stare straight ahead. I bunch my hands into fists while he clenches his jaw and his face blooms pink, then purple. His collar button looks in danger of exploding open from the pressure. I stand up straight and brace myself for another hit.

On this there will be no compromise. Pain and humiliation are necessary to my rebellion. This coward who sees fit to hit me will have to face his power-lessness and strike me again.

Lydia steps forward. "Sir, she's unable—."

I bite my cheek, willing her to stop. This is my battle, not hers. The one thing that might shake my resolve is if he hurts her. I can't stand by and watch her suffer.

The Banker throws up his hand. "Enough! No food!" He stomps from the room mumbling about Bank Security ripping him off, never telling him about any speech issues, selling him defective merchandise.

That's me—defective merchandise.

My brain is loose inside my head. It rattles every time I move. The Banker orders us to clean all the light fixtures and chandeliers, a job I'm sure he chose especially for me. I'll have to spend most of the day on a ladder. I don't know how I'll manage, but I will not let Lydia do my share of the work.

I make it through the morning, but dread having to endure watching the other Contracts eat their lunch. I sit by the tree, hoping to keep my distance from the food, but Nathan sits on one side of me, Lydia on the other. As she nibbles the crust of her sandwich, she throws a few furtive glances my way.

The thin bead of cheese spread on white bread looks so good and smells even better. I ogle their sandwiches for a while before I force myself to keep my eyes down.

Nathan nudges me. I lift my gaze. He raises his eyebrows and a hint of mischief plays at the corners of his mouth. "Hey, Roberta, was that the Banker calling for you?"

She glances back toward the kitchen door. "I didn't hear him."

"Yeah, I heard him too," Jonah says.

With a frustrated sigh, Roberta stands and hurries inside. Nathan tears off a piece of his sandwich and hands it to me. "Take it, quick."

I shake my head.

"We won't tell," Jasmine adds.

I can't have any of them getting in trouble or going hungry because of me. I shake my head again, then turn away from their circle.

After lunch, Lydia and I haul our supplies to the dining room where, over the table, a huge wrought iron chandelier hangs, dotted with tiny bulbs under smoked glass shades. My aching legs wobble as I climb the rungs of the ladder. The room spins around me as though I'm on a carnival ride. Several times I have to reach down and grab the top rung and cling to it until the dizzy spell passes.

I reach up to unscrew a burnt out bulb. Everything fades to dull grey and stars float across my field of vision. I clutch the ladder but my arms go limp. I can't hold on. Sound is sucked from the room and a dusky tunnel narrows my vision. I push at the darkness with all my strength, trying to beat it back, but it's strong—so easy to give in to it. Blackness enwraps me like a wool blanket, peaceful and warm.

And then the blanket is ripped away by pain. My hip. My arm. My head.

"Rielle, Rielle!" Lydia's voice is faint. She's miles away. Answering requires more energy than I possess. Everything grows brighter and louder as though someone is cranking up the world's volume.

"Clean this up, Lydia!" the Banker shouts.

His voice claws at my ears. I slowly open my eyes, blinking hard to force them to focus. Two forms tower above me...one is the Banker...the other is a woman I haven't seen before. Someone else kneels beside me. Lydia. She holds my hand.

"Arthur, I told you this would happen!" The new woman's voice. "She could have broken the chandelier. Do you know how hard it was to find that? It's an antique. Unbelievable!"

I squint up at the woman. She waves her arms animatedly, the diamond bracelet on her wrist glittering. "Maybe she can't speak, have you thought of that? Why do we need someone who cleans our toilets to talk anyway? I don't have time for this. I'm getting a massage in a half hour." She rolls her fawn-like brown eyes and presses her plump, candy-coated lips together.

She plants her left hand on her hip. A large rock—no, a boulder glimmers on her ring finger. The Banker's wife? She must be, but I can't imagine a more unlikely couple. She's taller than him, slender, yet softly rounded and at least ten years his junior. Why would someone like her be with someone like him?

"Nina, I—" the Banker's voice hits a higher pitch.

With an exasperated sigh she cuts him off. "I don't want to hear it! I told you I refuse to deal with *them*. You take care of this!"

She spins on stiletto heels, glossy black hair whipping around her shoulders. Her shoes click on the marble as she storms away.

"Lydia, get to it, NOW!" The Banker claps his hands loudly.

Lydia drops my hand and picks up glass shards with bare fingers.

The Banker opens the garden doors and shouts, "Nathan, get in here and clean *this* up." He points at me.

Nathan jogs into the room.

"Take *that* into the kitchen and get *it* something to eat," the Banker says as he walks away, waving his hand in my direction. "This mess had better be gone by the time I get home from work!"

Nathan extends his hand. "Can you get up?"

Getting up sounds like an unconquerable task. I just want to lie on the cold marble and sink into oblivion. I take his hand and attempt to pull myself up, but the moment my head lifts off the floor, everything spins again. I flop back down, knocking my head against the tile.

Nathan threads one arm under my knees and the other under my neck and scoops me off the floor. I want to protest, but I can't. His strong arms feel safe. It's the first time I've felt safe since I left home. I lean my head against his chest. The gentle sway of his gait nearly lulls me to sleep on the short journey to the kitchen. He sets me down on a chair at the table in the corner.

"Roberta, could you please get her something to eat?"

Roberta leans over the sink, peeling potatoes. "Oh, now I'm waiting on her, too. She can't get it herself?"

"Forget it," Nathan mumbles.

I lay my head on the table and close my eyes, enjoying the coolness of the laminate against my cheek. The microwave beeps. Nathan's boots pad the floor, dishes clank on the table. I inhale the warm smell of chicken broth. Saliva floods my mouth.

"Here. You'll feel better once you eat."

I open my eyes. In front of me, a bowl of soup steams beside a plate of crackers. Nathan sits in the chair next to me.

With supreme effort I lift my head off the table, my entire body as limp as the noodles in my soup.

Nathan scoots the bowl closer to me. "Come on, Rielle, you need to eat something."

I pick up a salt-topped cracker and nibble on the corners. The bite of salt on my tongue encourages me further. Nathan watches as I devour the crackers and start on the soup. Oh, the soup. The warm liquid fills my mouth and runs down my throat. Have I ever tasted anything more delicious?

"Are you okay?" Nathan asks when I slurp up the last drop.

I nod.

"Are you sure?" He tilts his head and searches my gaze as though he's inspecting the swelling around my eye. He clenches his teeth. "Come on. I'll help you get up to your room."

I nod again, the dizziness beginning to pass. I smile at him in thanks.

I head to the stairs for the women's quarters. Nathan follows. I take two steps on my own, but my hip is stiff from the fall and I stumble on the third step. Nathan catches me. Too exhausted to be embarrassed, I allow him to carry me the rest of the way. He lays me on my bed, pulls off my shoes and covers me with the blanket. I watch him close the door as he leaves.

When I open my eyes, the rising sun paints the sloped ceiling blue. As the first morning rays pour through the window I come to a sweet realization. I won. And even sweeter—the Banker lost. I'm stronger than he is. I paid a price—a gash on my cheek that will certainly leave a scar, too many bruises to count and an aching body, but it's worth it. I own my silence. It's mine and no one can steal it from me.

CHAPTER SEVEN

My New and Dismal Normal

THE ALARM CLOCK BUZZES. I POUND MY FIST twice on the snooze button. In the early morning greyness I lie under damp, clingy sheets, my forehead beaded with sweat. I kick the covers down to the end of the bed and wait for the oscillating fan on the windowsill to blow my way. I close my eyes when the breeze finds me, rippling my nightgown like a flag in the wind. A few seconds of refreshment and it pivots away, back toward Lydia's empty, already made bed. And the heat slides over me again.

Lydia kneels beside her bed, head bowed and hands folded. She insists on waking early every morning to pray. Fruitless ritual. I prefer to get a few extra minutes of sleep. At least that offers me some perceivable benefit. It's not like God is listening. Or maybe God is listening, but just doesn't care. Maybe this is all a test and I'm failing. Maybe in 400 years my people will be freed.

I can't wait that long.

Sometimes I wish I was good like Lydia.

I sit up, switch off the alarm, then shuffle to my dresser and pull on my uniform. How long have I been here? Weeks, months, centuries? It must be the end of July. The fourth was a couple weeks ago. Lydia and I watched bursts of fireworks from our bedroom window.

My days are as simple as instructions on a shampoo bottle. Wake, work, sleep, repeat. Until I die. Death. Wouldn't that be nice? A long sleep without an alarm to interrupt. I'll bet it's cooler six feet under. I hope they bury me with my hair down. I should find a scrap of paper and leave a note for Lydia. I don't want to spend eternity with a heavy brown knot sticking out of my head.

I'd probably run into my parents on the other side at some point. I'd be happy to see them. First, I'd give them a hug, then I'd throttle them. It wouldn't matter since they're already dead, but they'd get the message.

"Morning, Rielle." Lydia grins and rises from her knees.

As usual, I don't answer. I issue an irritated sigh.

I stumble like a drunkard down the hall to the bathroom, wash the salt from my face, twist and pin my hair into a bun. I hate looking in the mirror these days. In the months I've been here, I've lost weight and not in a good way. In a concentration camp kind of way. I'm pasty, gaunt, frail, sunken. My uniform hangs on my shoulders. I look waifish, robbed of any femininity.

I huddle around the sink with Jasmine and Roberta, brushing my teeth. When I'm done, I cup my hand under the faucet and rinse my mouth. Back home I used to put my mouth under the faucet. I tried that when I first got here, but Roberta spat toothpaste into my hair. "Well, stay out of the way then," she said.

I glare at her in the mirror. She sneers, then heads downstairs.

"Time to go," Lydia calls from the hall.

I slick water over my hair to keep it in place and follow Lydia down the stairs. A sweet, smoky smell greets me in the stairwell. My mouth waters. I can almost taste salty bacon on my tongue. It isn't for us, though. Our breakfast always consists of plain oatmeal and a cup of water.

I scoop a spoonful of grey mush out of my bowl, leaving a rounded crater behind. I scrape it off the spoon with my top teeth, chew twice and swallow to get it off my taste buds. I choke down the entire bowl and guzzle the cup of water.

The Banker's shoes clack down the hall. We scramble into line for his inspection. He lumbers through the swinging kitchen door, his bulbous torso supported by stubby legs that look like they might snap under their heavy burden.

Clasping his arms behind his back, he saunters down the line inspecting each of us up and down. He stops in front of me. I stiffen. "Absolutely slovenly, Rielle. Didn't your parents teach you anything? No, no, of course they didn't." He scowls. "Bunch of lazy thieves. Fix your hair."

Heat rushes to my cheeks. I reach up to feel a few tendrils of hair falling onto my forehead. Dumb cowlick.

The Banker continues, spittle spraying from his mouth. "Roberta, thanks to Rielle, you will get the night off from dishes." His eyes narrow to petty slits. "Rielle will take care of kitchen clean-up this evening on her own. Maybe that will help her remember that laziness and slovenliness are not tolerated in this house."

He turns his attention away from me and assigns chores. As usual, a solid twelve hours of work awaits us, plus the kitchen clean-up duty I also acquired. Even when the house appears perfectly clean, the Banker manages to find work for us. Anything that involves a toothbrush and bleach brings a gleam to his eyes.

We work quietly for a few hours, but silence doesn't sit well with Lydia. I can see it building up in her as the day wears on. Her sudden intakes of breath, as though she's about to say something, end in a sigh and slack shoulders. Inevitably, she can't take it anymore and bursts into chatter. I nod now and then to show her I'm listening.

This is the only time I feel guilty for my silence. Lydia could use some company. Certainly my vow of silence makes her work even more unbearable. She bubbles with friendliness. Poor girl. Being assigned to work with me must be torturous.

Eventually, Lydia starts talking about her family. Even though I've banished thoughts of my family to a box I store in the dark corners of my memory, when she speaks of her sisters, that box looms front and centre, and the lid peels open.

Silas. Alyssa. Little Alyssa—alone. Who is taking care of her? I touch the scar on my cheek. My chest tightens. What if—what if someone's hurting her?

And what about my parents—in prison? I can't feel sorry for them. They had a choice. I did not. They knew the consequences and barrelled headlong into them. I hate my parents. I love them. I miss them. My feelings don't make sense. It's all pain. Throbbing, inescapable pain.

"Are you okay?" Lydia asks.

I nod, flash a half smile and scrub with renewed vigour. Maybe hard work will drive these thoughts back into that box and seal it closed.

By the time the lunch bell rings, sweat has stained the underarms of my light grey dress charcoal. We sit under the live oak's outstretched branches, eating peanut butter sandwiches and guzzling as much water as our stomachs can hold. The pads of my fingers are already rubbed raw. My fatigued arms shake as I lift my cup to drink. The water sloshes. Twenty minutes later, we're back to work.

Three o'clock is hopeless hour. That's when it seems like we've been cleaning for days, but are nowhere near finished. We take twenty minutes for dinner: some concoction with cabbage, rice, tomato sauce and a chewy mystery meat that has the taste and consistency of canned dog food. Not that I've ever eaten canned dog food—at least not until now. I wolf it down like it's a big, juicy cheeseburger.

It's well after dark when Lydia and I finish scrubbing off the dirt that splashed onto the stucco fence during the last rainstorm. My knuckles are cracked from the water, and every muscle and joint aches. I limp back to the kitchen behind Lydia, bucket and scrub brush in hand, knowing my workday isn't over.

Lydia opens the sliding glass door to the kitchen and halts abruptly in the doorway. I have to shimmy around her to get in.

My mouth falls open. Dishes are piled in the sink and strewn over the counters—mountains of steel, stoneware and glass. Roberta! She must have dirtied every dish in the kitchen.

"Oh—!" Lydia leaves the word hanging like a coat hook ready for just about anything to be hung on it. She might have added "heck" or "shoot" or "fudge" if she were angry enough. I would have used the real words, not the flimsy stand-ins.

I can't decide whether to cry or scream or fly into a fit of maniacal laughter. What I really want to do is kill Roberta. Slowly. With my bare hands.

Lydia and I carry our buckets to the utility room. She places her hand on my shoulder. "I'll help you clean up."

I shake my head. It's my punishment, not hers.

"With two of us working, it'll go quickly." She rubs her neck and looks down. She knows as well as I do that if the Banker sees her helping or if Roberta reports it, he'll see it as disobedience and we'll both be punished.

I fold my arms and shake my head again.

"If you're sure." She takes a couple steps and glances back at me, her brows furrowed, then walks out of the utility room.

I drag myself to the kitchen and start scrubbing.

While I clean, I entertain myself by dreaming up creative ways to get back at her. The Banker doesn't like my hair falling out of the bun. How'd he like a bald Contract? I smile to myself as I imagine shaving Roberta's head in the night, leaving a pile of kinky orange hair on her pillow.

I scrub until everything sparkles. Unless it's perfect I'll find myself cleaning up after Roberta for a week. I wait in the kitchen, guarding my work, worried that Roberta will sabotage it if I walk away. The Banker finally marches through to inspect the kitchen. He tells me what a terrible job I did and dismisses me.

By the time I make it upstairs, Lydia is already asleep. I strip off my clothes and collapse into bed. One day of my life over, with many, many more to go. I dream of snow, falling cool and clean on the ground, glittering and dancing in the moonlight.

And then, unfortunately, morning arrives again.

Before the Banker assigns the day's chores, he makes an announcement. "I am having a meeting here tonight." He puffs out his chest. "Nathan, I will need you on hand. Dress accordingly."

Nathan bows his head in agreement.

"Jasmine, you will be required, of course. And Rielle, you will serve us. I want the rest of you in your rooms for the evening." The Banker's critical gaze scans me from head to toe. "Jasmine, make certain she's presentable. Six o'clock!"

I glance at Jasmine and Nathan, searching their faces for an explanation. They seem to know what the Banker is talking about. I, on the other hand, have no idea. And what does he mean, "look presentable?"

The Banker spits out the rest of the day's assignments. My workload is half its normal size. Odd. Not that I'm complaining, but I have a sick feeling that scrubbing tile grout with a toothbrush would be more fun than what the Banker has planned for me. When he dismisses us, I turn to Lydia, hoping for an explanation.

"Lucky you." She quirks one side of her mouth into a half-smile.

What does that mean? I bunch my brow together to form the most puzzled expression I can muster.

"He's having guests over, probably some bank executives, and he wants to impress them. Nathan and Jasmine and one of the other girls always serve." She's holding something back. I can see it in her eyes, but I have no way to press her on it without talking.

My anxiety rises with the sun, miserable and oppressive by the afternoon. Lydia would tell me if this evening's event will be really bad. Wouldn't she?

As I polish the last stretch of the stair railings, the Banker's wife breezes past me. She saunters toward the garage door in a curve hugging dress and glossy pink stilettos. Lily, probably five or six years old, dashes down the stairs, her beautiful black hair waving behind her and a beaming smile lighting her face. "Mommy!"

Inez hurries after her.

The Banker's wife's clicking heels speed up.

Lily locks her arms around her mother's legs. The Banker's wife doesn't embrace her in return. Instead, she raises her hands as though touching the small girl might contaminate her. "Inez!" She snaps. "I don't have time for this. Take her."

Inez peels the little girl's arms off her mother. "Come, Lily."

The Banker's wife marches out the garage door.

Tears roll down Lily's cheeks. Inez lifts Lily into her arms and carries her upstairs.

After completing my chores, I return to the women's quarters in search of Jasmine and further instruction. I catch her coming down the hall wrapped in a towel. "Shower's open. It's all yours," she says.

It's as though I'm walking through a dangerous neighbourhood at night— on high alert, suspicious of everything. I whisper to myself in the shower. "It's going to be okay. Don't see demons where there are none. It's dumb to be scared." So the Banker wants us clean and smelling pleasant for his guests. Nothing strange about that.

Since no one is lining up to use the shower after me, I could take my time, but I'm jittery and anxious and hop out a few minutes after I get in. I wrap the towel around me. Now what?

I return to my room where a garment bag lies on my bed, topped by a pair of obscenely high heels. He can't expect me to wear those. I stare at the bag warily, as though it might jump up and bite. My hair drips onto my shoulders. I'm terrified to open it. What if the outfit inside is as offensive as the shoes that sit on top?

I unzip the bag to expose a charcoal grey dress. At first glance, it appears sophisticated. Understandably, the Banker doesn't want me wearing my usual house dress for guests.

A muted knock draws my attention to the door. "Rielle, it's Jasmine."

I open the door. Jasmine's hair hangs in a perfect black sheet around the shoulders of her bathrobe, framing her expertly make-upped face. Not unusual for her. Since the Banker takes her to work with him, she always has to look professional.

"Come with me," she says.

I follow her back to her room. She motions to the desk in the corner, littered with a plethora of hair and make-up tools, bottles and accessories, and then tells me to have a seat. As I ease myself onto the chair, I realize what the Banker has asked of her.

She dries, curls and pins my hair. It takes forever. Then she coats my locks with a thick layer of hair spray, creating a dense cloud that lingers around my head. I cough.

Done. Finally. I start to get up and she pushes me back down. "Not yet." She dabs foundation on a sponge and rubs the cool goop over my face, then a layer of blush on my cheeks before she goes after my eyes with a black pencil. It feels thick and heavy on my skin. She comes at me with the mascara and I lean away. "Sit still," she says. My eyes flutter as she combs the applicator brush over my lashes.

With a frustrated sigh, she tucks the mascara brush back into the tube. "Well, that's as good as it's going to get."

That sounds bleak.

I stare at the make-up containers, afraid to look in the mirror.

She tucks an escaped strand of my hair back into place. "Now, go get dressed and meet me downstairs."

I stalk back to my room and gawk at the dress for a few more minutes, while evaluating my role this evening. Why did the Banker choose me for this? I'm not the best mannered or the most gracious. Those traits rest with Lydia. The Banker never tolerates accidents and will be far more critical of my performance with someone important present.

I sigh and my shoulders slump. There's no way I'll meet his high expectations. Never have before. Doubt tonight will be the first time. How many meals will I miss over this?

CHAPTER EIGHT

Eye Candy

I PULL ON THE DRESS. THE WIDE PLUNGING neckline barely catches my shoulders and the waist tapers inward, into a straight, hip-hugging skirt that doesn't reach past mid-thigh. It looked harmless on the hanger.

The dress lied to me.

I yank the back of the bodice down in an attempt to raise the neckline, but it slides right back into place, bearing an obscene amount of cleavage. I slip on the strappy heels, which fit, but throw me off balance. A twinge of panic quickens my heart rate. I have to wear this in front of people? And these shoes. How can I serve food when I can barely walk?

I go to the mirror behind our bedroom door, afraid to look. I half hope it will reveal an Amish girl's dress. Maybe it's not as bad as I think...

I was wrong. It's worse.

Heavy eye-liner rounds my eyes and thick mascara coats my already dense lashes. Everything is too much—the plum lipstick, the blush streaking my cheeks. Perhaps the Banker is entertaining a troupe of clowns. I'll fit right in. I can't imagine anyone else finding the look attractive. The only improvement comes from the foundation; it covers my scar and the dark circles permanently haunting my eyes.

The true humiliation, though, is the dress. Naughty French maid without the hat. The shoes bring the whole look together.

I suck back the angry, humiliated tears threatening to erupt. I'm seized by a strong desire to run to the bathroom and scrub it all off.

As I gape at my train wreck reflection, Lydia opens the door and pokes her head inside. Her eyebrows lift. "Oh, you're dressed."

I nod. For some reason, her acknowledgement causes more tears to spring to the surface.

"Don't cry! You'll ruin your make-up." She hands me a tissue. I dab the tears before they can escape.

"You look really, really—pretty." She smiles, forcing her eyes wide open as if that will prevent me from detecting her lie.

I shake my head. Not pretty. Obscene.

"It's going to be okay. He wants you to look nice for the guests. You'll serve drinks and food, and then you'll be done. Mainly, he wants you to stand there and look pretty so he can impress everyone."

I know she's trying to reassure me, but her words bring no comfort at all. Who could be comforted to find out they are nothing more than eye candy for a bunch of bank executives? It's demeaning in the extreme. It's one thing to do the Banker's work, another to be his entertainment.

Lydia adjusts the shoulders on my dress, tugging the neckline up, but it slides back down as it had for me. "You can do this. Just get through it. It doesn't happen often. I don't think anyone likes to visit with the Banker unless they have to."

I slink down the stairs as though walking to my own execution.

Jasmine awaits me, sitting at the kitchen table. "You look great." She grins. "You clean up really nice."

I grind my teeth.

Her encouraging smile turns serious. She stands, smoothes her dress and squares her shoulders. "You need to smile and be polite. It's in your best interest." Her tone is hard, cold, unsympathetic. "The Banker can make your life miserable if you embarrass him in front of important people. I don't like it either, but I suck it up and do it. Now, stand up straight and pull your shoulders back."

I do as I'm told. What choice do I have? The Banker owns me and he can show me off if he pleases. Another defeat to add to the pile.

"And smile," she says, flashing a beauty pageant grin.

I tighten my lips into the widest smile I can conjure.

"Good. Now we're ready. Follow me."

I trail her to the living room where every surface is clean and gleaming—the marble floors, polished wood, crystal vases full of white roses and gardenias, their perfume mixing with the lemony scent of furniture polish.

Jasmine tells me where to stand, what I'll be serving and when and how to serve it. She leads me back and forth across the floor with an elegant and confident stride to help me learn how to walk in my shoes. First my legs are too straight, and then I bend them too much.

"Don't stomp. Toe, heel, toe, heel," Jasmine says.

A man in a suit marches into the room, startling me. I lose my balance, trip over my own feet and grab onto Jasmine to keep from falling. I didn't realize a guest had already arrived, and here I am looking like an idiot trying to walk in high heels.

A familiar laugh resounds from the suited man. I look again. It's only Nathan. Heat radiates from my cheeks as I right myself. His hair, still wet, is parted and combed smooth.

He buttons the jacket on his black suit and adjusts his grey striped tie. He chuckles. "Try not to do that with a tray of food."

I groan internally at the thought.

"The usual?" he asks Jasmine.

"Yep."

I cock my head to the side and toss them a questioning glance.

Nathan pounds his fist into his hand for effect. "I'm security."

So, Jasmine is the Banker's assistant, Nathan's security and I'm the waitress slash eye candy. Excellent. How did I end up with the butt end of this deal?

Roberta rushes into the living room and glances around, as though conducting an inspection, then rearranges the flowers in the vase on the end table. She steps back, assesses the bouquet, and seeming satisfied, spins around. When her gaze finds me, her mouth curls up into a familiar mocking smirk. "Look at you Rielle, don't you look—cute."

Not in the mood for her jabs, I ignore her.

"Roberta, give it a rest," Nathan says.

"What?" Roberta puffs out her bottom lip. "I was just paying her a compliment. Rielle, you do cheap and easy so well."

My cheeks heat to molten. If ever I wanted to speak it's now. I would start with "Go to hell, Roberta." Oh wait, we're already there. I bite my cheek to keep my mouth shut.

"Don't worry about Roberta," Nathan says. "She's just jealous that the Banker doesn't want to see her in that dress. Can't say she's ever been asked."

Roberta narrows her eyes and throws an acidic glare at Nathan. "Ah, Nathan." She has a glint in her eye, the type my baby sister used to get when she spied a balloon. "I wonder how Jessica's doing."

Crimson flushes Nathan's face. He balls his hands into fists, his knuckles turning bone white. He takes a step toward Roberta, but Jasmine throws her arm in front of him.

"Roberta, this is not the time," Jasmine says through clenched teeth.

"You're right. I'll save this for later. I have some hors d'oeuvres to prepare." She struts back to the kitchen.

My curiosity piqued, I forget about my horrid outfit for a moment. Who's Jessica?

Nathan paces back and forth across the room—a caged lion.

"Don't let her get to you. Just forget it," Jasmine says.

It takes Nathan about ten round trips of pacing before he regains his composure.

The Banker marches into the room, his hair slicked to his skull, and complains about the filthiness of the living room. It's absolutely spotless. Not a speck of dust anywhere. I don't know what he sees. Maybe complaining makes him feel better. Or perhaps he wants to set up Lydia and me to take the blame if the evening goes poorly.

When the doorbell chimes, I go rigid. I'm on. The Banker follows me to the door. Every step I take is careful, deliberate. Slipping on the glistening marble floor would be too easy in these heels. With a deep breath, I open the door and nod a greeting to three suited men, and present them with my faux smile.

The Banker invites them inside. They step over the threshold in glossy black shoes.

The Banker shakes the hand of the first man, with whom he seems to be acquainted. He's an old guy with silver hair and more wrinkles than my fingers have after I dunk them in bleach water all day.

The second man looks familiar. I've seen his mousy grey comb-over somewhere before, but I can't figure out where.

Neither smile, instead, they grunt stern greetings at the Banker.

The third man, the youngest of the three, is probably my parents' age. He offers the Banker a wide smile under bright, friendly eyes, and shakes his hand heartily. The Banker's triple chins lift and his eyes sparkle at the enthusiastic greeting.

They all find seats in the living room and engage in small talk while Jasmine mixes drinks at the wet bar and I go back and forth to the kitchen, bringing the various delicacies Roberta has prepared. It takes all my concentration to stay vertical in these heels, especially with food in hand.

Admiral Wrinkles, the oldest man, is generally unpleasant and chooses not to participate in most of the conversation. Sir Smiles-a-lot, the youngest man, actually says "thank you" when I serve him. Captain Comb-over is a pig whose eyes lock on my chest every time I bend over to offer him food. I glare at him, but he doesn't seem to notice, since his eyes never find my face. Jasmine clears her throat to get my attention and shakes her head slowly.

When they're finished eating, I stand against the wall and try to wipe the annoyance from my expression as I watch them. Why does Captain Comb-over look so familiar? I've seen him somewhere and not that long ago. He hasn't been at the Banker's before, at least not since I got here. Did I see him on the road? At one of the stops along the way? No. A picture—that's it. I've seen a picture of him. A billboard! The one in the Fort Worth parking lot promising, "Prosperity for all!" He's a politician.

Admiral Wrinkles checks his holo, then clears his throat and says, "Arthur, we have something of a sensitive nature we need to discuss with you."

The Banker leans forward in his chair. "Yes?"

"We would prefer that all superfluous persons vacate the room," Admiral Wrinkles says.

The Banker snaps his fingers and points toward the door. "Nathan, Jasmine, Rielle."

It's all over. I'm done!

I follow Nathan and Jasmine toward the door.

"Why don't you have that one stay?"

I glance over my shoulder. Captain Comb-over swirls the liquid in his glass, his eyes glued to me—not me—my body. He continues, "We may as well have something pleasant to look at while we conduct our business."

Nathan stops and eyes me, his face paling. Jasmine disappears into the kitchen.

The Banker flashes a smug grin. "You like her?" He lifts his brows conspiratorially. "Rielle *James*."

Three pairs of eyes dart to me, then back to the Banker. He nods knowingly. Admiral Wrinkles cracks a smile.

What was that all about? Why would the Banker tell them my name? And why does it matter to them?

Sir Smiles-a-lot shifts in his seat. "This is sensitive information. The fewer who know, the better."

"That one's nothing to worry about. I have complete control over her. Besides, she can't even speak," the Banker says. "Have a seat Rielle. Nathan, you're dismissed." He sweeps his hand to shoo Nathan from the room.

Conflict rages in Nathan's eyes.

"Now," the Banker barks.

Nathan leaves, head down.

"Rielle, sit." The Banker motions to the sofa. The only seat left is beside Captain Comb-over.

I swallow hard as I ease onto the cushion, my arm brushing Captain Comb-over's.

Sir Smiles-a-lot presses his lips together and runs a scrutinizing gaze over me, as though conflicted about whether or not to allow me to stay. He must determine I pose no threat because he looks away as Admiral Wrinkles begins.

"Arthur, we have need of your expertise. Are you familiar with the ECPU?"

The Banker picks up his highball glass off the coffee table. The caramel-coloured fluid sloshes and ice cubes plink against the glass. "Of course, it works on the system I designed. It's all one and the same." He sips his drink and straightens his back, looking down his nose at the other men.

Captain Comb-over forms a sly grin, revealing rows of yellowed teeth, like kernels of corn on the cob. "We hoped that was the case." He places his hand on my knee and squeezes.

My breathing hitches. I want to push his hand away, but the Banker's eyes narrow in warning. I fist my hands and lock them at my side.

Admiral Wrinkles pulls a bulging envelope from his suit jacket and hands it to the Banker. The Banker peels it open and thumbs through its contents—a thick wad of Proper bills. Propers replaced the dollar when the world's economies united. That was before they eliminated most physical money altogether and opted for chips instead. Clearly some people still have access to Proper currency.

The Banker's lips twitch and he shifts his expression, as if he's trying to look unimpressed even though anyone can see he's enamoured with the wad of bills. "First I need to know what you want before I can determine the price."

Captain Comb-over inches his hand higher on my thigh.

Bile climbs my throat.

"We want to ensure that things go our way," Captain Comb-over says, tilting his head toward the younger man.

The Banker sits back in his chair and lays his hands on the armrests. "That is a tall order."

"You can't do it?" Admiral Wrinkles asks.

"Oh, I can do it, but this will only suffice as a deposit." The Banker fingers the bills in the envelope again.

"You will have five times that upon completion," Captain Comb-over says.

The Banker takes a long sip of amber liquid. "Ten."

Whatever they want, he seems confident they'll pay any amount for it.

Admiral Wrinkles pounds his fist on the sofa. "Done. Then our business here is complete." He stands and motions to the others to do the same. "See to it that it's close, but not so close as to demand a recount. Perhaps sixty per cent?"

Captain Comb-over's fingers stroke my inner thigh. I clamp my teeth together, so tight my jaw aches. He stands and joins Admiral Wrinkles, and his hands are finally off of me.

I release a tremulous breath.

Like an over-turned beetle trying to right itself, the Banker heaves himself out of the chair. "I will set it up and notify you when it's ready. You can consider it a success."

Admiral Wrinkles strides toward the door, seeming anxious to leave. Captain Comb-over and Sir Smiles-a-lot each shake the Banker's hand and join Admiral Wrinkles at the door. I cross the room, open the door and nod politely as they march outside. The Banker and I stand in the open doorway watching their car pull out of the driveway. When they're gone, the Banker releases a long breath and his stomach falls forward.

I close the door and he turns to me, shaking his head. "Very disappointing, Rielle. Because I'm in a good mood, I won't take away any meals. Go. Get out of my sight."

What did I do wrong? Who cares. The pig, Captain Comb-over is gone. And I get dinner. That's all that matters.

With the torture finally over, I shuffle back to the kitchen, allowing my shoulders to relax. I'm done with good posture. I push the swinging door open and stride into the kitchen, kicking off my shoes as soon as the door closes behind me. If I could burn them or find some way to torture the Banker with them, I would.

Nathan and Jasmine jump up from the table.

I'm surprised to see them there. I figured they would have gone to their rooms to get comfortable, like I'm planning to do.

Jasmine wrings her hands, her face lined with worry. "Is everything okay?" I nod.

"What did they talk about?" Nathan asks.

Even if I could tell him, what would I say? It was hard to concentrate with that jerk touching me. They paid him money for something. What and why? I have no idea. It was as though they were speaking in code. I shrug.

Nathan releases a heavy sigh and runs his fingers through his hair.

Jasmine glances at Nathan and folds her arms. "Well, I'm glad everything is okay. You can bring the clothes to my room after you change."

Nathan leaves through the sliding glass door and I follow Jasmine upstairs. I turn on the shower and strip off the sleazy dress. Under the stinging hot water, I scrub make-up off my face and hairspray from my hair, and scour every spot where that pig touched me. I dump the dress and shoes on Jasmine's bed and hope never to see them again.

I return to my room to meet Lydia's worried, questioning gaze. "How'd it go?"

I roll my eyes. I hated it. I hate the Banker and his friends. Nothing's changed, except that I feel a little less human than I did yesterday. I resent being an actor in the Banker's pretentious games, a piece of flesh for his friend's amusement.

"Were they—nice—to you?"

Why does everyone seem so nervous?

I nod and plop down on my bed.

"You're sure?"

I nod, this time in quick, tight motions to emphasize my point. I survived and now it's over. I want to put it all out of my head and never think of it again.

And then I recall something Roberta said. I breathe on the window and, in the condensation, write "Jessica?" with my finger.

Lydia squints at the glass. "Oh, Jessica. She used to be my roommate." A hint of sadness tugs at her features.

I throw her a quizzical look.

"The Banker sold her before you came."

I can see there's more, but it probably casts someone in a poor light. Sometimes I wish Lydia were more of a gossip.

I breathe on the window again, but this time I write, "Nathan?"

She opens her mouth into an *O* and draws a breath. "Oh. I see. Nathan and Jessica had a thing going and the Banker found out." Lydia shifts uncomfortably on her bed and seems to be considering something. "Roberta told the Banker about it."

She drops her gaze and twirls a loose thread from her sheets around her finger as tears fill her eyes. "I didn't even get to say goodbye. I woke up one morning and she was gone."

CHAPTER NINE

The Grand Piano

IT'S THE END OF AUGUST. I THINK. HARD to tell what day it is. Could be Monday or Thursday or Groundhog Day. Every day's the same, nothing to look forward to and definitely nothing I'd want to look back on.

Get out of bed.

My sore legs refuse to budge.

Get out of bed.

"The dead one has risen," Roberta says as I step into the kitchen.

Roberta reminds me of a cat. Her eyes have the same shape. She would be the type of cat with a kindly old lady for an owner. The old lady would lovingly groom her and feed her cans of tuna fish. And then one day the old lady would die. A week later someone would find Roberta nibbling on her toes, having already eaten the juicier parts.

The Banker left yesterday for an overnight business trip, which makes this day better than most. Lydia studies the chore list he left.

I peek over her shoulder. The Banker is receiving an out of town guest, so he wants everything to sparkle. The entryway, main hall, living room and the largest guest bedroom must be cleaned before the end of the day.

We decide to divide and conquer. Lydia heads upstairs to clean the bedrooms and I work on the main floor. Starting with the living room, I dust, polish and vacuum. As I haul my cleaning supplies to the dining room, the doorbell rings. I wait for a second to see if anyone will come for it. I never like to answer the door because it usually involves talking and all I can do is stand there and look ridiculous.

The bell chimes again. I drop my supplies, smooth my hands over my dress and swing the door open. A gust of hot air hits my face.

"Arthur Hayes?" a young man in faded navy blue coveralls asks. Behind him, a white cube van with *Quality Movers* stamped across the side is parked on the driveway.

I step back and motion for him to come in. As I turn to go in search of the Banker's wife, high heels tick on marble stair treads. She descends the stairs in fitted white capris and strappy gold heels laced around her ankles. Her loosely-draped tangerine blouse falls off one shoulder, flowing as she moves, giving the illusion that she's floating rather than walking.

Her gaze falls on me, a heavy load that bears down on my shoulders. Her eyes soften, sadden for a split second before her mask of indifference returns. She looks past me. I step out of her way before she can walk into me. She smiles warmly at the man who clutches a holo in his hand.

The tangle of gold bangles on her wrists tinkle as she moves her fingers over her holo with a flourish. Sunlight beams through the door, catching facets of the diamonds and emeralds decorating her fingers. Her pinky finger sports a simple ring of thin gold topped with a crumb of ruby that looks out of place among the other jewels. A lot like me standing next to her.

"Where would you like it?" the man asks.

"Follow me." The Banker's wife waves her hand and the mover follows her.

I return to the dining room, pick up my rag and spray polish on the table. Why does her indifference bother me so much? I like it when the Banker ignores me. In fact, I find it comforting. But when his wife does the same, it sets off an ache in my chest. Perhaps I expect her, as a mother, to be like my mother, even though I rarely see her with her children. Mom was a warm blanket fresh from the dryer.

The movers carry several smaller pieces into the empty and seldom used solarium before hauling in a huge and oddly-shaped object covered with padding and sheets. It takes three of them and a dolly to move it. I'm glad I haven't cleaned the foyer floors. Their rubber soles leave a pattern of black tally marks all over the marble. I sigh. More work.

As I polish the hutch, I listen to the movers' clanking tools interspersed with a few colourful curses. They must be assembling whatever they brought in. They labour for nearly an hour before they carry their tools out the front door. The moment they're gone, the Banker's wife flies out the door to the garage and the house is quiet again. I listen for the grinding of the garage door opener and the gasoline-devouring roar of her car engine before creeping to the solarium, curious and thirsty for something new and out of the ordinary. Anything to break up the monotony.

I gasp and stop mid-step. Light streams into the room from floor-to-ceiling windows and captures the deep, rich wood grain of an exquisite grand piano placed in the centre of the room.

My fingers tap my thighs of their own accord, as though dancing over ivory keys. An instinct. A long time ago, I begged my parents for lessons and a piano to practice on. They came through. I never had to be reminded to practice. I played for pure pleasure.

The piano exerts a magnetic pull on me. I glance over my shoulder, then take a silent step toward it. Playing always relaxed me when I was stressed, cheered me when I was sad. I realize now what a sacrifice it must've been for us to keep the piano when it could've been traded for a few months' worth of food or a mortgage payment.

What I wouldn't give to sit on that leather bench and allow my fingers to dance over the keys, not to feel like a slave for a few moments. A few more steps and I'm so close I could touch it. A melody fills my thoughts—a song I wrote—its shadow rings in my ears.

Mom loved that song. I played it for her the night before Bank Security came for us. It had been another quiet dinner. Lots of sulking on my part. I finished ahead of my parents, but after Silas, who wolfed his food down and skulked off to his room. Intent on making my escape, running away from family time, I dashed upstairs. Mom called behind me, "Rielle, would you play your song for me while I do dishes?" I looked back at her. She stood in the doorway to the kitchen, a stack of dirty plates in her hands. More worry and fatigue burdened her eyes than usual.

I sighed with irritation, backed down the stairs and planted myself at the piano, positioning my feet over the pedals. I closed the music book in front of me. I didn't need it. My song was etched into my brain.

My fingers glided over the keys, smoothly, lightly. I played the song through twice, then pulled my hands away from the keyboard and waited. Mom always clapped at the end, but she didn't clap this time. She murmured in the kitchen. I couldn't make out what she was saying, but her voice sounded wrong.

I stood, went to the kitchen and found Dad holding Mom, her face buried in his neck.

"I'm so sorry," Dad whispered.

Between sobs, Mom said, "Don't say that. You did the right thing."

"I should've helped you and the kids first. Now it's too—"

"No! I'm proud of you." Mom lifted her head to look into Dad's eyes. "Never think otherwise." Mom tensed as she caught sight of me. Dad's arms fell from around her and she wiped her tears away, attempting to form a smile.

"What's going on?" I asked.

Dad opened his mouth to speak, but Mom cut him off. "Same old thing." She walked over to me and threw her arms around me. "You know how much I love you, right?"

"Yeah. Me, too." I stared at Dad over Mom's shoulder as she patted me on the back. He stared at the floor, mouth turned down. Mom squeezed me harder.

"Are you sure everything's okay?" I asked.

"Everything is going to be fine," Dad said.

Mom stepped back and took my face between her hands. "You're my strong girl."

It's easy to see in hindsight. They knew what was coming. They lied to me.

I swallow the lump in my throat. How could they just stand around crying and do nothing about it? They just let it all happen.

I slowly reach for the piano's crystalline veneer. I can almost hear crisp, clear notes rising from the beautiful instrument. I yank back my hand, hold it to my chest. I'd be punished for sure if I even breathed on it. I back out of the solarium, still gaping at the piano. It's difficult to be so close to something, and yet, a million miles from it. To see and never touch.

I get a bucket of soapy water and go to the entryway to scour away the movers' scuff marks. I find myself scrubbing the same spot over and over as I daydream about which songs I'd play. For the rest of the day, I ache for the piano as though it's a sixth member of my family.

Late afternoon, the Banker returns from his trip with a suitcase full of new toys for Lily and Caleb. They tear into the packaging and scatter parts all over the living room—interlocking bricks, doll brushes, toy guns for action figures and roughly a million twist ties that anchored them inside their boxes. By dinner, Lydia and I have cleaned up what looked like a toy store explosion.

After choking down some sort of stew concoction, I slip into pajamas and lie on my bed, sweltering and watching the light fade from the ceiling. Lydia climbs into bed about an hour later. The whir of the oscillating fan and Lydia's rhythmic breathing both lull me. As I drift toward sleep, thunder rumbles in the distance.

A cool gust of wind blows through the open window, cutting the sultry night air and raising goose bumps on my arms. I lift my arm to my face and stare through the darkness at the strange, foreign little bumps. With all this heat, I forgot what goose-bumps looked like.

Silvery lightning flickers, then darkness returns. Thunder growls again. Closer this time. I crawl to the window, press my face to the screen and allow the cool air to caress my cheeks. The smell of rain gushes through the mesh—cut grass and damp wood, fresh and heavy.

A few raindrops slap the scalloped oak leaves. A few more patter down. And then the clouds empty an ocean of rain over top of us. Thunder crashes, lightning flashes and the wind whips a fine mist through the window onto my face.

Beyond our bedroom door the stairs groan, each in turn. Then the floor creaks. I tiptoe to the door, open it and peer into the hall. Roberta gasps and throws her hand over her chest. Her surprise transforms into a glower. "What are you doing up?"

I could ask her the same question. Lightning illuminates her wet hair and pajamas, the shoes on her feet. What was she doing outside at this time of night?

I ignore her question, close the door and return to bed. Weird. Why would Roberta go out during a storm like that? I sigh. Who knows? It's not like I've ever understood Roberta, why she treats us like dirt when she's when she's a Contract, too.

I close my eyes, pull the sheet over me and breathe deeply of the cool, misty air—cleansing, invigorating, optimistic even, as if the rain could somehow set everything right. Maybe it'll wash away all the evil in the world and I'll wake up in the morning at home in my own bed.

Snow falls in my dreams again, but this time each flake carries its own musical note, forming a beautiful and painful melody. Alyssa holds out her arms to me. I can't reach her.

My chest aches and my arms feel empty when I wake to another day. Why can't I just go to sleep one night and never wake up? While most people probably hope for a long life, I hope for an early death. How can I spend the next 70 years like this?

"Good morning, Rielle. You're not looking too good," Lydia says.

I draw a deep breath and shake my head.

"The Banker wants to meet with all of us early. You'll have to hurry and get ready."

As if our days aren't long enough already. I force myself out of bed, pull a clean dress over my head, wash up and fix my hair.

The Banker is waiting for us in the kitchen, tapping his foot as we fall into line. He glares at us with his small eyes, black beads sewn tightly onto a pillow. His stomach seems to protrude more with each passing week. It looks like he'll be giving birth to triplets any day.

The kitchen door opens and a young man, maybe a couple of years older than me, strides confidently into the room. He smiles, a light and easy grin, almost playful, then sweeps his gaze down the line of Contracts. His blue eyes settle on mine for a moment then move on to Lydia.

The creased pant legs of his dark denim and the crispness of his pinstriped dress shirt—all too perfect, as idealistic as a magazine cover. He stands straight and tall, shoulders squared, beside the Banker with his hands clasped behind his back.

The Banker clears his throat. "My nephew, Justin, has come to stay with us while he attends graduate school. He'll be living in the suite on the south end of the house. I expect you all to treat him with the utmost respect. His words are as good as mine. I don't want to hear of any disobedience."

Wonderful—this nephew gets to order us around, too. Just what I need. Another master. We can barely keep up with the Banker's whims, now we get the privilege of placating his spoiled nephew.

The Banker continues by introducing all the Contracts to his nephew. He ends by pointing at me. "I overpaid for that one. They claim she was able to speak before she came here. Perhaps it's for the best. They're full of nonsense anyway.

"I am going to show Justin around the property. Nathan, get his belongings out of the car and take them to his room. Lydia and Rielle, make sure the room is absolutely spotless and unpack his things. I want this to feel like home. Roberta, there will be one more person for every meal, ensure there is a place setting for him and plenty to eat. Get to it!"

We disband. Lydia and I head straight to the guest room, still spotless from yesterday and dust the bookshelves and smooth the bedding to look busy. Nathan squeezes through the door with two large suitcases, one suspended from each arm. He tosses them both on the bed. We unload them, refold the clothes and organize them in the drawers.

Around midnight another thunderstorm blows in, bringing cooler air with it. I dream about camping at Mille Lacs with my family—a happy dream for once. Silas drifts on an air mattress, while Alyssa plays in the sand on the beach, her bright orange life jacket reflecting the sun's glare. I jump into chilly water. The cold penetrates my thick hair, cooling my scalp. I float, feeling nearly weightless. Tendrils of my hair sway like seaweed.

The alarm clock yanks me from paradise. I stare at the white ceiling, willing myself to get out of bed. The coolness of last night's storm evaporated with my dream.

"Is this heat ever going to end?" Lydia, still in bed, stares at the ceiling too, her arms and legs spread like Da Vinci's *Vitruvian Man.*

I suppress a smile. I know it's bad if Lydia resorts to complaining. I roll off my mattress, already sweating.

"It's cool for five minutes while it rains and then the sun comes out and it turns into a sauna. I think hell might be directly under Texas."

I chuckle, glad that I'm not the only one who hates this place with a passion.

We're assigned to clean the entryway tile grout with toothbrushes and bleach.

Yay. My favourite.

At least there's air conditioning in the main house. After a couple of hours, my knees ache from the cold tile beneath them. I long for a reason to stand and stretch, so when footsteps thump toward us, I seize the opportunity to lift myself off the floor.

Great. The nephew. Here come the demands. Although, at this point, I'd welcome any excuse to stop scrubbing.

His blue eyes glint as he smiles. "Good morning, ladies."

"Good morning," Lydia says.

Good? How could any morning here be good?

He looks at me, waiting for my reply. One side of my mouth lifts; that's as much of a smile as I can manage.

"I'm Justin. In case you forgot." He extends his hand to Lydia. She throws me a wary sideways glance and shakes his hand.

"I met a lot of people yesterday. Could you please remind me of your names?" he says.

"I'm Lydia, and this is Rielle."

He holds his hand out to me. "She can't introduce herself?" He clasps my hand in his firm grip and gives it two shakes.

"She can't speak, sir." Lydia shifts from one foot to the other, locks her hand onto her opposite arm.

"Oh. I forgot." His lips curl into a crooked smile. "She can't, or she won't?"

"Is there something I can do for you?" Lydia asks, clearly trying to steer the nephew away from that sore subject.

"No, just trying to get acquainted." He strides away.

We go back to scrubbing grout lines.

Lydia dips her toothbrush in the bucket and swishes. "He seems nice. Maybe he won't be so bad."

I shake my head. I don't like him. What did he mean "can't" or "won't?" What kind of a question is that?

The Banker pulls out all the stops for the next few evenings. He must be desperate to impress Justin, ordering complex dishes—beef wellington, *coq au vin*, a soufflé—which means that in an addition to our regular duties, we're required to help Roberta in the kitchen. And she's in a miserable mood. I think she's nervous she'll make a mistake by burning something or not seasoning it right; at least that's what I'm nervous about.

While Lydia and I eat dinner with the other Contracts, the metal-on-metal whir of the sliding glass door silences the pleasant, hushed conversations. The Banker throws open the door so hard it slams against the sill.

"Lydia! Rielle!"

I swallow a mouthful of dry biscuit. It sticks in my throat. I force the lump down and it hits my stomach like a brick. The Banker's anger is so much worse when it catches me off guard.

"Get in here!"

CHAPTER TEN

Everyone Knows Banks are Generous and Kind

COLOUR DRAINS FROM LYDIA'S FACE. We rise to our feet and walk into the kitchen together, heads down. I brace myself.

"Of all the good-for-nothing! Lazy!"

What did we do? I mentally scramble through our chore list. Did we forget to do something? No, we did everything he asked us to do. I glance at Lydia; her eyes are glassy. I hate when he yells at Lydia. It distresses me more than when he yells at me. I want to step between the two of them, to shield her from his anger.

He marches out of the kitchen. We rush to keep up as he waddles toward the large urn decorating the entryway, lifts it out of the way and points to the floor underneath. "What is this?"

I can't see anything. What did we do? Is it damaged? I stare at the urn, searching for damage, then glance at Lydia. Does she see anything? Lydia stands as still as death, except for her chest, pumping with quick, shallow breaths.

The Banker yanks Lydia by the hair. She stumbles forward and he shoves her toward the floor. She falls to her knees. As I reach for her, the Banker traps me in his biting glower. I stop short. He slams Lydia's face to the floor, rubs it against the tile. "Filth!" Spit droplets spray from his mouth.

I strain my eyes, searching for the filth. A button-sized dull spot spoils the stretch of gleaming marble.

"I'm sorry. I forgot to move it. I'm really sorry." Lydia's voice trembles.

Guilt seizes me with the same force as the Banker's grip on Lydia's hair. My face should be the one smashed against the tile. I should be the one to apologize. I cleaned that area. I'm the one who forgot to move the urn.

"You damned lazy Contracts. I feed you, I house you and this is the thanks I get? Clean the foyer again—and do it right this time!" He lets go of her hair and storms upstairs.

I help Lydia up and lead her to the pantry to retrieve our supplies. In the privacy of the pantry Lydia allows her tears to fall. I wrap my arms around her, wanting to tell her I'm sorry, that it should have been me with my face to the floor. She shakes with sobs. I pull away and point upstairs.

Lydia wipes her tears away, her cheek already swelling and a bruise purpling beneath her skin. "No, the Banker said both of us."

I point to my chest. This is my fault, not hers.

"Rielle, we're in this together. I'm not going to sleep while you work. You'd do the same for me."

I nod, of course I would. Lydia is my family now.

The job took most of the day, the first time. We scrub. Our tears mix with the bleach water. Exhausted and discouraged, we make sure it'll pass inspection this time. The kitchen clock reads 3:12 when we pass through to put our supplies away. We drop into bed still wearing our clothes, and it seems like only seconds later, the alarm buzzes.

Time to start again.

After a few days the Banker calms down, and things settle into their normal pace. Apparently, school hasn't started yet for the nephew, so he sleeps in everyday, wanders the grounds in a fuzzy brown bathrobe and plays with his holo. He likes to drink root beer and eat cheese-dusted tortilla chips while he watches the deep screen. At least he's tidy. I check for crumbs but never find any.

He ventures out to the backyard basketball court daily. He shoots hoops in his bathrobe and boxer shorts, announcing his plays as if he's a sports broadcaster. "He shoots, he scores, the crowd goes wild. Woo!"

What an arrogant idiot.

Whenever a Contract happens by, he tries coaxing them to play with him. Today it's our turn. "Lydia, you play basketball?"

Lydia stops and looks at me. I shrug.

"No—no, I don't play basketball."

"Rielle, you play?"

I shake my head. I would love to play, but that's not an option.

"Come on ladies, I'll be easy on you." He smiles and dribbles the ball between his legs.

We keep walking. It irritates me that he assumes he's better than us. We could probably beat him, but we'd have to throw the game because he wouldn't want to lose to Contracts. Smug jerk.

I hate the nephew—Justin, or whatever his stupid name is. We never get to rest, and this guy spends his whole day loafing around. Leisure time—fun, boredom—what's that? I wouldn't know anymore. Maybe someday I can forget about those Friday nights when my family watched movies together. How Mom would make popcorn and we'd spread blankets and pillows on the floor, and sack out in our pajamas. The violent longing leaves a bitter taste in my mouth.

Maybe, when I forget, it won't bother me so much. Will I ever forget? Part of me wants to, but another part of me wants to hold onto every precious memory of my freedom. Knowing that I will never get to do any of those things again brings on a new bout of despair. I really hate the nephew. I avoid him if I can.

I knock on the nephew's door. His room is next up for cleaning.

"Come in."

He's at his desk, hunched over his holo, his gaze intent on the image. Behind him, a news program blares on the deep screen. The news anchor's three-dimensional form, from the waist up, sits atop Justin's dresser. It looks as if her bottom half is buried inside the mahogany drawers.

He doesn't turn off the program. Strange. The Banker is quick to turn off the deep screen when I'm around. Perhaps the nephew doesn't know the rule.

I pretend to ignore the program as I strip bed linens.

"…bloody protest in front of the OneEarth Bank offices in New York," the anchor says.

I shake a pillow out of its case.

"What began as a peaceful protest ended with two dead and at least eighteen injured as a group protesting what they call 'the enslavement of American citizens,' turned violent when Bank Security opened fire on the protesters."

I shove the pillowcases into the laundry basket, grab a rag and move to the dresser where the deep screen base is mounted. I slowly rub the rag over the wood.

"Samuel Brenay, a OneEarth Bank representative, is in the studio with us today. Welcome Mr. Brenay."

Samuel Brenay grins. "Thank you for having me, Janet."

"Mr. Brenay, what is your response to the allegations these protesters are making?" the anchor asks.

"Well, Janet, these accusations are unfounded, completely preposterous." He releases a dismissive chuckle. "The banks are not enslaving people. In fact, their actions are hugely benevolent. They don't want young people suffering for their parents' mistakes. The Community Service Contracts are an effort to rehabilitate them, so they can be reintroduced into society."

The anchor rolls a pen between her fingers. "But critics are saying you haven't released any Contracts yet."

"We are unsure at this time how long the rehabilitation process will take. We are constantly evaluating this. But please remember, these aren't people like you and me. They've been brainwashed into thinking we are the enemy. They're dangerous right now, and it would be irresponsible to set them loose in our communities. We care about the safety of the American people and we are doing everything in our power to preserve our way of life."

"Thank you for your time, Mr. Brenay. In other news. How the ECPU will benefit voters in the upcoming presidential election…"

The news is just the way I remember it. Depressing. I don't want to hear anymore. It's somewhat encouraging to know that a few people have noticed what's happening to us, but they were shot for taking a stand. The lies that Brenay guy is spreading turns my stomach. Lydia and I are so dangerous. Yeah, right. Maybe the Banker was doing me a favour by keeping the media from me.

"Depressing, isn't it?" the nephew asks, startling me.

I shrug. I'm not going to admit to listening. Why would he find it depressing? It's working out just peachy for him. Maybe he found the protesters depressing.

I scoop up his dirty clothes, piling them on top of the sheets. I pivot to leave, but turn back to eye his grubby bathrobe, the one he wears for everything including playing basketball. It has to smell ripe by now. I point to the pile of laundry, then to his robe.

"You think it needs washing?" he asks.

I nod.

A playful grin spreads across his face. He lifts the lapel to his nose and inhales deeply. "No, I think we can get another week out of it."

I let a repulsed gasp escape my lips. Probably unwise, but I couldn't help myself. I sweep out of the room.

Disgusting idiot.

I close the nephew's door behind me, balancing the full laundry basket on my hip. At the end of the hall, the Banker's office door eases open. I press myself into the shadowed doorway to the nephew's room. Roberta hurries out of the office with a small, red metallic object dangling from her fingers. She shoves it into her pocket. Strange. Contracts aren't allowed in the Banker's office. This is the second time I've seen her skulking about. Is she up to something? Or perhaps the Banker's favourite Contract has special permission.

A few days later, I'm polishing the silver in the dining room when the nephew walks into the solarium and plunks himself down in front of the piano. The piano that no one has ever played. The one I wish every day I could play.

He's finally put on some real clothes. It must've been exhausting for him.

The nephew taps the keys, high, low, high, low and then a clipped staccato version of "Mary had a Little Lamb". I wrinkle my nose at the sound of it. He's desecrating that fine instrument.

I rub a cloth over a tarnished sugar bowl, recalling the hours I spent practicing music, all the lessons and nerve-wracking recitals. I look down at my hands, red and calloused, my fingernails broken and stubby. Once, these hands made beautiful music. Seems like a million years ago

Hopelessness envelopes me, crushing my chest. Those dreams, their passion, their consuming fire in my life, are now extinguished. After all the time and emotion poured into them, the only thing these hands will ever do is scrub floors and disinfect bathrooms. Tears well, but I push them back. I'm a captured bird, wings clipped.

I sense eyes on me. For a moment, I forgot that I'm not alone. I lift my gaze to find Justin's stare fixed on me.

Oh, not good.

I scrub the sugar bowl more vigorously, my heart racing and my cheeks hot.

"What do you think of my amazing musical skills?" he calls.

They suck, just like you.

Maybe it's a good thing I don't speak. Who knows what would spring from my mouth. I work up what I hope is a genuine-looking smile and shrug.

"Do you know how to play?"

I pause. Should I be honest? I don't want to share this part of me with him. Him of all people. But if he found out I'm lying, that would be bad too. There's no good way to answer that question, so I give him a non-committal shrug.

"You do play."

I keep my head down and concentrate on applying silver polish to the coffee urn in a circular motion.

"Why don't you come over here and play something. I don't think this piano has ever been used."

That's true. I itch to touch the keys, but I shake my head. If the Banker found out, I'd be punished.

"Why not?"

This is a game for him. Pressing my lips into a tight grin, I hold up my cleaning rag and return to work.

His voice lowers. "My uncle said you have to listen to me. I'm asking you to play." His smile fades, replaced by an expression I can't read. Does he feel badly ordering me around? No, he's probably just annoyed that I didn't play the first time he asked.

I tighten my fist around the rag. My heart thumps erratically, both with fear and excitement at the prospect of playing, and at the thought of the nephew—Justin—watching me. I set my rag down on the table and walk to the solarium. I have to play.

As I approach, I wipe my hands against my skirt. It would be a shame to soil the keys with my grimy hands. Justin stands, leaving the bench empty for me. I stop, taking in the beauty before me—the piano and the boy. His designer clothes are perfectly pressed—obviously Lydia's work—and his clean, honey-brown hair is combed down in the back, but intentionally messy at the bangs. With only a bench length between us, I can smell him—cedar and vanilla.

I can smell myself too—ammonia and sweat. I drop my head and inspect my dress. It's smudged with dirt and cleaning fluid. Even if it were clean, it's plain, utilitarian. To sit at this beautiful piano next to this handsome boy offers a study in contrasts. Pearls and pigs, mud and diamonds come to mind. I ease myself down onto the bench, while trying desperately to find a way out of this.

He waits, his brows pulled together, seemingly puzzled by the delay. I correct my posture, lengthen my neck and hang my fingers over the keys. The ivory cools my fingertips. I hold my breath. I don't want to give my gift over to this boy.

"Rielle!" Roberta screeches from the hall. I gasp and jump. If she sees me sitting here—

Justin groans. "Roberta."

I spring to my feet, dash back to the dining room and snatch up my cleaning rag before she rounds the corner.

Roberta hitches her hand on her hip. "You're not done in here yet? What's taking so long? I'm serving the family dinner on the patio. Go help Lydia clean the table and chairs. They're dusty. And do it quickly. Dinner is in an hour."

Justin taps middle C. "Hey Roberta, that's a lovely singing voice you've got there."

Roberta stiffens. "Oh, I'm sorry, sir, I didn't realize you were in here. Sorry for disturbing you."

I bite my lip to stifle a grin, then gather my supplies and dart toward the kitchen. I cast a glance over my shoulder at the piano and the boy sitting at it. He looks disappointed. He must be bored.

That night we have our dinner inside. The Banker doesn't want us eating anywhere near him and his family. It's a nice change of pace to sit in chairs and at a table. Jonah starts in with a new set of jokes. With the exception of Roberta, who wolfs down her food and darts upstairs, we all laugh quietly and enjoy each other's company. Nathan even cracks a smile. Does he still miss Jessica? Was their relationship serious or just a crush the Banker overreacted to? All questions I will never get to ask.

CHAPTER ELEVEN

The Eraser

AS WEEKS PASS, THE HUMID WEATHER THAT PLAGUED US all summer subsides. It's laundry day, and Lydia and I have a system worked out. I gather laundry, we both fold and she irons. I'm hopeless when it comes to ironing. The clothes end up more wrinkled than when I started.

I carry my basket to the Banker's bedroom to collect dirty clothes and towels. I knock on the door and wait. I knock again. When no one answers, I twist the knob and step inside.

It takes a few seconds for my eyes to adjust to the dark room. A strange earthy odour thickens the air, heavy and moist, a hint warmer than the rest of the house. I cross the room to draw curtains and open shades, picking up the dirty laundry littering the floor and shoving it into the basket.

I haul my heaping basket into the bathroom to find the granite counter strewn with empty prescription bottles and a scattered mosaic of colourful pills. The Banker's wife usually keeps her small pharmacy tucked neatly into the corner of the counter.

The Banker is such a neat freak that I'm surprised he'd let his bedroom get so dishevelled. Should I tidy the counter before I finish gathering the laundry? No. I'll come back once I get the load going.

I shuffle into the darkened shower room to retrieve towels. I step into a puddle. My feet slide forward and I lose my balance. I grab the towel bar to keep from falling. I flip on the light and lift my foot. A coat of syrupy crimson fluid paints the sole of my shoe. I lower my foot. Red covers the whole floor.

The Banker's wife leans against the wall, her clothing blood drenched and her cheeks streaked with blood and tears. Deep gashes criss-cross the back of her hands and trail around her wrists. A razor blade and tweezers, both blood encrusted, lie next to her.

I gasp and freeze. Is she dead? I drop to my knees beside her, blood soaking into my dress.

Her eyes pop open.

She's alive!

I pull clean towels down from the towel bar and wrap them around her hands. Red soaks through the pristine white cloth.

"Leave me alone, Rielle," she whispers, her eyes droopy and glassy. "I deserve to die."

I shake my head. I need to slow the bleeding and get help. My hands tremble as I apply pressure to her wounds. She winces and tears stream down her cheeks. She stares into my eyes. "I'm just like you, you know." She slurs her words.

I doubt that.

"I just wanted to get it out but I couldn't find it. I want the chip out!" She tries to shout, but it's only a strained whisper. "My parents are in prison, like yours. It's our deep, dark family secret. I was already married to Arthur, but my dad said, 'don't take it Nina, no amount of money is worth your soul.' So I took the chip and I live in this mansion and my parents rot in prison." Her body convulses with sobs as I wrap her hands tighter. I place my hand on her shoulder and force eye contact.

"My parents were right." She closes her eyes. "They were right. They were right."

I run from the room. Dashing down the stairs, I plough headlong into someone and fall backward. The Banker is home early.

"Rielle! What are you doing?" His eyes widen as he looks me over. "What is going on?"

I jump to my feet and dart upstairs, back-tracking over my own bloody footprints, toward his bedroom. He follows. I turn the corner into the bathroom and he gasps.

"Nina? No!" He hovers over her, staring. He doesn't move. Is he too stunned to act—too horrified to know what to do next? He glances away from her and his gaze grows distant, cold.

"Go get Nathan." His voice is calm and dull.

Shouldn't he call an ambulance?

The Banker grinds his teeth. "Go!"

I stumble over my own feet, sliding down the last few stairs, and run to the kitchen. Roberta opens her mouth to comment, but promptly snaps it shut.

Through the glass door I spy Nathan atop a ladder, pruning a tree at the back of the yard. I fling open the sliding glass door and sprint across the yard. The moment he sees me, he scrambles down the ladder and runs toward me.

"Rielle, what happened to you?" He clutches my arms, searching for a source for all the blood.

I shake my head and point back toward the house.

"Did someone hurt you?" His voice turns stern.

There's no time for questions. I grab his hand and tow him back to the house. I lead him upstairs and into the master suite. His reaction mirrors that of the Banker.

"Don't stand there gawking. Carry her to the car. Now!" the Banker shouts.

I pull a blanket off the bed and wrap it around Nina's shivering form. Nathan gathers her into his arms. I follow the Banker as far as the entrance to the garage and watch Nathan ease her into the car and secure the seatbelt around her.

The Banker strides to the driver's side, his chins quivering. "Not a word to anyone! And I want that mess erased before I get back." With that, he cranks the gasoline engine. The scent of exhaust sullies the air and then the car squeals out of the garage. I stand there for a moment, unable to move, staring after them as the garage door closes and cuts them off from sight.

I lift my quaking hands, turn them palm up. Nina's blood is all over me. Adrenaline pulses through my veins. A deep breath. Get a hold of yourself. Erase the mess. The Banker's words ring. Erase the memory of this. That's my job.

Nathan turns to me. I meet his concerned gaze for a moment, then I look away. I walk upstairs, clutching the railing for support. The smell of blood hits me like a backhand slap when I enter the bathroom. I twist on the sink taps. Leaning on my elbows, I plunge my blood-caked hands under the warm, gushing water and watch streaks of crimson swirl down the drain.

Finally alone, I allow a few tears to escape. They fall into the sink, mingling with the blood. Nina's revelation dominates my thoughts. Her parents were like mine. How many times have I wished my life would end? I never considered ending it myself. Did that mean I still held out hope that I'd see my family again? I just can't give up on Silas and Alyssa like that.

I dry my hands and inspect the aftermath. Where to start—how to start? I begin by organizing the pills, like a preschool sorting game. Pinks with pinks. Green capsules with green capsules. And then I attempt to match them to their appropriate bottles. Perhaps they can figure out what she took by calculating what remains. As I sort, Nathan walks in, lugging an awkward contraption, cords and hoses and a pile of rags.

"I thought you might need the carpet cleaner. It was out in the shed."

Perfect. I was wondering how I'd "erase" blood from white carpeting. I flash Nathan an uneasy smile in thanks.

He sets down the carpet cleaner, grabs a rag and wets it under the faucet. "Rielle, what happened here? Did she hurt you?"

I shake my head and peer down at myself. Blood crusts my arms and blackens my dress where I knelt next to Nina. From the hem, blood drips and snakes down my legs. It's probably hard to tell if I'm hurt or not. I must look like something out of a horror movie.

Nathan picks up my left arm. I try to pull it away, but his grip tightens. With the warm cloth, he wipes off the blood, inspecting as he goes. He moves on to the right arm and then on to my face, gently stroking the cloth across my cheek.

I relax for a moment as he washes away the blood. And for one moment I don't feel alone. It reminds me of Alyssa when Mom used to wash food from her face. She tried to wriggle away, but grinned at the same time. To be taken care of, even for a few seconds, soothes my soul. When he finishes, he seems satisfied that I'm not hurt.

"I want you to answer my question. What happened up here?"

I pick up the bloody razor blade and trace it over the tops of my hands and down my wrists to demonstrate.

He clenches his teeth and the outline of his jaw muscles tightens. "Damn it, Rielle, *tell* me. I know you can talk. Lydia said you talk in your sleep."

I do? She never mentioned it. I guess since I refuse to speak consciously, it's coming out unconsciously. Well, in any case, the Banker said not to talk about this and that shouldn't be a problem for me. I turn away from Nathan and reach for a rag.

He sighs. He picks up a rag too and squats down to help sop blood off the floor. This is my job. I touch his shoulder and shake my head.

"I'm going to help you clean up, Rielle. You don't have to do this by yourself."

I shake my head assertively. Why should both of us suffer?

"Staying." He sets his lips in a firm line.

Okay, he looks determined. Help would be nice, especially since I don't know how to run the carpet cleaner. So, I wipe the counter and cabinets while he works on the floor.

That afternoon, he cleans and recleans the carpet, dumping out bucket after bucket of bloody water until no more red will come out. I scrub the tile grout with bleach to remove the bloodstains. We erase the incident. Nathan packs up his equipment and leaves without saying another word. At dinner,

Roberta implores Nathan and me to share our secret, but tonight, he's as quiet as I am.

I spend extra time in the shower, scrubbing away the day's evils. Roberta bangs at the door, but I ignore her.

I sit on the shower floor, wrap my arms around my legs and weep as the water pours over my head. So many things are wrong here. My home was a place of peace and hope. This is a place of turmoil and despair. Everything here is dying—the plants from the lack of rain, the Banker's wife and parts of me.

One world. One currency. One bright future.

CHAPTER TWELVE

Under New Management

I FALL ASLEEP AND SUFFER NIGHTMARES about my parents locked in a cold, dank prison. I never imagined them that way before, but thanks to Nina, that's all I can think about. Mom cries while Dad picks at the lock. He keeps saying, "I'm not giving up."

In the morning after we line up for our day's assignments, Justin arrives and informs us that the Banker will be gone for a few days. He's leaving Justin in charge.

Justin divvies out jobs. Even the boys get indoor work today. Finally, he comes to me. "Rielle, you're needed in the music room. I'd like to learn to play piano."

My mouth pops open. Is he serious? He can't be. There's got to be a catch. I glance at Lydia questioningly. She shrugs. It's the easiest assignment I've had since arriving here and something I'm actually good at. A shock of excitement rolls through me. I get to spend my day at the piano!

The other Contracts disband in various directions, except for Nathan. He looks at me, his eyes wide. Why? Should I be alarmed? He glances from me to Justin, then stalks through the kitchen door.

"You ready?" Justin asks.

I nod, far less confident than I felt moments ago.

I follow Justin to the music room. He plucks a music book from the bookshelf, then sits at the piano and places the book on the music rack. I join him on the bench and flip to the first lesson. Smiling to myself, I survey the teddy bears that decorate the first page. Justin should enjoy this. Now, how to begin without speaking?

But he speaks first. "So you do play."

I draw my brows together.

He chuckles. "Your fingers gave you away."

I lift my hands and inspect my fingers, rough and calloused, not like any pianist's hands I've ever seen.

"Not the way they look. The way they move. Sometimes you move your fingers like you're playing imaginary keys. I remember my mom doing that when I was a kid."

I clench my hands into fists. I was doing that? I don't like Justin noticing. He leans closer to me, as though to tell me a secret. "I wonder if we can get you to talk today, Rielle."

I lean away from him. Lydia has told him I can't speak. What makes him think this is a choice and not a disability? Maybe he thinks I don't speak because I'm traumatized.

Now I get it. I'm a project, something to satisfy his boredom. He must be a psychology student. If he thinks he's going to fix this broken little Contract, he's got another thing coming.

I shake my head and point at the book, matching notes to keys, expecting him to do the same when I finish.

"Why don't you speak?"

I roll my eyes and sigh. What is his problem? Does he want a piano lesson or not? I tap my finger on the book.

He smiles. "If you aren't going to talk, could you at least play me a song?"

Of course, I can play him a song. I sit up tall and elegant, extend my arms and drape my fingers over the keys. From the corner of my eye, I watch his anticipation at what's coming. I suppress a devious grin and plunk out the same staccato "Mary had a Little Lamb" he played the first time he tried to lure me to the piano.

I internally apologize to the piano. It's a betrayal to play this beautiful instrument that way, but I'm not giving the Banker's nephew the satisfaction of hearing what I can really do.

He throws up his hands in surrender. "Okay, I get it. Teach away."

I circle my finger around a middle C in the book, then touch the key on the piano and the lesson moves on without any more trouble. I've never taught anyone to play, but I enjoy it.

The next day holds the same routine. Justin goads me to speak, I stubbornly resist, and he concedes to the lesson.

On day three of the Banker's absence, I wake up looking forward to the next lesson. Finally, something I can do well—one thing I don't have to struggle through. He doesn't even try to get me to speak; we just get to work.

Part way through the lesson he pulls his hands off the keys, resting them on his legs, and watches me tap out a few notes. "How can you possibly play with such small hands?"

I shrug. It's never been a problem. They aren't that small.

"I mean, look." He holds up his hand and flays his fingers. He grasps my wrist and pulls it up to his, pressing our palms together. I smile. His hands are a lot bigger. Folding his fingers over mine, he looks into my eyes, holding me in his warm gaze.

My heart speeds. I want to look away, but for a moment I can't. I yank my hand away and point to the book. His eyes don't leave me. He brings his hand up to my cheek. "Rielle, what happened here?" His fingers graze the pink scar that adorns my cheek. I flinch away from his touch. "Did you get that after you got here?"

I suck in a breath and tap my finger on the book.

"Did someone hurt you?"

I bite my bottom lip.

"It was my uncle, wasn't it?" Justin's cheeks flush.

I play out the notes on the page and point again. He ignores my pointing and stares at me. I look at him, pleading with my eyes for him to let this go. Why does it matter to him?

He turns away from me and peers out the window for what seems like an eternity. He gets up off the bench. "I'll see you tomorrow."

He walks out of the room.

Justin's workload is so much lighter than the Banker's that by the fourth day, everyone is in good spirits. Even Roberta is less witchy than usual. It'll end soon, though; the Banker's due back tomorrow. Will his wife come home with him? Is she okay? Every time I pass their bedroom, the image of her bloodied hands flashes in my mind—along with her revelation about her parents.

I help Lydia make sure everything is clean and tidy, and then I settle into the music room for another lesson.

As I wait for Justin on the piano bench, I silently touch my fingers to the keys, hearing each note of my song, Mom's favourite, in my head.

Justin rounds the corner into the room, out of breath. "I'm ready." He slides onto the bench, nestles against my side and flashes me a playful grin. The scent of vanilla and cedar rolls off his wet hair. I breathe it in and then edge away from him. He sidles toward me until he's beside me again. I scoot all the way to the end of the bench, but he follows.

My heart stutters, hard and fast, and then seems to stop for a moment. He's too friendly. It makes me jittery. I jump to my feet and throw him a hard glare.

He chuckles. "Okay, okay." He moves over, takes my hand and tugs me back onto the seat. "I'm confident you're going to speak to me today."

Keep dreaming. I shake my head, push him over until he reaches the edge of the bench, then I flip open the book.

"I'm upsetting you."

Definitely. But I ignore him.

"I'm sorry, Rielle. I'm just kidding around with you. I don't really have any friends here and I guess I'm starved for company. I'm not going to hurt you."

I inhale deeply and begin again. Pointing a quaking finger at the book, I will the trembling to stop. I touch the keys as usual, Justin following suit. I try not to look him in the eye, but his enthusiasm is gone. He's been nice to me. I need to pull it together.

My fingers rest on the keys as he pivots to face me. He reaches over and picks up my hand, wrapping his warm fingers around mine. "Rielle, I'm not going to hurt you, please believe me."

A high-pitched screech erupts behind me and sends a shiver down my spine. I whip my head around to see Nathan perched on a ladder outside the window, a squeegee in his hand.

Justin gave us all indoor duties. Why is Nathan washing windows? He stares through the glass. Not at me. Not at Justin. At our hands. I yank my hand away from Justin's and fold my arms across my chest. Nathan issues an innocent smile and mouths the words "sorry," before he continues washing.

Justin's shoulders drop. He stands slowly, glances out the window at Nathan, then back at me. "Thanks for the lessons, but your torture is over. My uncle comes back tomorrow and I'll be starting school."

He walks away, but when he reaches the doorway, he stops and turns toward me. "Rielle, you're a good teacher. And I just want you to know. I'm so sorry for what's happened to you." He wheels around and leaves the room.

I linger on the piano bench. Could he really be sorry for me? Abrupt tapping on the window demands my attention. I look up. Nathan scowls and points toward the kitchen. What now? I stand. My legs feel thick, heavy with dread as I shuffle toward the kitchen. I push through the swinging door. Nathan waits on the other side, legs planted and arms folded. "Good lesson?" he asks, his tone hostile and accusing.

I consider his words and nod.

"What was happening between the two of you?"

My mouth falls open. What's he talking about?

"He's our owner's nephew. Hear this. These people use slaves. And in case you've forgotten we are their slaves—not their friends."

I know that. He doesn't have to tell me. I shoot him an irritated glower.

"Come on Rielle, he doesn't hold my hand like that. Get a clue!"

His accusation stings. I didn't do anything wrong, did I? I know my place. How can I forget? I brush past him and stomp upstairs to my room. I was stupid to have enjoyed the piano lessons, stupid to take pride in anything, stupid to think I have any value at all.

Remember your place. Slave.

I'm face down, crying into my pillow when Lydia returns to our room. She doesn't say anything. The bed depresses beside me. She rubs my back as I sob. As minutes pass, her hand begins to tremble and a few of her tears fall onto my back. She pulls away and crawls into her own bed, jostling with quiet sobs. We all try to be strong, but on the inside we're cut and bleeding, just like the Banker's wife—Nina.

When the Banker and Nina return, Nathan carries Nina into the house. She looks catatonic, her eyes open but vacant. The Banker informs all the Contracts that his wife is ill, and needs time and quiet to recuperate. The only person allowed in her room is Roberta, who will bring meals for her.

The children and Justin start school, and our workloads return to normal. Autumn cools the weather and colours the yard in warm yellows and oranges.

I do my best to avoid Justin. The last thing I need is more commentary from Nathan. I keep my head down, do my work and try to avoid punishment. To be ignored in this place is the best I can hope for.

The week before Thanksgiving, the Banker gathers us to make an announcement. He's so excited that his jowls quiver as he tells us that his brother, Justin's father, will join his family for Thanksgiving. He demands the house be in perfect order. We have to scrub the tops of baseboards and mop the ceiling. The Banker has new dining room furniture brought in and orders fresh lobsters for Thanksgiving dinner. He yells at us to start and end every day. By Tuesday evening, my knuckles are cracked and bleeding.

On Wednesday afternoon, the Banker hovers over us as we work. He paces the room, stopping every now and then to point out something we missed. We never miss a speck, but we go back and clean things over again to please him.

The doorbell chimes. I stop, my rag clutched in my fist.

"Lydia, get the door. Rielle, put that away. No. Wait. There's no time." He grabs the rag out of my hand and shoves it into a potted plant. "Justin! Nina! Kids!" he shouts.

The children bound down the stairs, Inez behind them. Nina appears in her bathrobe and a pair of slippers at the top of the stairs, then slowly descends, gripping the railing with both scarred hands. The Banker's family, Inez, Justin, Lydia and I, gather in the entryway. He motions for Lydia to open the door.

She swings the door open. A wide smile warms the face of the man on the other side. "Uncle Rex!" Lily and Caleb shout, bouncing up and down.

I expected a fat, squat twin of the Banker, thinking that Justin must have inherited his good looks from his mother, but Uncle Rex is nothing like his brother. Completely opposite, in fact. Uncle Rex stands a head taller than the Banker. He's lean and strong with friendly blue eyes, the same shade as Justin's.

"How are my favourite niece and nephew?" He drops to his haunches, throws open his arms and they run at him. He closes his arms around them and gives each child a hearty squeeze. He rises to full height, seizes the Banker's hand in a vigorous handshake, and then wraps Nina in a careful embrace. Her eyes are glassy when he releases her.

He combs his fingers through unruly silver hair, smoothing it down, but it pops back up. Uncle Rex's gaze moves to Justin and he lights up. "Justin!" He pulls him into a tight hug. "It's so good to see you." He pats Justin's back. "My boy hasn't given you any trouble, has he Arthur?"

A broad grin lifts Justin's cheeks.

"Of course not, no trouble at all."

The Banker snaps his fingers. "Lydia, Rielle, take Mr. Hayes' things upstairs to the room across from Justin's."

Lydia grabs the handle of his suitcase, while I clutch the strap of his garment bag.

"I'll get that," Justin says. He pulls the suitcase away from Lydia.

Uncle Rex lifts the strap off my shoulder. "And I'll get that."

Flustered, the Banker says, "The two of you show him to his room and unpack his things."

Uncle Rex pats the Banker's shoulder. "I'm fine, Arthur. Justin can show me to my room."

Justin leads his father upstairs. My chest aches with envy. His father seems proud of him. I've seen that look before, when I brought home a good grade on a test or after a piano recital. What I wouldn't give to have Dad's proud gaze on me that way again, telling me I've done a good job.

Once they're out of sight the Banker glares at us. What did we do? Were we supposed to tackle them and force them to let us carry the luggage?

Lydia and I return to the kitchen. She cleans out the refrigerator while I tackle the floor with a scrub brush. Leaning back on my knees, I dip the brush in a bucket of soapy water and peer out the window. Justin and Uncle

Rex walk past. As Justin talks, deep creases cut into the skin between his brows. His hands move as much as his mouth does. Uncle Rex's head inclines toward Justin. Justin touches his own cheek and shakes his head before opening the back gate for his father, and then following him through.

I touch my cheek with water-wrinkled fingers. Was Justin talking about me? No, why would he be?

Lydia and I serve dinner. The Banker sits at the head of the table, his chest puffed out, surveying the silver and crystal adornments. Uncle Rex doesn't seem to notice any of it. They engage in conversation about school and business while they eat. Uncle Rex lifts his last forkful of steak to his mouth, sets his fork and knife on his plate and then dabs his mouth with a cloth napkin. "Delicious, Arthur. Absolutely delicious."

The Banker sits up taller. "Thank you." He shoves a heap of mashed potato into his mouth.

Uncle Rex sighs. "Oh, but Arthur, I wish I would have known."

The Banker looks up, his mouth full of mash and his brows furrowed. He swallows the lump of potato. "Known?"

"Known that you were struggling for money. You know, little brother, you can always borrow from me. I've got plenty."

I stifle a chuckle at his false sympathy.

The Banker's face turns molten red. "I have plenty of money. More than I can spend, actually. I don't know where you would get that ridiculous idea." His jowls swing back and forth in vigorous denial.

Uncle Rex strokes his chin. "I was just looking at your malnourished Contracts. You obviously can't afford to feed them."

The Banker bristles. "Oh on the contrary, they're just wiry. They eat like kings here."

"And the way they're dressed." Uncle Rex shakes his head and lifts one eyebrow. "Nursing home staff come to mind." He chuckles. "But of course you are getting older and all that extra weight you carry around, Arthur…"

It takes every ounce of self-control I possess to suppress a smile.

The next evening Roberta prepares Thanksgiving dinner. The Banker instructs her to leave a portion of the lobster, turkey and trimmings in the kitchen for us. We stand at the serving counter, gawking at the food. I eye the others, wary about taking any of it. What's the catch?

Lydia and the others all have the same perplexed look on their faces. One by one, starting with Roberta, the others fill their plates. I'm the last to get my helping. I take my seat at the kitchen table, but no one has started eating yet. Nathan prays and then everyone stares at their plates.

Jonah picks up his forks. "One world. One currency. One bright future." He laughs and shoves a flake of turkey in his mouth. I dig into my meal.

The Banker bursts through the door, Uncle Rex behind him. I freeze mid-chew.

CHAPTER THIRTEEN

The Amazing Sandwich

"I TRUST YOU ALL ARE ENJOYING THE meal I provided for you?" the Banker says.

No one speaks. Eyes wide as empty bowls watch him.

Nathan speaks up. "Yes, sir. Thank you."

"See. There. They eat like kings," the Banker tells his brother before they exit the kitchen.

I devour my dinner. For the first time in months, I'm full.

After dinner, the Banker makes me join him, Justin and Uncle Rex when they go to the games room. I'm here to pop the caps off of beer bottles for them. With a full stomach, I struggle to keep my eyes open.

They shoot pool. The Banker makes several wagers, all of which he loses, forcing him to dig Proper bills out of his wallet.

Uncle Rex hovers over the green felt, lining up a shot. "Arthur, you were always a poor businessman."

The Banker leans on his pool cue. "What are you talking about? My bank is quite profitable."

"Oh, not your bank. Your home. I always give my Contracts a day off once per week. I get much more productivity out of them if I give them a day off now and then." He slings back his elbow, then thrusts it forward, knocking a ball into the corner pocket. "It's just good business. Protecting your investment." Uncle Rex chuckles and slaps the Banker on the back.

In the morning when Lydia and I go downstairs to receive the day's edicts, the Banker waits for us, tapping his foot. We fall into line. He tells us we all have the day off, then marches out of the kitchen.

Huh? Am I dreaming? I glance at Lydia. She looks to Nathan.

I'm starting to adore Uncle Rex. He has such a powerful influence over the Banker—why?

Oh, who cares? I get a day off!

"I'm going back to bed," Jonah says.

Sounds like a fantastic idea. I return to my room, strip off my uniform, let my hair down and fall into bed. The next thing I know Lydia's nudging my shoulder.

"Rielle, do you want some dinner?"

I detest the idea of opening my eyes, but the moment I'm conscious, a growling complaint rumbles from my stomach. I shuffle down the stairs, wolf down some Thanksgiving leftovers with the other Contracts, then go back to bed.

It takes awhile for me to fall back to sleep. I stare at the ceiling as the sun sets. My mind drifts to my family. Silas is likely in a reform school. But what about Alyssa? Are my parents okay? Will I ever see them again? Thinking like this makes me restless. I get out of bed and search for something to do— anything that could scrub their images from my brain.

I follow Lydia's voice down the hall to Jasmine and Roberta's room. Lydia motions for me to come in. I quickly scan the room. No Roberta. So I sit beside Lydia on the floor, leaning against Jasmine's bed and listening to her and Lydia talk about their favourite books. If only I could add in a few of my own. But I'd have to talk for that.

On the Saturday after Thanksgiving, my alarm clock rouses me at the usual time. Back to work. The Banker hurries into the kitchen, a sheen of sweat on his forehead, and clears his throat. "I will be at the office today, so I expect you all to make my brother feel welcome, even in my absence. You are to wait on him hand and foot, be constantly available for whatever he requests. If you are not needed, then I expect you to complete the work on your lists."

He barks out our work lists, which are longer than usual. He's obviously making up for the day he lost—and for the lobster.

Uncle Rex is nowhere to be seen, so I set to work wiping out the kitchen cabinets with the goal of finishing before Roberta returns to the kitchen to prepare lunch. But I'm not fast enough. She marches in with a smirk that tells me she's going to make the rest of my morning miserable. She steps on my hand and kicks me twice. "Oh, sorry, Rielle, I didn't see you there."

As I contemplate "accidentally" strangling Roberta, Uncle Rex and Justin walk into the kitchen.

"Good morning, ladies," Uncle Rex says cheerfully.

I stand up and bow my head in greeting.

Uncle Rex flashes Roberta an enthusiastic smile, as though he's happy to see her. "Roberta, Justin and I are going to take a horseback ride around the estate. When we return, we'd like to take a late lunch in the gazebo. Would you be so kind as to make us some cold turkey sandwiches from that delicious turkey you prepared—make that three sandwiches. Also, please put a healthy dollop of cranberry sauce on top."

Roberta lights up in a butt-kissing grin. "Of course. When would you like it?"

"Around two o'clock. That would be lovely. Thank you. Oh, and please include a big pitcher of ice tea with three glasses? And, Rielle, could you please bring our food out to us, if it's not too much trouble?"

I nod in agreement and watch Uncle Rex and Justin slip through the sliding glass door.

At a quarter to two, I finish in the kitchen and go upstairs to wash up before trekking out to the gazebo with a tray of sandwiches and drinks in hand.

The gazebo stands in the far corner of the yard opposite the shed, flanked on either side by large weeping willows, which partially hide the structure. I didn't even realize it existed until autumn hit and the leaves fell.

I step onto the patio, balancing my tray of drinks and sandwiches. The smell of decaying leaves mixed with a hint of wood smoke reminds me of fall at home. A light breeze, cool and dry, presses my dress against my legs as I march up the flagstone walkway. I pass the first curtain-like branches of the willow—a fountain comes into view—a sculpture of a Grecian woman pouring water from a jug. The trickling water lends the area a peaceful tone.

I approach the door to the screened gazebo. Uncle Rex and Justin lean toward one another, deep in conversation. I don't want to interrupt, so I slow my pace. Justin rests his chin on his fist, his brows furrowed, while Uncle Rex speaks. As I contemplate whether or not I should knock to announce my presence, Justin notices me.

He beckons me with his hand. "Rielle, come on in."

I push at the door with the toe of my shoe, terrified of spilling the tray. Justin jumps up and holds the screen door open. I set the tray on the table and then unload the glasses and plates of sandwiches. After pouring the iced tea, I tuck the tray under my arm, ready to leave.

"Rielle, would you please join us?" Uncle Rex says.

Is he serious? I glance back at the house, unsure. Will I get in trouble?

Justin pulls an empty chair away from the table. "It's okay, Rielle."

Remembering the Banker's request to attend to his brother, I nod and ease my weight onto the wicker chair. Justin serves me the extra turkey sandwich, then pours me a glass of iced tea. I stare at the food and drink in disbelief. They want me to join them for lunch?

After Uncle Rex prays to bless the food, he sets his holo on the table, runs his fingers over the screen, and a miniature piano hovers over the device. A tiny pianist with a shaved head and a silver sheath hugging her curves, sits at the keyboard and dances her fingers over the keys. It's a song I've played before. *"The Secret Life of Daydreams"* by Dario Marianelli. My fingers wiggle, tapping each note against my leg.

Uncle Rex and Justin take their first bites. I watch them for a moment to make sure this isn't some sort of trick. Maybe they'll change their minds. Scrutinizing Justin's reaction, I slowly pick up my sandwich. Justin smiles. I sink my teeth into it—fresh bread, cold turkey, thick mayonnaise and the sweet and tart flavour of cranberry sauce. Amazing. Maybe it's because I so seldom eat good food, but this is probably the most delicious turkey sandwich I've ever tasted.

I savour every morsel, chewing longer than normal to keep the taste on my tongue. I wash it down with a tall glass of iced tea with cut lemons, the ice clinking against the sides as I drink the last drop.

"Rielle, tell me, where are you from?" Uncle Rex asks. His expression holds the hint of assurance as though he knows the answer, but asks anyway.

My cheeks warm. I can't answer his question even though part of me wants to as a thank you for his kindness. Instead, I look down at my lap, hoping Justin will explain that I don't speak.

"Remember, Dad, she can't speak."

"Oh that's right. Can't or won't?" He chuckles.

Like father like son. Why do they assume this is a choice?

"Rielle, Justin and I were just discussing the law. In a recent landmark case, a couple who owned Contracts got divorced. The judge ruled that the Contracts were owned equally by the husband and the wife, regardless of who purchased them. That makes Nina just as much your owner as Arthur."

The comfortable feeling the turkey sandwich left me with evaporates like July rain. Instead of one owner I have two. Brilliant.

"So, if Aunt Nina gives her an order, does it carry as much weight as Uncle Arthur's orders?" Justin asks. Something in his expression arouses my suspicion. He, too, knows the answer to the question he posed. Did they rehearse this before I arrived?

Uncle Rex lifts his hands and then lets them drop. "Absolutely! You see, Rielle, law is a little hobby of mine, especially when it comes to Contracts. I've been watching the legal progression of this whole mess from the beginning. It's absolutely fascinating how you can take a free kid from an upstanding family, rob them of their rights and sell them into slavery—and it's all completely legal!" He sits back in his chair. "Absolutely fascinating."

I suddenly realize my mouth is gaping. I snap it shut and clench my fists under the table. Fascinating? My lot amuses him.

"Do you want to know what the key to pulling that off is?"

I don't. I open my hands and stare at lines, the letter "M" etched into my palms.

"Take away one right at a time. Start with something small. And every now and then take another and before you know it, you're no longer a person. You're a possession.

"Dad, I don't think Rielle finds this as entertaining as you do."

"I assure you, my dear, it is the darkest type of amusement, like one gapes at a train wreck." Uncle Rex sips iced tea and sets his glass on the table. "Your people were perfect."

My gaze jumps from my hands to Uncle Rex's face. Anger burns under my skin and speeds my pulse. Perfect? My people?

"Your parents taught you from a young age to accept your lot. Doesn't the Bible teach you to "work as unto the Lord," even when referring to slaves and masters? You were taught to always obey those in authority, so you don't rebel.

"Families like yours make the perfect slaves because you will never do anything to free yourselves. You work hard for your master, all the while telling yourselves that you are really working for God."

I stare at him, stunned. Why is he telling me this? Is he trying to get my goat like he does with the Banker? Or to make me feel worse for what I've already lost, like somehow I sat back and allowed it to happen?

I turn my attention to the miniscule pianist hovering above Uncle Rex's holo, irritated. No, seething. Seething over Uncle Rex's musings. Seething over the way that tiny person is playing—technically perfect, but dynamically flat. Emotionless. Robotic. Anger sours my stomach. She's living my grand piano dreams and I'm here.

Justin reaches over to touch my arm, but I jerk away. I push my chair back and rise to my feet. He hasn't dismissed me, but I don't care. If the choice is between Uncle Rex's verbal beating or the Banker's physical one, I'd take the physical one any day.

"You shouldn't leave without being excused, but it's so nice to see you still have some fight within you. You may need it. Go in peace, my dear." Uncle Rex nods, his eyebrows raised approvingly.

I run back to the house, wishing it were a longer distance. Acidic rage pours into my veins. I didn't *let* this happen. They arrested my parents.

They stole my dreams from me. They sold me! I want to run or scream or punch something to make the blazing anger go away.

As much as I enjoy watching Uncle Rex make the Banker squirm, I can't say I'll be sad to see him go. Sunday morning, Lydia and I wash Uncle Rex's clothes and pack his bags. Nathan carries his luggage to the car. Roberta cooks an elaborate lunch, which Lydia and I serve before it's time for Uncle Rex to leave. I stand against the wall and stare off into the distance, refining my piano piece in my head while they eat.

"Brother, whatever happened to that Contract?" Uncle Rex asks waving his hand in my direction.

Please don't let him be talking about me.

The Banker scans the room as though there are twenty Contracts to choose from. "Which?"

"This nice looking young lady, with the light brown hair. I'm referring to that unsightly scar on her face."

I press my back to the wall, wishing somehow I could disappear into it.

The Banker scratches the back of his head. "Oh—yes. Ah, Rielle. Terribly clumsy. Not very bright. Can't even talk, you know. She fell."

I contemplate crawling under the table to get out of the spotlight, but I keep my eyes fixed on a distant point, pretending I'm not listening.

Uncle Rex shakes his head slowly, clicking his tongue in disapproval. The smile evaporates from his face and his eyes grow serious, intense. "A fall?" He rests his elbows on the table and leans over the table toward the Banker. "She has such a lovely face. Who wouldn't want her serving at their table? Now it's sullied—damaged goods. But I guess accidents are hard to prevent, aren't they?"

The Banker's face matches the tomato soup in his bowl. An awkward silence hangs between them.

"I had wondered if someone had struck her." Uncle Rex says. "I'm so relieved to hear it was an accident. Our parents taught us better than to strike women. I should've known better than to think you capable of such barbaric behaviour."

Roberta strides through the doorway carrying a tray of desserts. The first and only time I've ever been happy to see Roberta.

After lunch, I go upstairs to strip the linens from Uncle Rex's bed. The Banker's shouts echo down the hall from his office. I loiter in the doorway to the guest bedroom and listen. "For the last time, no, absolutely not!" the Banker shouts.

Uncle Rex steps into the hall, so I hurry into the guest room before the Banker can emerge.

"I'm sorry you feel that way," Uncle Rex says as he walks away. "Goodbye, brother."

A few minutes later, the front door slams closed. I pull the curtain aside. Uncle Rex's car backs out of the driveway.

I try to forget about what he said, but his words linger. Have I given in to all of this too easily? Have we all? It's true; no one put up a fight or made any fuss at all. We sat back and took it. They made new laws. We obeyed them. They led us quietly into our own enslavement, like pigs into a slaughterhouse.

What good would fighting have done? There are so many more of them than us. But I keep coming back to one thing: would it have been better to die protecting our freedom than to live as slaves?

CHAPTER FOURTEEN

The Most Miserable Time of the Year

I DREAD CHRISTMAS. I WANT LIFE TO GO ON AS USUAL and forget that there's a holiday at all, but that's impossible. Morris and Nathan spend an entire day erecting trees in various rooms including a towering, two story evergreen in the foyer. The Banker assigns Lydia and me to decorate them and nearly every surface in the house with something festive. When we're done, the house is a Christmas wonderland—beautiful, I have to admit. Beautiful and bitter.

There won't be any parties, candlelight church services, or choirs singing Silent Night for Contracts. No gifts and no family. A familiar, crushing ache attacks with ferocity.

On the twenty-third, the Banker's chores list contains a couple of days' worth of work. He basically wants the house perfect for their family Christmas celebrations. Lydia and I spend the morning scrubbing tiles and bathrooms. My hands ache from hours of cleaning, and two hairline cracks open on my knuckles. Every time I bend my fingers, the scabs open up again, stinging and oozing blood.

After lunch we separate. Lydia tackles the bedrooms, and I dust and vacuum the main floor. After dabbing fresh blood from my hands with the inside hem of my dress, I remove the sofa cushions. I push the vacuum attachment into the corners, sucking up dust and lint. Toward the middle of the sofa, something clanks up the vacuum tube, and the whoosh of suction turns to a whistle. After turning off the machine, I peer into the hose. A shiny metallic object is lodged inside. I reach in, pinch it between my fingers, and pry it out.

It's a Proper coin. I turn the tarnished bronze piece over in my hand. I haven't seen one of these in years. It tumbles from my hand onto the floor and rolls under the couch. I get down on my hands and knees and reach into the darkness, patting the floor until I hit something.

It moves.

I gasp and yank my hand back like I've stuck my fingers in a hornets' nest. What was it? A spider? A scorpion? Pressing my cheek to the floor, I strain my eyes to find out. A pin sized red dot glows at the back of the couch. The dot is still for a moment then moves sideways. I crawl to the end of the couch and watch it emerge. A metallic bug skitters across the floor—the kind Bank Security released in my living room the day they took my family.

I jump to my feet and dash after it. As it scurries away, I mash the device underfoot. I drop to my haunches to examine it. One silvery leg still pulsates, but its devilish red eye is extinguished.

A shiver ripples down my spine as I pinch it between my finger and thumb to pick it up. Bank Security used the bugs to search my house. Why would there be one of them here? Is Bank Security spying on the Banker? No, that can't be. He's one of them, not a Resistor like me. Maybe the Banker is using them to watch us—to make sure we're doing our work while he's gone. Seems like something he'd do. I carry it to the trash can, toss it in and hurry back to work, now paranoid that the Banker is watching everything I do.

Christmas Eve arrives, although it doesn't look like Christmas. No snow. No icicles. Just dead brown grass and naked trees shivering in the wind. A dark mood hovers over the Contracts. We eat white rice with bits of hamburger mixed in. Everyone's quiet. No jokes from Jonah tonight. He concentrates on stirring his rice, his eyes glassy. Nathan's face is stoic, distant. Jasmine wraps her arms around her middle and stares at the ground, looking fragile, as though she's a paper-thin sheet of glass that might shatter if touched.

Once the lights are out, Lydia cries into her pillow. I sit on the edge of her bed and stroke her hair as sobs wrack her body. I want to take away her pain. My pain too. Put it in a box and ship it away. Cut out my heart so I can't feel anymore and erase the memories that make me ache for home—ache for Christmas with my family.

If I had known a year ago that I was spending my last Christmas with my family, I would've done everything differently.

Dad lost his job that October because he didn't take the chip implant. I overheard my parents discussing where we'd live if the bank took our home, but didn't let on that I knew. While my friends discussed the latest holos they wanted for Christmas, I wondered if my parents would be able to afford any presents at all. Even if they could afford them, where would they shop? No one took Proper currency anymore. Store window signs read, "Chips only."

My parents sat us down, their faces lined with worry. They attempted to sound upbeat about the coming holiday.

"Christmas is going to be a little different this year." Dad forced a smile. "You all know we are in a bit of a tough spot, but we think this will be a great Christmas. You know Christmas isn't about gifts…"

Mom picked up where he left off. "It's going to be fun, we're going to make a tree out of construction paper, and then we'll make presents or find things we already have to give to each other." She smiled, but raised her eyebrows too high. Her eyes were sad.

Alyssa was too young to understand what was going on. Silas said, "There's still going to be turkey."

Of course, Silas, who seemed to grow nightly, would be most concerned about food.

"Yeah, of course. We've already signed up with the food bank for a hamper," Mom said.

Dad threw her a disapproving glance.

"Then it's all good," Silas said.

Unlike Silas, I made a point of displaying my disappointment. I always made my distaste about their decisions regarding the chip clear. I refused to help decorate the paper tree they taped to the wall. When Christmas morning arrived, I had a small box under our make-shift tree. I opened it to find a locket my mother had owned since she was a child and had been my grandmother's before that. Tears filled her eyes as she helped me put it on. I gave her an unimpressed, "Thanks."

My throat tightens as I remember the locket. I place my hand on my chest where its warm gold used to lay, and hold back my tears. I should've hugged her. I should've told her how much I loved her. All I wanted was a new holo like my friends were getting, not a hand-me-down locket.

What I wouldn't give to have that locket now.

Our only chore on Christmas day is to clean up piles of torn wrapping paper and toy packaging. Roberta has to cook Christmas dinner, and Lydia volunteers us to help.

"'Tis' the season," she says.

After dinner we return to our room to mourn some more.

A couple of days after Christmas, the Banker gives me the best gift of all: he leaves. He and his family take off to a Caribbean theme park for a week long vacation, which means a sort of vacation for us too because Justin gives us less work. The news makes everyone happy, except for Nathan, who seems leery of the arrangement. "Excellent," he says with a heaping dose of sarcasm.

Seriously, would he rather have the Banker around?

The first day the Banker is away, Nathan hovers over everything I do. He carries the bucket of water when I go to mop the kitchen and returns every five minutes to see if I need fresh water. I almost forget myself and shout "no" at him after the twelfth time he asks, but I bite my lip. Finally, he goes off to do something else.

Justin strolls in through the back door as I scrub the floors. He greets us cheerfully, drops his holo on the table and ambles over to Roberta's side. "Hey Roberta, how about some spaghetti for dinner? Maybe a big Caesar salad and some garlic bread?"

"Yes, sir. I can do that."

"Great. Make enough for everyone."

Roberta blinks several times and shakes her head. "Everyone? As in—?"

"As in everyone. You, me, Rielle, Nathan. Everyone."

"Alright." She draws the word out, stunned.

He walks out of the kitchen. Ten minutes later Justin's voice crackles through the intercom. "Roberta?"

Roberta stops chopping an onion. "Yes?"

"I forgot my holo in the kitchen. I know you're really busy. Could you tell Rielle to bring it up to my room?"

"Yes, sir." The intercom cuts off and she starts chopping again. "You heard him. Go!"

I stand and drop my rag in the bucket, dry my hands on my skirt and pick up the holo. It instantly forms to the shape of my hand.

"You know the rules. You better not turn it on!" Roberta calls as I march through the swinging door. I roll my eyes.

Once the kitchen door closes behind me, I glance around to see if anyone is watching, then swipe my thumb across the metal, mainly to spite Roberta. She's a Contract too and I hate it when she orders me around.

I expect it to require a fingerprint to proceed, but an image pops on. A news site glows before me with a headline that turns my legs numb. "Angelique Terror Cell Strikes Again." Angelique? My aunt? No. It can't be. I have to remind myself to keep walking as I read the subheading. "For the second time in as many weeks the Angelique terror cell has attacked a Bank Security facility."

My heart pounds. The day Bank Security came for my family rushes back to me, the memory clear and detailed. Trenchcoat asked about Aunt Angelique. The question caught me off guard. Why would he ask about my reclusive aunt? Come to think of it, he seemed dissatisfied with my answer.

Aunt Angelique is a free spirit, a bit of a hippie. Silas and I sometimes referred to her as Auntie Granola. She made a ton of money working for some software firm, then took early retirement. Dad and his sister were close, so he insisted we visit her at least once a year. She proudly lived "off the grid." She grew her own food and subsisted on the amount of electricity her solar panels provided.

As a child, I loved visiting her. Silas and I ran around in the woods, climbed trees and swam in the lake bordering her property. When I got older, the lack of net access at her place made me beg my parents to allow me to stay home when it came time for a visit. The last time I saw Aunt Angelique, we argued about whether or not blow drying my hair was a good use of finite resources.

Sometimes Dad joked around about joining her in the woods and living off the land. "You can go, but I'm not," I'd throw back at him. If we'd gone, maybe Bank Security wouldn't have found us. Maybe I'd be climbing trees with Silas right now, or hoeing the garden with Mom and Aunt Angelique. Still hard work, but I'd be free.

The memories blind me. I stumble on the stairs and back into the depressing here and now.

I try to read as much as I can as I slowly climb the stairs. The article says that the "terrorists" have been raiding Bank Security facilities where Contracts are awaiting transport. They've kidnapped forty-five to date.

Kidnapped? No, I would say rescued. These aren't terrorists. These are heroes.

I realize I'm taking far too long to bring Justin his device, so I quicken my pace. I swipe my thumb across the edge of the holo again to deactivate it and knock on the door.

Justin opens the door and reaches out his hand. "Thanks, Rielle."

I nod and turn to walk away.

"Did you see the headline?"

I glance back at him and shake my head.

He takes the holo, activates it and turns it toward me. I divert my eyes to the floor. He sighs. "Thanks."

I issue a polite smile and return to work with one question dominating all my thoughts. Could my aunt really be involved in these rescues? And if so, why hasn't she come for me?

At dinner, Justin joins us under the live oak tree while we all feast on spaghetti, salad and fresh baked French bread. The moment he sits down all conversation ends and everyone stops eating, staring at him, forks in hand.

"You guys mind if I join you?"

Six pairs of eyes dart around the circle. Nathan answers. "No. It's a free country." Jonah snorts and I press my lips together to suppress a smile. Silence, obvious and awkward, saturates the air. Forks clink against plates and the slurp of spaghetti sounds deafening.

Morris twists his fork in his spaghetti, rolling up a third of his noodles in one bite. He does this a couple more times and his plate is empty. He gets up and stalks toward the men's quarters. Within a few minutes the others begin trickling back into the house. Lydia and I are the last ones, but we leave before Justin finishes eating.

In the morning, Justin marches into the kitchen to hand out chores dressed in some sort of western looking get-up, complete with cowboy boots. I stifle a chuckle. Is today dress-up day? I look him over from top to bottom. It doesn't look too bad on him. Kind of suits him. In fact, I like it. A lot. I stiffen at the uninvited, stray thought.

He goes down the line announcing jobs, first the boys, then the girls. He pauses before he gets to me. The others scatter to their various work sites. I wait.

"And Rielle, I want to do some riding today. Your chore is to join me."

Nathan halts, one foot through the sliding door.

Justin continues, "You'll need to dress for a day outdoors." He turns to Roberta. "We'll need you to pack us a lunch. Make sure you throw in a few apples as well." Roberta glares at me.

Please don't spit in my sandwich.

I head toward the stairs to change into my outdoor uniform, but before I can place my foot on the first tread, Nathan seizes my upper arm in his large hand, pulling me to a stop.

"Sir," Nathan says. "I'd be glad to go riding with you. I've been along most of the trails and could be your guide. Of course, I'd make sure I complete my other work as well."

Panic bears down on me. What is he doing? He's going to get in trouble. Our assignments are never, ever negotiable.

"That won't be necessary, but thanks for the offer," Justin says.

All three of us stand there for a tense moment.

Please let me go, Nathan.

Nathan leans closer to me. Worry plagues his eyes. "Be careful," he whispers. Did Justin hear? His hand slowly loosens from my arm.

I bound upstairs and pull on the blue jeans the Banker provided after Uncle Rex commented that we all dressed like nursing home staff. Bless Uncle Rex.

My oversized shoes, however, may be a problem. Thin, flat soled canvas shoes offer no protection if the horse steps on my feet, but that's all I have.

A little fresh air and adventure will make up for the pathetic footwear. Outdoors. Riding. No work. I'm getting out of prison for the day! I peer out my window at the world beyond the fence.

The fence!

I almost forgot. Lydia said if I went beyond the fence, sensors would activate my tracker chip. I rub my fingers over my left hand, the one containing the chip. There's no way I can go with Justin, unless…maybe he has a way to deactivate the chip. I dress for riding, hoping he has a plan. I bounce down the stairs jittery with excitement.

A broad smile spreads over Justin's face when I return to the kitchen. "Ready?"

I bite my lip, hold out my left hand and furrow my brow questioningly.

He stares at me for a second before understanding washes over him. "You're worried about your chip?"

I swallow hard and nod.

"Not to worry. I've got it covered." He digs into his breast pocket and pulls out his holo along with a thin band that seems to be made of the same metallic material. He walks up to me and reaches for my hand. I yank it away.

"It's okay, Rielle. Just a bracelet."

I glance from him to the object in his hand.

"It scrambles the tracker chip's signal. We use them whenever we need to take Contracts outside their usual boundaries. We don't need to make our horseback ride a matter of national security." He chuckles.

I extend my left hand, and he slips the bracelet around my wrist. It's huge on me, but when he runs his fingers over his holo, the bracelet heats and contracts until it forms to my wrist.

Justin leads me through the yard toward the wrought iron gate at the back. A huge shed that looks as though it was once a small barn, decades older than the house, sits at the back corner of the property. I've only ventured into it a couple times. Unlike the rest of the Banker's possessions, it's ill-kempt, full of gardening tools, dusty boxes, an out-of-commission truck and a rotting boat that clearly would never float. Nathan and Jonah squat on the roof of the shed, tearing shingles off and tossing them to the ground. We pass them on our way to the gate. Nathan stops and watches us. I avoid his stare. What's he so worried about?

Justin opens the gate for me. I walk through and he closes it with a tinny clang, cutting off my view of the yard. A vast expanse of land stretches before us. Justin and I are alone out here. Just the two of us. No witnesses. No Nathan to step in if something goes wrong.

My pulse climbs. Is Justin taking me away to harm me? He promised me once that he wouldn't hurt me. Was that just a ruse to make me trust him, to follow him when I shouldn't? Would anyone come looking for me if I didn't return? Would anyone bat an eye if a Contract disappeared? I know the answer. No one would care.

If I know that—so does Justin.

CHAPTER FIFTEEN

The Grand Freak-out

I LAG BEHIND SO I CAN KEEP AN EYE ON JUSTIN. I gnaw on my lip. Dead girl walking.

Justin glances back at me. "What happened to your smile? Rielle, you're going to bite your lip right off. Relax. Enjoy the day!" He seems to be in good spirits, but I can't trust that.

We walk about a quarter of a mile before I spot a large white building ahead. As we draw closer, a fence and grazing horses come into view.

Morris runs out to greet us wearing a bracelet like mine. "Good morning, sir. You've come for a ride?"

"Yeah, we'll need two of your best."

"I'll go saddle 'em up," Morris says. He jogs back to the barn.

Justin hangs one foot on the bottom rung of the fence and rests his arms on the top rung. "Have you ever ridden before?"

I nod. I did some riding at summer camp, but I'm unsure if those glue factory rejects count as horses.

A breeze rustles the dry grass, highlighting the silence between us. This is one of those times when people usually make small talk like "nice day isn't it?" or "we could use some rain." Justin whistles a tune while I survey the landscape.

The barn sits at the edge of a large plateau. To the north a rounded hill rises, covered in white and gold limestone, dotted by tufts of grass and twisting junipers. Beyond the stable, to the south, the land slopes downward sharply, then drops off. A stand of trees springs up from the valley beyond. The faint trickling sound of moving water climbs over the ridge.

About ten minutes later, Morris leads two horses out to us. He calls the large honey-coloured horse Goliath, and the smaller one, a brown and white Appaloosa, Cherokee.

Justin tosses me an apple from his pack. Surprised, I fumble before clasping it between my hands.

"You should make friends with that horse before you ride her."

I flatten my hand, supporting the apple as the horse bites into it. I stroke her smooth muzzle while she chews down the apple and sniffs for more, nuzzling my arm. I always enjoyed riding; this might actually be fun. In fact, if Justin tries anything weird it gives me a means of escape, although his horse looks faster than mine. He could probably catch me.

Gathering the reins in one hand, I wiggle my right foot into the stirrup and grab the horn. Justin comes up behind me and places his hands on my waist. I shoo his hands away.

Justin laughs as I fling my leg over the horse's back.

He mounts his horse, draws his reigns to one side, angling his horse to face me. "Are you going to talk to me today, Rielle?"

I shake my head. He keeps beating that dead horse.

"We'll see." He turns Goliath and nudges him forward with his heel.

I want to hate it because it's my prison, but there's no denying the beauty of the Texas hill country. The rolling hills and scrubby bushes look like something out of a western movie. I expect a wad of tumbleweed to roll across our path. Justin rides in front of me and points out animals along the way. An armadillo scurries alongside the trail and a small deer nibbles grass in the distance. The deer here look a little like us Contracts—underfed and over-worked.

The brush beside the trail rustles, and a scrawny deer leaps in front of us. Goliath startles and dances sideways. Justin gathers the reins tighter. "Whoa, boy." The horse rears. Afraid my horse will spook too, I cling to the saddle horn as Cherokee backs away from Goliath, but she remains calm, steady. She simply distances herself and watches, snorts and stomps her front hoof, as Justin calms Goliath.

I pat Cherokee's shoulder. The last thing I need today is a skittish horse.

We ride on, following the winding river. Wind jostles the tree branches and gravel crunches beneath the horses' hooves. I draw in a deep breath of mesquite-tinged air, close my eyes and allow the horse's rhythmic gait to carry me along. With my eyes closed, I could be anywhere with anyone. It could be Silas in front of me. We could be at Lake Mille Lacs where my family liked to camp when we were still allowed to travel. For a moment, I feel free.

I let the feeling wash over me, but I can't allow myself to linger too long on the illusion of liberty. My owner's nephew is in front of me. I need to be cautious. I open my eyes and I'm back in Texas. A million miles from home.

As we plod along, my longing for freedom doesn't diminish, it grows stronger. I crave the wind in my hair, the thunder of hoof beats and the thrill of flying over the ground. Is it worth the risk to try? Or would he think it's some lame attempt at escape?

I'm sure Justin can keep up.

I squeeze my legs around Cherokee and she breaks into a trot. I catch up to Justin and bounce beside him. I smile so he knows I'm not trying to run away, then dig my heels into Cherokee's side. She speeds and I pull ahead. Justin grins as he catches up to my canter. I lift my eyebrows and grin back. Leaning down and clutching the saddle horn with one hand, I give the horse a kick. I hold tight with my legs as her long, lunging strides yank me forward.

Though I anticipate speed, this horse is faster than any I've ever ridden. I grip the horn as tightly as I can, but the thrill turns my muscles to jelly. I start giggling as my weight shifts to the side. I let go of the saddle horn and pull back on the reins. Cherokee nearly bounces me off her back. She slows, returning to a walk. I lay my head against her mane, shaking with hysterical laughter, nine months of tension draining out of me.

Justin urges his horse alongside mine. "Are you okay?" His eyes are wide with concern.

I nod, laughing so hard tears roll down my cheeks.

He chuckles. "You're laughing? Oh, geez, I thought you were hurt."

I shake my head, trying to control my laughing fit.

"I've never heard you laugh before. It's nice."

The comment has me cracking up again. I don't know why. It's not funny, but I can't stop.

"Maybe we should stop for lunch." Justin steers his horse down a shallow embankment toward the river. My horse follows.

Justin dismounts. I tug on the reins, then slide off the horse. Exhausted from the ride, my legs buckle under me. I hit the ground, land on my backside and break into hysterics again. Sprawled on the grass, I allow a few more giggles to escape. Justin takes off his hat and crouches next to me. "Are you alright?" He seems concerned for my safety or my sanity. Maybe both.

I suck in a deep breath, look into his eyes and smile. He has nice eyes. Friendly, appealing, genuine. He stands and holds out his hand. I grasp it and he pulls me to my feet. After I dust off my pants, we lead the horses down to the river so they can drink. They bury their muzzles in the slow moving liquid. We let them gulp for a minute, then pull them away from the water and loop their reins over a low tree branch.

Justin unbuckles the flap of his saddle bag and retrieves our lunch pack. I follow him over the stone strewn shore to a flat, sandy spot near the water. He spread his arms.

"This is the Guadalupe River."

A wide expanse of sage green water meanders past us. Towering cypress trees line the river banks, dipping their exposed finger-like roots into the water. Branches from trees on opposite sides of the river reach toward each other. Two lovers who can never be together. It must be beautiful in the summer when the foliage creates a canopy over the sleepy water.

Justin pulls our lunch from the pack and opens each sandwich, inspecting their contents. "Just making sure Roberta didn't do anything to your lunch." He hands me my portion. "All clear."

I smile and take the sandwich from him, then nod in thanks and settle onto the ground to eat.

I angle myself toward the river, draw my knees into my chest and take small bites, listening to the peaceful trickle of water and watching it ripple over rocks and swirl in eddies. Justin stares at the river as he eats too, seemingly deep in thought.

He finishes his sandwich and takes a long drink from his water bottle. He twists the cap back on and says, "Rielle, will you please speak to me?" Other times when he's asked, his tone has been playful, this time it's serious, pleading. As if it's the thing he wants most in the world.

I press my lips together and shake my head. Same tired subject. Lydia and Nathan know about me talking in my sleep, but they wouldn't have told him. So why, when everyone else has accepted that I can't talk, does he continue pressing me to speak? I *was* enjoying myself, but all good things must come to an end.

"No one will know. We're all the way out here. I won't tell anyone."

Is that why he brought me out here, to persuade me to talk? I shake my head again. I glance back toward to the horse, longing for an excuse to return to her.

He brushes his fingers over the stones on the ground beside him, picks one up and turns it over in his hand. He sighs and flings the stone into the water. He inches closer to me.

I straighten my back. Alert. Ready to run.

He looks into my eyes too long. His probing gaze sets my heart pounding.

"Aubrielle Angelique James, please talk to me."

My head snaps up and my mouth falls open. That name. How could Justin know that name? Only three people in the world have called me by my full name—my parents when I was in trouble, and Silas to irritate me. The name on my Contract is Rielle James. It's not like Bank Security bothered to check my birth certificate.

Justin lifts his hand and touches my scarred cheek. "Now are you going to talk to me?"

I jump to my feet and back away, afraid to turn my back on him. I stumble over the rocks, lose my balance and fall backward. I land hard and jagged stones cut into my palms.

Justin scrambles after me. "I'm sorry, Rielle. Don't freak out. I'm sorry."

Tears overflow as I inspect my bleeding hands.

He reaches for my hands. I yank them away and clench them into fists, sending a shot of pain up my arms. I struggle to get to my feet. He reaches for my arm, but I slap his hands away. I stand on quivering legs and glare at him through my tears. I march over to Cherokee and untie her.

"Rielle. Stop. Please."

I work at untangling the reins from the branches. Justin takes hold of my wrist. I stop. He hands me a napkin from our lunch. "I'm sorry."

I smudge away my tears, my cheeks hot, so hot the tears might boil off if I leave them. How could I let him see me cry? Why do I have to be so weak?

I stare down at the ground. He tries lifting my chin, but I whip my head away. He pulls my hand closer and tugs at my fingers. "Let me see your hand."

I look away from him, fix my eyes on the trees on the other side of the river and keep my fists clenched even though it hurts.

"I just want to help you."

I don't respond. I shut down like I do when the Banker hits or yells at me. Justin's voice is in another world. I'm in my own.

"Alright. I'll take you home," he says, barely above a whisper. He shuffles toward his horse, his head hanging and shoulders slumped.

I want to stop crying, but I can't. I weep quietly most of the way home, at first for what happened and then out of regret. I did freak out.

Justin rides ahead of me, wilted. He looks back at me a few times as though he wants to say something, but he never does. Between my excitement and Nathan's worries, it didn't take much to set me off. I'm a rubber band stretched as far as it can go. And then, snap. This should have been the best time I've had in a year and I cut it short with my outburst.

I hold the reins gingerly. The heels of my hands scraped raw, still ooze blood. Chores will be interesting with scraped up hands. Nothing like bleach on raw skin.

The sun perches atop the eastern hills as Justin leads me back through the gate to the Banker's yard, removes my bracelet and tucks it in his back pocket. As we approach the house, I spot Nathan leaning against the wall beside the door to the kitchen.

Oh, no. Nathan will see that I've been crying. He's going to think…

I rub my cheeks and eyes with the back of my hand, take a deep breath and correct my posture.

Justin halts. His stare stops on Nathan too. "Great," he mutters under his breath. He turns to me, glances down at my hands. The creases between his brows deepen. "I hope you know that this wasn't what I intended. I'd never hurt you."

He makes a quarter turn and stalks toward the garden doors off the dining room.

I free my hair from the bun, let it fall down around my shoulders and sweep across my forehead like a veil, hoping it will hide me from Nathan. I keep my head down as I walk past him and into the house, but he follows me inside.

"How was the ride?"

Desperate to avoid eye contact, I give him a thumbs-up then dart for the stairs, but he steps between me and the stair case. I try to push past him, but he stands his ground. I just want to hide in my room and sort this thing out. Why can't he leave me alone?

"Look at me and tell me you're okay."

I bite my lip. I know what's going to happen. I'll look up, and he'll assume the worst. His fingers under my chin, he lifts my head. With no other option, I peer up at him.

He steps back and his eyes narrow as they move over my face. His teeth snap together and he draws in a breath through his nose. "What did he do to you?"

I shrug and shake my head. I even attempt a smile, but it's as flat as a popped balloon.

"Then why are you crying?"

The stress pushes more tears past my swollen eyelids. Will they never stop? I swipe my cheek with the back of my hand, punishing my tears for exposing me like this.

"Why does he keep singling you out? He doesn't do this to any of the other girls. What's his fascination with you?"

I never stopped to consider—why me? When he wanted piano lessons, it made sense because he figured out I play. But horseback riding?

Nathan jams his fingers through his hair. "I can't protect you. All I can do is stand by and watch him walk away with you, not knowing if he'll bring you back. It kills me!"

He spins around and flings open the glass door. It slams into the casing, the glass vibrating as if it might shatter. He storms out the door and slams it again.

Cringing, I glance around the kitchen, hoping there are no witnesses. Especially not Roberta. He can't behave this way. If someone tells the Banker…

I shuffle upstairs and to my room. When I walk through the door Lydia jumps to her feet and releases a heavy sign. "Oh, good. You're back."

I cross the room and begin stripping off my dusty clothes.

"What happened? Are you okay?"

I nod and dig my pajamas out of the drawer.

"What happened to your hands?"

I sit down on my bed and flip my palms up so she can see.

Her eyelids peel wider. "Did he hurt you?"

I shake my head. No. This is a result of my own stupidity.

Lydia leaves the room and returns with some petroleum jelly. I smile in thanks and rub it over my palms. With a shiny coat over the damaged skin, I snap the lid closed.

"Are you sure everything's okay? You look like you've been crying."

I need to get a handle on my tears. They're giving everyone the wrong idea. I would assume the same thing if Lydia returned in this state, and I'm pretty sure I'd want to wring Justin's neck. I breathe a large circle of condensation onto the window and write, "Fine. Don't worry," then mop the writing away with my fist.

"If you're sure." She still looks uneasy.

I settle into bed, but lie awake thinking about my day, the same questions circling my mind. Why me, and how does he know my full name?

Nathan implied Justin has some sort of interest in me. I doubt that. Justin's the type of guy who could be with any girl he wanted. How could a mute slave possibly interest him? Yeah, me in my scrubs, my hair in a tight bun on a magazine centerfold. Hot. I'm sure.

And then there's the issue of my name. Perhaps the Banker has paperwork with my full name. Would they have sent my birth certificate to him? That would explain it. Justin probably came across the papers in the Banker's office with my name on them. But then, why would he be poking around in the Banker's office? Seems unlikely too. The Banker calls me Rielle and he doesn't seem like the type for cozy nicknames.

Maybe I'm making a huge deal out of nothing.

At least I don't have to worry about spending any more time alone with Justin. After my behaviour today, I doubt he'll take me on anymore horseback rides. And Nathan will calm down once Justin finds a new pal to hang out with.

CHAPTER SIXTEEN

Flash Flood

IN THE MORNING, JUSTIN JOINS US FOR breakfast. As soon as Justin sits down next to me, Nathan stops eating and glares at him. Worried that Nathan will get himself into trouble, I stare at him until he makes eye contact. I slowly shake my head. Lydia glances at me and then at Nathan. She starts chattering at him about yesterday's work, her voice high with anxiety. She found a scorpion behind the toilet in the guest bathroom.

Nathan looks over at her instead of Justin. Thank you, Lydia!

Jonah comes to the rescue with a few new jokes, breaking the iceberg that's settled over the group. With the exception of Nathan, everyone returns to their normal banter.

"So what do you like to do in your spare time—I mean what did you like to do—before?" Justin asks the group. The conversation stops like a car hitting a brick wall. Stunned faces stare at Justin and then at each other. The hum of the refrigerator erupts, a jet engine in the silence. Justin shifts in his seat, sighs and looks down at his plate.

Lydia swallows a mouthful of biscuit. "I wanted to be a nurse like my mom, so I used to volunteer at a nursing home."

"Knit. I liked to knit. Hats. Scarves," Jasmine says in a small voice.

Silence hangs in the air like a heavy fog.

Jonah lifts his chin, blinks away a hint of sadness. "I used to go fishing with my dad on the weekends."

Roberta gets up and carries her plate to the sink. She doesn't need to share. I can make an educated guess at her hobby. Probably torturing small animals.

"How 'bout you, Nathan?" Justin asks.

Why does he have to poke the angry bear?

Nathan folds his arms. "Computers."

Really? Not what I would've guessed. All muscle bound with broad shoulders, I would've pegged him for a guy who lives and breathes sports.

Justin leans forward and grins. "Games?"

Nathan fixes a dead pan glare on Justin. "No." Nathan drops his fork in his plate and rises to his feet.

"Before you all leave…" Justin digs his hand into his pocket and pulls out a handful of folded paper strips.

Paper? Who uses paper?

He hands out the scraps.

The others unfold their papers and their eyes move over the writing inside. One by one they pick up their plates, set them in the sink and head in different directions, except for Nathan. He lingers in the doorway to the utility room.

I dump my plate in the sink before I lean against the counter and unfold my scrap of paper. Nathan steps closer.

I scan the short message, "Horseback riding." I do a double take. What? I can't believe it. Now I understand why he wrote them down instead of announcing them.

Nathan watches me suspiciously, moves closer and peeks over my shoulder. I hold the paper to my chest, and scamper past him upstairs to my room to change. I dig my jeans out of the dirty clothes hamper. I'll have to wear them again.

I can't believe he wants to go riding with me again after yesterday's disaster. I get a second chance and this time, I'm not going to screw it up. Justin clearly isn't taking me out there to hurt me. After all, he had the opportunity yesterday and he was nothing but nice, even when I wasn't so nice. Today I'm going to take his advice. I'm going to relax and have fun. Leave my freak-out self at the Banker's place.

I wriggle my head though the neck of my T-shirt. Footfalls pound against the stairs. I glance at the door, expecting to see Lydia, but Nathan fills the doorway.

I gasp. He's not supposed to be in the women's quarters. I form an irritated expression, march over to him and point down the stairs. He needs to leave before he gets caught.

He walks into my room, catches my elbow and flings the door shut.

I throw hard glances between him and the door. The skin on his forehead crinkles. "Don't go. Tell him you're sick or something, but don't go," he whispers.

He grasps my hands between his fingers, lifts them, turns them over to expose my palms. He examines the now scabbed scrapes. "Do they hurt?"

I shake my head. How can I reassure him? I don't want him to waste his time and energy worrying about me, but there's no way to tell him without speaking.

He gently strokes his thumbs over the heels of my hands. "Don't go." His eyes bore into mine. "Please."

I want to tell him how much his concern means to me. Having friends who truly care about me in this horrible place count as miracles I don't deserve. But I have to go. I don't have a choice. I pull my hands out of his, ball them into fists and hide them behind my back.

He releases a long breath and hangs his head.

Guilt pours over me. I pick up his hand, unfurl his fingers and look him in the eye. I write one word at a time on his palm.

"I'm fine," he reads. He looks up again. "I have a hard time believing that. I just don't want to see these people hurt you, Rielle."

I write "thank you," on his palm, then brush past him and return to the kitchen where Justin waits for me. I need to get him out of here before Nathan comes downstairs, so I grab our lunch pack off the counter and hurry out the back door.

"Hey, what's the rush? I can carry that," Justin calls after me. Let's get this over with. The sooner I'm back the less time Nathan will have to spend worrying.

I stop at the gate. Justin fixes the bracelet on my wrist, then snatches the pack out of my hands and opens the gate. The horses are already saddled when we reach the stable. Justin tosses me an apple. I feed it to Cherokee and settle into the saddle before Justin has a chance to help me. I nudge the horse forward while he mounts Goliath.

Hooves pound and crunch against the gravel behind me. "Will you slow down? I need to talk to you." Justin gallops up beside me and yanks back on the reins. His horse slows to match my horse's pace.

I look over at him and instantly find his blue eyes. My heart quickens. I force my gaze to the horizon.

He plods alongside me. I sense his eyes on me, but I don't dare look at them again. They make me feel—I don't know—nervous and excited and confused all at the same time.

"I thought through what happened yesterday. I realized I'm coming at this from the wrong angle. And I'm so sorry. I'd like to start over. I asked you to trust me, but have given you nothing in return. You don't know anything about me. Why would you trust a stranger?"

I venture a glance at him, considering his words. Why does he care if I trust him? And why should I trust him? His family owns me. I don't trust the Banker and I don't trust him. Never will.

"Did you know that my dad's not a banker? He's in oil. They're the only ones the bankers can't control because the bankers need their oil." He chuckles. "They wouldn't want to lower themselves to driving solar cars."

When the shortage drove gasoline prices up, out of the range of normal people like my family, gas powered cars became a status symbol.

Hey, look at me. I'm so rich, I can trash the environment.

Justin pauses, apparently waiting for a response, but I keep my face emotionless and disinterested. It doesn't matter what his daddy does for a living. Just another rich slave owner.

"I'm taking industrial engineering and my favourite color is green. The Dallas Cowboys are my favourite football team and I have a weakness for pizza."

He isn't a psych major after all. So much for that theory. I gnaw on my cheek. Thanks for the information because everyone who likes the Dallas Cowboys is trustworthy. What's he want me to do? Oh Justin—the color green—that's my favourite colour too. Now I can talk to you.

If he thinks that telling me any of this is going to make me trust him, he's going to be sorely disappointed.

"When I'm not in school, I live with my dad outside of Eagle Pass, Texas. My mom took off when I was six and it's been just me and Dad ever since."

I rub my thumb along the leather reins. He lost his mother too. I shove aside a pang of empathy. His mother chose to leave. My mom never would've left us. Her choices were stolen from her. I turn my head away from Justin and toward the river. The breeze carries the heavy scent of damp wood and earth over the ridge, ruffling the few stray hairs that escaped my bun. They tickle my cheeks, so I push them behind my ears.

He sighs. "I grew up with this kid, Luke. We were best friends all through school. We got into some trouble together. One time, we took all these construction signs and used them to barricade the highway coming into town. There was this traffic jam." He laughs. "People just sat there until the police came and took the signs away. They never figured out who did it."

I sneak a glimpse of him. His mouth is turned up in a smile, but his eyes are sad.

"Luke's a Contract now, out on the west coast somewhere."

I take in his expression, disarmed. I don't like thinking of him as a person with a past and a future. He's…human…like me.

No! He's not like me! Of course he'd be sad at losing his best friend. Doesn't stop him from ordering me around. What a hypocrite. I'm not a person to him. Just a Contract. A slave. An object. Usable and disposable.

I ignore him as he yammers on about random aspects of his life until we reach the same spot on the river where we ate lunch yesterday.

He tugs on the reins and Goliath slows to a stop. "What do you think? Should we try this again?" He dismounts his horse and unties the lunch pack from the saddle.

I sweep my gaze over the river bank. My cheeks warm as I note the spot where I fell and skinned my hands. Today, I'll do better. No freaking out.

Sunbeams thread the bare branches, forming thin shadows on the riverside. I jump down from the horse and tether her to a tree branch beside Goliath. Justin hands me my peanut butter sandwich, and I pick my way over the loose stones to a flat boulder. I brush silt from the sun-warmed rock and sit, folding my legs under me. I check my sandwich for signs of Roberta's ire before digging in.

The breeze rustles the tree branches. I pin another strand of hair behind my ear and bite into the sandwich. Something about the sunshine, fresh air and lapping water makes it taste extra good. I'm halfway done when Justin points at the river. "See how the trees dip their roots into the water?"

I nod. The tree roots resemble straws. I imagine them sucking up the river water.

"Water moccasins like to nest in the roots."

I draw my brows together.

"It's a type of poisonous water snake."

A shiver ripples down my spine. I can almost feel the slimy things slithering around my legs, obscured by the murky water. Note to self: never swim in that river. Not that I'll get the chance.

"What do you say we walk up the river a ways?"

I nod and swallow my last bite of sandwich.

Justin lifts himself off the ground, slaps his backside to knock off the dust. He extends his hand to me. I grab hold of it, strong, but soft, not calloused like Nathan's. He pulls me to my feet. His hand remains around mine until I let go, long enough for my heart to double its pace.

He meanders up river and I follow close behind. "Please talk to me." His voice holds a hint of desperation. "You can ask me anything you want."

He looks back at me in time to see my eyes roll. "I'll get you to talk to me."

If he knew what my silence meant to me, he wouldn't be so confident.

He points across the river. "See that washed out bridge?"

My eyes trace his outstretched arm toward the opposite river bank. Twisted re-bar and concrete remnants poke from the overgrown foliage.

"A long time ago a terrible accident happened here. A bus full of kids from a summer camp stalled on that bridge when a flash flood came through. A wall of water hit the bus. Toppled it like a Matchbox car. The water was so high that the kids who managed to get out of the bus were clinging to the treetops."

I peer up at the towering Cypress trees. He has to be exaggerating. The water couldn't possibly reach that high. Could it? I imagine screaming children tossed about in the raging water. Trapped. Terrified. Out of control. Not knowing if they were going to live or die or see their families again.

That horrifying image tightens my chest. I know how those kids felt. I'm trapped. I'm drowning. The current is carrying me farther and farther from home, and I'm too weak to fight it. But those kids, if they wanted to survive, couldn't stop swimming. They would've had to fight the current with all their strength. How? How do you keep fighting when you feel you have no strength left?

Justin continues. "Flash floods are fairly common around here. Even if it's not raining where we are, rain up in the hills can cause it to flood down here in the valley."

We return to our horses and resume our ride. Justin continues his public service announcements. "You have to watch out for rattle snakes. We've also got brown recluse spiders and black widows. They're both poisonous."

Goose-bumps rise on my arms. Poisonous snakes and spiders. Flash floods. Is there anything here that can't kill me? Texas is a death trap. Why would anyone choose to live here?

"Oh, and watch out for the centipedes. They have a stinger on every foot, so if they end up on you...well, you can do the math."

Thanks. Now I'll never be able to sleep again. Why is he telling me this? I have enough nightmares without him giving me fodder for more.

In the early afternoon, Justin changes course and leaves the well-worn trail behind. He veers into a dense bushy area where the branches scrape my arms. He leads me into a clearing, and a two-story salt block house comes into view. Yellow paint bubbles and peels from the siding to reveal weathered grey wood beneath.

Justin slides off his horse and winds the reins around a leaning fence post that seems as though it might topple if Goliath gives a slight tug.

I stay on Cherokee, glancing from Justin to the house, then back to Justin. Where are we?

"Come here. I'll help you down."

I don't need his help. I grip the reigns tighter and Cherokee dances backward, as though she senses my apprehension.

"There's something I want you to see."

This morning's discussion with Nathan consumes my thoughts and makes my heart pound in my ears. I allowed Justin to bring me all the way out here where no one would be able to find me and no one would hear me scream. An abandoned house would give him all the privacy he needs to do whatever he wants to me. I should've listened to Nathan. I should've played sick.

Justin takes hold of my horse's bridle. "C'mon Rielle." His hands follow the reins to my fingers, white knuckled around a knot of leather. He looks into my eyes. "Don't worry."

I hug the horse tighter with my legs. Justin presses his lips together. His tone turns stern, almost parental when he says, "Come down." He begins to pry my fingers away from the reins. "Rielle, I'm not going to hurt you. Just get off the horse."

I press my teeth into my bottom lip.

"I will drag you off that horse if I have to."

I throw a nervous glance behind me. Can I find the way back on my own? I search Justin's face for deception, waiting for a demon to appear and give his true motive away. I don't see a devil. More like a concerned angel. Wide blue eyes. Honest eyes? I think. But I don't know. An odd sensation nudges me. I don't trust him, but part of me wants to trust him.

I'll probably live to regret this.

I sling my legs over the side of the horse and jump down. I follow Justin up the back steps of the old house, onto the creaky porch. He turns the knob and swings the door open. I take a step backward and then another. Justin motions for me to go in. "Ladies first."

Turn my back on him? I think not. I step backward again.

He pushes out an exasperated sigh. "Rielle, please. Quit making this so difficult. I'm not going to hurt you. I just want to show you this and then we can head home." He holds out his hand.

I scrutinize his hand like it's one of those water snakes he talked about earlier. I extend mine. He closes his fingers around it in a firm grip and tows me into the house.

A haze of rotting eggs and sour milk hits me as we step inside the small kitchen with white painted cabinets and brown floral linoleum. It's a museum of the ordinary—everything as a normal family would have it. A round kitchen table surrounded by four chairs stands in the middle of the room, a tea kettle tops the stove, a hand-tied rug sprawls on the floor in front of the sink.

He leads me through a doorway into a small family room at the front of the house. Dust motes dance in a ray of sunlight that sneaks through the gap in the curtains. We walk past a plaid sofa and loveseat, arranged around an old flat screen TV. If it weren't for the dust and cobwebs, it would be cozy and inviting.

Justin walks to the fireplace and rests his arm on the mantle. "A family like yours used to live here. Resistors. They refused the chip too. Bank Security came for them. They had the house surrounded with the family inside. After a short standoff, security rushed the door, but found the house empty. If you go upstairs, their clothes are still in the drawers. It's like they disappeared. They've never been found. The Bank gave my uncle the property after that."

Disappeared? No, this family escaped, but where did they go? Bank Security monitors everything. Resistors can't come into a populated area without being noticed. Chip detectors are set to detect not only chips, but biometrics. If it detects a human and no chip, alarms go off like someone just stole the crown jewels. It happened to me once—at the movie theatre of all places.

I ease my weight onto the sofa. It feels sadly familiar to be in a regular house. I run my hand over the velvety material, freeing more dust. I breathe in and out, awash in memories. Mom holding Alyssa. Silas. Dad. I close my eyes. For a moment I'm home. The sofa depresses beside me and Justin's warmth touches my arm. I lift my eyelids. Justin is next to me. Close. Too close. I jump to my feet.

Ocean blue eyes look up at me. "You're not going to talk to me are you?"

I shake my head. Never. He'll eventually accept this just as everyone else has.

He drops his head, blows out a long breathe. He's silent for a long minute. "We need to get back." He stands and I follow him out the back door to the horses.

Once back in the saddle, stress falls away like autumn leaves off a tree. I'm relieved to be on my way home. Home? The Banker's house is not my home. I have no home. I shouldn't be happy to return to it. Better the devil you know, I guess.

As we ride away, I twist in the saddle to take one last look at the house. Why did he take me there? I want to ask him, but I can't.

Justin doesn't speak. He plods along half a horse length in front of me. My thoughts center on the family who lived in that house. They're out there somewhere—free. But where? How would they find food and shelter? Maybe Bank Security caught them, and they're no better off than me and my family.

Justin's voice interrupts my thoughts. "What a beautiful evening." He cranks his neck around so he can look back at me.

I've been too deep in thought to notice. I survey the landscape. Justin's right. The lower curve of the sun rests below the horizon, bathing the countryside in an orange and gold glow. Wispy clouds blush purple and pink, like threads of cotton candy on a blue backdrop.

A light breeze ruffles strands of hair that fell out of my bun. As I move to the rhythm of the horse's gait, I suck in a deep breath. The smell of wood smoke and the resinous scent of pine perfumes the air. I exhale, expelling my stress and anxiety.

Justin slows his horse and comes alongside me. "So. I've spilled my guts. I'm sure you're tired of hearing about me. Can I ask you some questions?"

I clamp my teeth together and tighten my grip on the reins. Is that his way of tricking me into speaking? Not going to happen.

He grins. "Just 'yes' or 'no' questions. You don't have to talk. Heaven knows, no one's going to make you talk."

It's about time he got the message, but even without the need for speech, I'm a little apprehensive. What does he want to know? Only one way to find out. I shrug and nod.

"I heard you lived in Minnesota. Had you lived there your whole life?"

I nod.

"It gets pretty cold up there in the winter."

I smile. If I were talking, I'd tell him that I miss the crisp winter air and the pristine white of freshly fallen snow.

"Did you do any camping with your family?"

I nod enthusiastically. We used to camp every summer. It was the highlight of the summer—until they took that away from us too.

"That really helped my dad and me through the time after my mom left. Dad and I would go on fishing trips. We'd camp and canoe for a couple of weeks every summer. One of our favourite spots was in Minnesota. Mille Lacs. You ever been there?"

Nodding, I place my hand on my chest.

"You camped there, with your family?"

I bite my lip and smile.

His eyes go distant for a moment before he looks at me again. "It must've been great to have a mom *and* a dad. You had good parents."

How would he know? For all he knows they were tyrants.

"You must be proud of them."

I tilt my head. My brows knit together.

"Aren't you proud of them?"

I shake my head. His words stir the anger at my parents that's always smouldering beneath the surface. Why would I be proud of them when they're the reason I'm here? Maybe I'd be proud of them if they had kept our family together. But they're in prison, I'm a slave, and who knows where Silas and Alyssa ended up. What's to be proud of? There's a part of me that feels sorry for them, especially after what Nina said about her parents. I don't like to think about that. Hatred I can handle. Pity? I just can't do pity. I clench my teeth and stare off into the distance, away from Justin's probing gaze.

"I would have thought…" Justin trails off. "Well, you should be proud of them, you know. They took a stand."

My dam of emotions breaks—rage, despair, heartbreak—all boiling over, threatening to escape my body as tears. I lock my teeth on my cheek until I taste blood to force them back. I'm not going to fall apart again!

Justin reaches out, grabs my reins and stops both our horses. "I can see I've upset you. Why? I don't know. You won't tell me. You know, I'd prefer if you'd just tell me where to get off instead of this guessing game I have to play all the time. Tell me to go to hell. It would be music to my ears."

I kick my horse to get her going again. I fix my stare on the horizon and control every breath—in, out, in. I press my tornado of emotions down inside me until they become a jagged ball in the pit of my stomach. Everything else is numb. No emotion. No thought. An empty shell.

Justin catches up with me. I feel him staring at me, but I pretend he's not there. If I look at him I'll boil over again.

"Rielle?" His voice is a distant droning. I force him out of my world. I'm alone, as always.

In silence, we ride back to the stable. I climb the rungs on one of the corrals and sit at the top, watching Justin remove the bridles from our horses. He lifts off each of the saddles, the muscles on his arms bulging under tanned skin. His sleeve slides higher and exposes his tan line. I check my arm. I've got one too.

When he finishes, I jump down and follow him back to the gate that leads into the Banker's yard. He stops, his hand on the gate latch. "Same thing tomorrow. You may as well dress for it when you get up."

Is he crazy? Riding with me cannot be a pleasant experience.

He chuckles. "Maybe third time's the charm."

CHAPTER SEVENTEEN

Texas Two-Step

JUSTIN OPENS THE GATE AND MOTIONS for me to walk through. He removes the bracelet, then we cross the yard to find the other Contracts lounging under the live oak. As we pass them, I feel Nathan's and Lydia's gaze target me like spotlights. I follow Justin inside. We dish up cold dinners and carry them outside.

I ease myself to the ground next to Lydia, cross my legs and smile at her. Only one side of her mouth lifts as she returns the gesture. Her wary eyes search my face. "Everything okay?"

I nod, trying to keep my expression jovial.

Justin sits between Jonah and Morris. Nathan, who's seated at Lydia's side, does his own inspection. I roll my eyes.

Nathan purses his lips and shakes his head. "So, what'd the two of you do today?" He fixes his glare on Justin as he puts a fork full of potato in his mouth. Every other conversation ceases. Crickets chirp and the wind rustles the oak. I glower at Nathan.

Justin shrugs. "We took the horses out. Rode the trails."

Nathan looks at me, furrowing his brow. I nod in agreement, pleading with my eyes for him to let it go.

Justin plunges his fork into a pile of green beans. "Hey Jonah, you have anything for us today?"

Jonah glances from Nathan to Justin. "I do have one. Why does a chicken coop always have two doors?"

"Why?" Justin asks a little too enthusiastically.

"Because if it had four doors it would be a chicken sedan."

"That is the stupidest joke I've ever heard," Roberta says.

"Really, Roberta? That's really the stupidest joke you've ever heard? You have some sort of rating system for these things?" Jonah saturates his voice with sarcasm. She aims a battery acidic glare at him.

With the attention off Justin and me, I start eating my dinner and listening in on the other conversations. Everyone seems lighter, freer with the Banker gone. Lydia smiles more. Morris lies back on his elbows. Jasmine sits next to Jonah; he nudges her with his elbow every now and then. In the Banker's presence Jasmine is stiff and emotionless, as if she's always posing. When he's gone though, that façade falls away. Tonight she looks vulnerable and raw, her legs hugged to her chest.

Several times, she drifts off, deep emotion dominating her beautiful eyes. Jonah always seems to be aware of her, his gaze moving from the others to linger on her. He smiles and nudges her again, but she drifts and barely flinches when he touches her. He seems almost desperate to keep her engaged. Not like someone with romantic interest, but like holding onto someone who is falling over a cliff. There's sadness in Jonah's face when she drifts off like that.

Nathan lifts his chin as if encouraging Jonah to continue. What's going on with her? Why the concern?

Jonah, though, is a master of his craft. He whispers something to her and she chuckles. What did he say? He whispers something else and she breaks into laughter. She laughs until tears spill down her cheeks.

Justin gets up and walks into the house, leaving his plate half full. A few minutes go by before he returns with his docking station. He fiddles with some buttons on the top, then music explodes from the speakers.

Jonah and Nathan begin bantering about a song.

"Come on. Best band of the decade," Jonah says.

Nathan smirks. "If you're a twelve year old girl."

They both laugh.

"So, they don't do much of that up in Utah?" Justin asks Lydia.

I turn my attention to them. What are they talking about?

"No, I think that might be more of a Texas thing," she says.

Justin grins. "It's easy. I'm sure Nathan can. Every southern boy knows how to two-step."

Nathan throws an irritated glance at Justin.

Justin scrolls through a song list and chooses a country western tune with a quick beat.

"I'll teach you how." Justin rises to his feet and holds out his hand, beckoning for Lydia to join him.

Lydia blushes. "I don't know. I have no idea how."

"I'm an excellent teacher," Justin says.

Lydia's cheeks pink a deeper shade as Justin takes her hand, pulls her to her feet and begins his two-stepping tutorial. Lydia laughs as she stumbles over her own feet, but she gradually finds her rhythm. I laugh along with her, glad it's her on the spot and not me this time.

With Lydia gone, Nathan edges toward me. He inclines his head, a crooked smile playing on his lips. "May I have this dance?"

My eyes widen. I shake my head. No way!

"Just give it a try. You can step on my feet all you want."

Lydia seems to be having a good time. It might be fun and Nathan still has his work boots on. I stand, my neck already warm and we haven't even started yet.

"Okay. One hand on my shoulder." He positions my arm for me, then picks up my other hand, closes his fingers around it. He seems taller when I'm this close to him.

He steps forward. "Now back." But my feet go forward. I end up on his toes.

I clamp my teeth together and throw him an apologetic glance. Within the first thirty seconds I trip over my feet and his at least five times. I grip his shoulder for support and stare at my feet in an effort to force them to do the right thing.

He chuckles. "You can't stare at your feet the whole time. Look at me. I'll lead you."

I lift my head and meet his warm hazel eyes. My stomach rises as though I'm falling. There's something about his gaze that whispers, "Everything's going to be okay. You're safe." I tear my stare away from his.

Jonah persuades Jasmine to join us, though he doesn't seem to know the dance steps.

The music stops for a moment before another song comes on. I'm tense, afraid to step on him again. I try to follow, but my rhythm is all off.

"Relax. And breathe."

I didn't realize I was holding my breath.

He jiggles my arms. "You're too stiff. Don't worry about me. You only weigh about ten pounds. Just move with me."

I inhale deeply, relax my shoulders and allow the music to saturate me. I find the beat and trust Nathan to move me at the right time. My feet begin to cooperate, my movements still jerky, but I keep my feet on the ground and off his toes.

He smiles down at me. "You're getting it."

I return his easy smile.

He rests his cheek against my hair. "You smell a little like horse."

I grimace and turn my head to smell my shoulder.

"Don't worry. I like the smell of horses."

I stumble again. He catches me and I start giggling, which only makes me trip again. The more I laugh, the clumsier I get. Laughter rumbles in Nathan's chest. When it's clear that I'm not going to recover from my giggle fit, he gathers me closer, picks me up and proceeds to dance, my legs dangling above the ground, swinging like a rag doll's.

"Is that better?"

I nod, still convulsing with laughter.

Nathan. So safe. His eyes seem to sparkle in the moonlight. His arms form a protective cocoon around me, a shield that no evil can penetrate. I can see where Jessica would be taken with him. He must miss her. A flood of sadness for Nathan washes over me. He probably wishes he were dancing with her. How difficult it must have been to find love, only to lose it. Jessica's probably out there somewhere pining for him, hoping for a miracle that might bring them back together.

"Hey, Nathan," Justin says. "How about we trade partners?"

Nathan's cheerful expression fades. "No, thank you."

Did he offend Lydia? She throws Nathan a knowing look. Justin's jaw tightens.

Nathan's treading on dangerous ground. I shoot him an uneasy look.

"I'm not afraid of him," Nathan whispers. "You need to stand up to him, Rielle."

I bite my lip and shake my head.

Justin stops dancing. "She's not going to learn if you're just swinging her around like that."

"I think you've spent enough time with her today," Nathan says.

My chest tightens. If the Banker hears about his disrespect, he'll be punished. I pinch Nathan.

"Ow!" He furrows his brow and assesses my expression. "I don't think Justin wants the Banker to know about any of this. He's not going to run off and tattle on me." Nathan flashes an impish grin.

When the song ends, Justin dashes to the docking station and hits the power button. Nathan sets me back on my feet, then bends at the waist into a gentlemanly bow. "Thank you for the dance. Goodnight."

I follow Lydia up to our room and dig my pajamas out of the drawer. Lydia stands next to her bed, wringing her hands as if she wants to say something, but just stares at me instead. I tilt my head, waiting.

She licks her lips and presses them together. "Is Justin…doing something to you…that you don't want?"

Oh no, not her too. I shake my head.

"Are you sure? I mean—you can tell me. Maybe we could tell the Banker." But then, as though she thinks better of it, she says, "Or maybe his wife." She doesn't seem convinced that either party would be helpful.

I appreciate Lydia's concern and want to assure her that she doesn't need to worry. I breathe on the window and write, "He's nice," in the mist.

"Really?" She eyes me like Mom used to eye Silas when he made excuses for skipping school.

I nod in the most emphatic way I can muster.

"Alright. If you say so."

I shuffle down the hall to bathroom with my pajamas under my arm, intent on showering away the horse smell. As I pass Roberta's room, she opens her door.

"Rielle," she says, as though she's happy to see me. I stop for a moment, stunned. I start to walk again, but she throws up her arm to block me. I glare at her.

She issues a fake, toothy grin. "I just want to talk to you for a minute." Her voice is high, sickeningly sweet. "Justin seems to like you." I know the tone. I had one of those gossipy friends in school who would cozy up to people to get juicy morsels of information.

I shrug, push her arm out of the way and keep walking. She follows me into the bathroom. I look at her like she's crazy.

"So. Where have you two been going?" She tries to sound light, but there's an imperative in her voice.

I fold my arms. Her expression turns frigid, calculating. "Tell me." The words come out as a growl.

I shake my head. Why does she want to know so bad?

"Tell me or I'll tell the Banker you've been snooping around in his office."

As if I'd tell her anything. I wouldn't even tell her the sky was blue if I thought for a second it would give her any satisfaction. The Banker can beat me if he wants. It wouldn't be the first time. I turn my back on her, pick up my toothbrush scrub it over my teeth.

Roberta's face flushes angry red. "You know Justin doesn't like you, right? He's just going to use you and drop you like yesterday's trash."

I ignore her, which seems to make her angrier. She grabs my arm.

"What are you doing, Roberta?" Lydia stands in the doorway to the bathroom.

Roberta lets go of my arm and snatches up her toothbrush. "We're just brushing our teeth." She squeezes too much toothpaste onto the bristles, then stuffs it in her mouth.

CHAPTER EIGHTEEN

Spider Duty

AFTER BREAKFAST, I WAIT WITH ALL the other Contracts for their day's chores even though Justin has already informed me I'll spend another day on horseback. Justin hands out slips of paper again, and everyone marches off to get started. Even Nathan strides out of the room in a hurry, which is a relief.

I follow Justin across the yard. A step before the gate, a twig snaps behind me. I spin around and Nathan steps out from behind the hedge. Justin stops and turns around too. I freeze. Nathan's going to get in trouble. He has no business being back here—other than me.

Nathan stands taller and folds his arms across his broad chest. "Where are you taking her?"

"You don't need to worry about it, Nathan." Justin waves his hand dismissively, opens the gate and motions for me to keep walking.

Nathan steps forward. "I do need to worry about it. Why do you keep taking her away? What are you doing to her?"

If I had a roll of duct tape, I'd seal Nathan's mouth shut. He'll be punished if he keeps this up. The idea of Nathan going hungry because of me—or worse—makes my stomach lurch. I walk over to Nathan, put my hand on his chest and shake my head.

"I won't let anything happen to her. She's safe with me," Justin says, his voice patient, understanding.

"I don't believe you. Why do you keep singling her out? Is it because she won't be able to tell anyone what you're doing to her?"

I watch the accusation sink in. Crimson colours Justin's cheeks. "You think I'm—"

"No! Ask her yourself!"

I stand between them wishing I could hold back Nathan's flood of words. He looks straight into my eyes. "Is he hurting you?"

I set my lips and shake my head. As Nathan stares at me, evaluating my answer, Justin says, "Why are *you* singling her out? I don't see you coming to Jasmine's rescue."

Jasmine needs rescuing? Last night's behaviour confirms that. But rescuing from what? I've never seen the Banker hit her like he does me, or pay much attention to her at all. Maybe he hits her while she's with him at work. Or maybe he has more creepy friends like Captain Comb-over putting his hands on her.

Nathan's mouth snaps closed and a faint flush crosses his cheeks. He stomps back through the yard.

"Let's go," Justin says, irritated. He heads for the stables at double pace. I have to jog to keep up.

I fidget with the bracelet that scrambles my tracker chip. If Justin tells the Banker, Nathan will be punished for sure. I'll probably be punished too. The Banker might even assume it's like it was with Jessica—that Nathan and I have some sort of relationship going on. Days without food. Beatings. And, what if? What if he sends me away to a new owner? I'd lose Lydia and Nathan.

Justin glances back at me as we near the stables. The annoyance drains from his face, replaced by concern. "Nathan's a good guy."

I try to read his face. He seems to mean what he says, but it doesn't help my anxiety. I feel like a cracked window. One touch might shatter me.

"He wants to protect you. I can respect that. Anyone who's looking out for your best interests is okay in my books. Don't worry. I won't be tattling to my uncle about it."

I breathe a sigh of relief.

"I would like to know one thing, though. Don't worry, you won't have to talk for this one, but I do want an honest answer. Okay?"

I nod.

"Is Nathan right? Does it bother you that I'm bringing you out here like this, that I'm *singling* you out?

I take a moment to think through his question. Sure, at first it made me nervous, but not anymore. There are a lot of things that bother me. I miss my family. I hate living in the Banker's house. Justin is the only bright spot in my life. When I'm out riding with him, I'm free. It's Nathan's anxiety that causes most of mine. If Nathan would stop worrying, I'd be far less stressed.

Finally, I meet his gaze and shake my head "no." Justin singling me out doesn't bother me.

Justin looks at me sceptically. "Are you sure?"

I nod. Whinnying carries across the pasture. Cherokee charges toward us, mane and tail waving in the wind.

"She's either happy to see you, or happy to see the apples." Justin flashes a crooked grin and tosses me a waxy red fruit. I flatten my hand and feed her the apple, stroking her muzzle. She bites it in half and chews. Drool drips from her mouth as she comes back for the other half. I wipe the slime off on my pants.

"Have you ever rode bareback?"

I force my eyes wider. I don't like the sound of that. What will I hold onto?

"Let's give it a try."

No way. I shake my head.

"Don't worry, Cherokee is well trained. You'll be fine."

Morris carries the bridles from the stable, slips one onto each horse and turns them over to us. Justin kneels beside the horse and threads his fingers together. "I'll give you a boost."

I place my foot in his hands, and he hoists me onto the horse. I feel naked with nowhere to put my feet and no saddle horn to hold.

"You'll have to hold on with your legs," Justin says.

I nudge Cherokee gently, afraid that if I nudge her too hard she'll start trotting and I'll bounce right off her back. Justin mounts his saddle-less horse, and we start down the trail. Maybe this won't be so bad.

We plod along while I get used to riding without a saddle. It's not too bad, other than the seat of my pants acting as a giant sponge for horse sweat. After about an hour, Justin pulls back on his reins to stop Goliath. "Do you know the way to the old house from here?"

I think back to yesterday, peer down the trail and nod.

"Then you lead the way."

I tap Cherokee with my heels and pass Justin. He rides behind me. By the time we arrive at our usual lunch spot, my thighs burn from gripping the horse. I'm going to be sore tomorrow. After lunch we ride on toward the old house.

I follow the trail, but Justin has to tell me where to turn off when we're almost there. "See the hill with that rock jutting out of the top. When you see it, you're close. And then take a left between those two trees." He points to a couple twisted junipers.

The old house comes into view. I steer Cherokee to the leaning fence post, prepared to dismount.

"Good job. Next time I won't help you, though. You'll have to find it yourself."

Next time?

"Well, we should probably head back. I've got an essay to work on." Justin tugs on one rein and Goliath wheels around.

Why did we come here only to turn around and go back? I turn my horse and follow him away from the house, through the stand of trees and back to the trail.

I sigh. Tomorrow the Banker is due back, and everything will return to normal. It would've been nice to see more of the hill country before his return. Trail riding, picnic lunches and fresh air beat scrubbing toilets any day. I hadn't realized until this moment, that the knot of anxiety permanently plaguing me in the Banker's presence had disappeared. Now it's back.

I savour everything on our way home—the way the limestone seems to glow in the evening light, the scent of dust and pine, the feeling of the breeze on my arms, the cadenced gait of the horse and the sound of the stones crunching under her hooves.

My heart sinks and my shoulders slump. This may be the last time I ever leave the Banker's yard. I want to kick the horse and bolt in the opposite direction.

Justin slows his horse and rides next to me. "I'm going to miss our rides."

I nod and steal another glance at the river.

"Did I say something wrong again or are you down because my uncle is coming back?"

I open my mouth and then catch myself, snap my mouth closed.

Justin laughs. "Were you actually going to answer me?"

The back of my neck heats and I shake my head.

"Well, I'm going to hope you're down because my uncle's coming back. It makes me feel better."

I smile at him.

"I think there's one more experience you need to have before I take you back. What's the Texas adventure without a little bit of country music?"

His mouth curls into a crooked smile. "Daybreak run San Antone to Austin," he sings, his voice low and smooth.

He cocks his hat and peeks at me out of the corner of his eye. "Rodeo left me my truck and boots, but my pockets, they got nothin'."

I throw him my best you-are-insane look. I try to hold it in, but can't suppress a giggle.

"I left my girl in Amarillo, my Amarillo rose. She said, 'Boy, stay with me.' But bull ridin's in my blood. I had to go." He belts it out, his voice echoing in the distance.

He pauses. He's done. Good.

But then he continues and sings the entire song with pride and enthusiasm.

Having him serenade me as we ride through the Texas countryside is more endearing than I would've thought. I've never been a big fan of that type of music, but between the setting and his silky voice, I think I could be persuaded...

The Banker waddles into the kitchen the next morning looking like a butter ball turkey roasted to a golden brown. His vacation hasn't made him more pleasant, though. Same old Banker. All the Contracts flee to their morning chores with heads hung. The pleasant atmosphere that had been ignited while the Banker was away has been smothered.

Today I'm assigned spider duty. I have to clear the mansion exterior of daddy-long-legs. Hundreds of them gather in clumps scattered sporadically over the exterior walls.

I retrieve a broom from the utility room and head outside where I find a pulsating clump, a tangle of thin brown legs. A pile of disembodied legs lie on the ground below the throng. I shudder. I hate spiders! And scorpions and centipedes and walking sticks.

The cluster of spiders have tucked themselves under the eaves, far beyond my reach. I stand on tip-toe and swipe at them with my broom. They begin to fall, but the breeze catches them and whips them around my head. They rain onto my back, into my hair. They slide down my face and land on my bare arms. I scream, stomping and batting at my head. Thin creepy legs are everywhere—tickling inside my shirt, crawling down my neck. I slap my clothes and scratch my neck. I jump up and down, like a two- year-old throwing a temper tantrum.

Nathan rounds the corner. "What happened?" he asks, out of breath.

I continue my frantic dance, now pulling down my hair to shake it out.

Nathan barks out a hearty laugh. "All that over a few daddy-long-legs? They won't kill you, you know. Just hold still for a minute. I'll see if there are any left." He combs his fingers through my hair, moves it to the side, touches the back of my neck. A shiver runs down my spine.

"I think you got them all." He shakes his head. "You scared me. I thought Justin got to you."

I roll my eyes, still feeling the prickle of spider legs all over me.

"You really shouldn't trust that guy. I don't trust him any further than I can throw him." His eyes grow distant for a moment and a his lips lift into a wistful grin. "Although I could probably throw him pretty far. Maybe I should give it a try."

I shake my head.

"Seriously though, I think he's up to something. When the Banker's brother visited, I overheard him and Justin talking when they were walking around the grounds. They were talking about buying your contract."

My heart leaps, the spiders pushed from my mind. What? Why would they want to do that? I tilt my head and knit my brows together, hoping Nathan has an explanation.

"That obviously didn't happen for whatever reason, so I got worried when he started taking you on those outings. I thought maybe since he wasn't able to buy, he was just going to—" He seems to search for the right term. "To just *take* what he wanted." He pauses. "Well, I need to get back to work. But think about what I said. I don't think he is what he appears to be." Nathan disappears around the back of the house.

It's a relief to finally understand Nathan's anxiety about Justin, but why would Uncle Rex want to buy my contract? Was that what their argument was about before Uncle Rex left after Thanksgiving?

It's kind of weird—the acceptance of being someone's property. If someone had talked about buying me a couple of years ago, I would've been insulted. I know that Uncle Rex treats his Contracts humanely, but I don't like that my heart surged at the thought of being purchased by him. Why? Was it the idea of better treatment? Or, being permanently in Justin's home? No. I can't think like that. I'm a slave. He's free. Period.

Still, why didn't it happen? Did they change their minds? And why me and why not Lydia? She can work circles around me. Could Nathan be right about Justin's interest in me? That's ridiculous. I'm sure there are plenty of girls at his university vying for his attention.

He couldn't possibly want me.

CHAPTER NINETEEN

Weightless, Yet Infinitely Heavy

WEEKS GO BY, FILLED WITH BACK BREAKING labour and the Banker's verbal abuse. With the Banker home, I rarely see Justin. He's gone all day at school and spends most of his time in his room in the evenings. I pass him in the halls a few times. He nods a greeting and his gaze stays on me long enough to make me blush and hurry away.

Vacuuming day is nauseatingly repetitive. Back and forth, back and forth. Some of the rooms are so huge I wonder if anyone's invented a riding vacuum. Not that it would matter. The Banker would never purchase one, but I can dream.

I turn my mind off as I clean the long upstairs hall. The droning whir of the vacuum cleaner allows me to hum the song mom liked so well to myself without anyone hearing. I save the area in front of the Banker's room until last because I don't want to risk disturbing Nina too early in the day.

We're always being told "don't disturb Nina." The Banker's adamant about it and Roberta guards the room like a rabid dog. Luckily, she's busy getting Nina's lunch ready, so she won't appear out of nowhere, frothing at the mouth and growling at me for making too much noise. I still haven't figured out how to vacuum without making noise.

As I pass the double doors to the master suite, hinges creak and the door swings open. Nina stumbles toward me. Startled, I freeze, the vacuum still humming. I back away.

She falls forward and grabs onto my collar. I stagger backward and bump into the wall. Nina leans in close and presses her cheek to my cheek. "Rielle, help me," she whispers. Nina draws back and peers into my eyes, her desperate gaze searching so deeply that I'm sure she must've found my soul. Tears overflow her lower eyelids as she brings one trembling hand up to cup my face. Blood coats her other hand. Again.

"Please. Please, help me."

Help her? I can't even help myself.

Then, like fingernails on a chalk board, a voice breaks through the hum of the vacuum cleaner.

"What do you think you're doing? Rielle, did you wake her?" Roberta stands at the end of the hall, a tray in one hand, the other hand on her hip.

The emotion drains from Nina's face. Her eyes go blank and her hand falls from my face. She steps back and tucks her bleeding hand into her bathrobe.

Roberta saunters toward us, balancing the lunch tray.

"Nina, did she wake you? Believe me; I will make sure she is punished. You need to get back to bed right away." Roberta throws me a hateful glare.

"No, she didn't wake me. I—I—I. I thought I'd come downstairs and have lunch in the kitchen, but I stumbled and Rielle caught me." I catch the hint of a suppressed Hispanic accent as she rolls the "R" in my name.

"You know you shouldn't be out of bed," Roberta says. She shoves the tray at my chest. "Take this." Tomato soup sloshes over the side of the bowl, and saltine crackers slide into sliced apples on the plate. Three pills clatter against a stoneware mug of tea. What are they for? Is Roberta why Nina needs my help?

Roberta wraps her arm around Nina's waist, shifting Nina's weight onto her. She drags her back to bed. Nina hangs her head, then glances back at me pleadingly. I follow them in and set the tray on the dresser, while Roberta tucks Nina into her bed.

Roberta doesn't look at me when she says, "You can leave now. Find somewhere else to vacuum. You've done enough damage for today. And close the door behind you."

I shuffle toward the door as Roberta coaxes Nina. "Now it's time to take your pills."

"No Roberta, please. I want to see my children. I don't want to sleep." Her voice quivers.

I throw Nina one last glance before I close the door behind me. I walk away from the room, towing the vacuum cleaner behind me to the other end of the hall. Justin's room is about as far from Nina as I can get.

I can't concentrate. I vacuum in the same spot over and over, too fixated on Nina to think of anything else.

I grip the vacuum hose, tighter, tighter. Did she realize who she was asking for help? She may as well be asking the doorknob to help her. What did she want from me? Maybe I should forget about it. Maybe she's lost her mind. I want to dismiss it, blame it on paranoia or medication, but I can't. Her eyes were lucid and her pleading real.

And, what did she do to her hand? Did she cut herself again? Whatever she did, she didn't want Roberta to know. If Roberta is a problem, she could tell the Banker, certainly he'd believe his wife before he'd believe Roberta unless—unless the Banker wants her drugged. Maybe she's ruining his perfect life.

I stop vacuuming. It's not like I'm making any progress anyway. Half curious, half concerned, I formulate a plan.

Pretending to need a fresh vacuum bag, I pass through the kitchen on my way to the utility room to see what Roberta is up to. She plucks chunks of meat from a chicken carcass, her hands coated in a glistening layer of grease. I rush back upstairs, insert the new bag, drag the vacuum into one of the spare bedrooms and turn it on. I check the clock. I've got about ten minutes. After that someone may notice that the vacuum isn't changing rooms.

I creep down the hall, leaving the vacuum cleaner roaring behind me, and ease open the door to the master suite. I peek inside, then squeeze through the narrow opening. A thin band of sunlight skirts the edge of the window blinds, casting a dim, strangled light over the room.

I ghost across the floor to the edge of Nina's bed. She lies propped up on two pillows, her eyes closed and her face stained with salt-crusted tear tracks. I pick up her undamaged hand. At my touch, her eyelids lift slowly, heavily. "Rielle? Please help me."

I ease onto the bed beside her. Finding her injured hand, I inspect it. The damage isn't as bad as last time—just a single deep gash cut into the fleshy area between her thumb and index finger. I retrieve the first aid kit from the bathroom, clean the wound and then bandage her hand, making it look messy, as though she wrapped it herself.

"Rielle, I found it."

I furrow my brow as I evaluate her expression. Relieved. Peaceful. Drugged?

"When I hurt myself awhile back…do you remember?"

How could I forget? I nod.

"They took an MRI of my hands, to see if I damaged tendons. When they showed the pictures to Arthur, I saw it!" She forms a weak smile. "I'd been cutting in the wrong spot. I knew where to find it this time."

She lifts her good hand from the blankets, her fingers pinched together. In the dim light, I have to lean in for a closer look. She clutches a tiny, blood-encrusted metal object between her fingers. What is it?

A fresh round of tears swell in her eyes. "I got it out."

I can't stop a gasp from escaping my lips as the realization of what she holds hits me. Her chip.

"Take it."

I don't want it. I shake my head.

"Please! Get it away from me. I don't want it. It's taken my soul," she says, her voice strained.

Her shaking hand hangs in the air, the chip held between her fingers. Is that all she needs, someone to take it from her so she doesn't have to see it anymore?

I extend my open hand and she drops the tiny object onto my palm. She presses her eyes closed. "Thank you so much. Thank you." Her breathing slows.

The chip, though nearly weightless, feels heavy on my palm. I close my hand around it. Opening the door a crack, I peek into the empty hall, then slink through the narrow opening and ease the door closed behind me. I tip-toe back to the spare bedroom where the vacuum still drones.

I open my hand to get a better look at the chip. It appears harmless, nothing but a minuscule piece of metal, but in a way it's a metallic demon. Other demons just like it stole everything from me—my home, my family, my freedom. Without the chip, we'd still be together and I'd be free. I should smash it with a hammer.

But what if Nina needs it? If she tries to go anywhere without it, they'll know she removed it. As I stare at it, something inside me urges me not do destroy it.

I kick off my shoe and tuck the chip under the insole.

I reach for the vacuum handle and then stop. I run my fingers over my left hand, the spot where they inserted the chip. Somewhere below the skin, the tracker chip hides. Could mine be in the same spot as Nina's? I massage the area where she made her incision. She got hers out. This thing that keeps me inside the fence…perhaps it's not as permanent as I once thought.

CHAPTER TWENTY

Welcome to Hell, Eli

CLEANING UP GLUE, GLITTER AND construction paper from Lily and Caleb crafting their Valentines tells me we're well into February. As the days pass, cool grey weeks flow into warm sunny days.

The Banker arrives to assign our duties with a stranger at his side. A boy, maybe fifteen years old. About Silas' age. The way he hangs his head, his light blond hair dangling in stringy clumps, the purple bruises oozing beneath his freckled skin, it's clear that this newcomer is a Contract.

"This is Eli. He was a trouble maker at reform school, so I picked him up for cheap." The Banker straightens his back, forcing his belly out. "They've assured me that he was strongly reformed before I bought him and shouldn't be any trouble. But I know how shifty Resistors are, so I expect you all to keep him in line. If he makes one wrong move, there will be no food for the lot of you. Now get to work."

Maybe it's the sadness in his eyes or that he's Silas' age, but Eli sparks some sort of sisterly protectiveness. My heart aches for the kid. Fifteen and covered in bruises. I thought you had to be sixteen to be placed in a contract. Do they usually sell them after they complete reform school? Maybe it's just because this boy didn't behave. I hope that's all it is.

As I scrub the children's bedroom walls, more questions fill my mind. What exactly did Eli do wrong? Were the bruises punishments for his behaviour, or just a regular part of life at reform schools? Subconscious worries flow to the surface. Is my brother okay or is he suffering?

With each passing day, my concern for Silas increases. After a couple of days they overtake every thought. Eli has the information I need. He can either put my fears to rest or confirm them. But as long as the Banker assigns him outdoor work, I only see him at meals and I can't ask him questions in front of the others.

How am I going to do this anyway? Asking him questions requires me to speak.

A week after Eli's arrival, I can't take it anymore. That evening, I wait in the shadows beneath the stairs to the men's dorm, hoping for a moment alone with him. As he passes, I step into the moonlight, startling him. I smile reassuringly, but he backs away. I point at a yellowed bruise on his arm. He flinches away from my touch and starts upstairs. I grab his arm and point again, more forcefully this time. He yanks his arm from my grip and hurries upstairs to his room.

Nice going. Now he thinks I'm a freak. All my pointing and grabbing, why didn't I start grunting while I was at it? My silence—my one freedom—is becoming my own prison.

Finally, the Banker starts giving Eli some indoor duties. More and more the Banker gives us duties together. So we work alongside each other in silence. It almost kills me to have the answers to my questions about my brother so close, but so unreachable.

I lie in bed at night, restless. Exhaustion can't overcome my anxious thoughts. There's only one way to get answers: I'll have to speak to Eli. But what will I say?

The clock reads 2:07 in blinding red digits and I'm not any closer to sleep than I was when I laid down. I sit up and watch Lydia sleep for a few minutes, then peer out the window. There's nothing to see but the breeze rustling the branches of the live oak tree. The elegant dance, rhythmic and peaceful, settles my mind.

As I consider giving sleep another try, the shed door opens. A shadowy figure creeps out and dashes across the lawn toward the house. Moonlight glints off a mass of red hair, tossed by the breeze.

Roberta.

The stairs creak and then footsteps patter down the hall.

What was she doing in the shed this time of night?

Great. I'm wide awake again.

After only a couple of hours of sleep, my alarm clock wakes me to beautiful spring weather. The Banker is intent on getting the yard into shape, so everyone gets outdoor duties. He sends Eli and me to weed the vegetable garden.

Perfect.

Eli and I retrieve a hoe, a rake and a spade from the shed, carry them to the garden and set to work. My heart races as I ponder how to begin. I've been silent for a year now. Does my voice even work anymore?

I glance around to make sure we're alone, crouch down near him and pluck a few weeds out of the dirt. I open my mouth to speak, but nothing comes out except air. I clear my throat. "Eli," I whisper.

His head snaps up, eyes wide.

I check over my shoulder for witnesses, then incline my head toward him. "I need to talk to you about something."

"I—I thought you didn't talk."

I pull in a deep breath, considering my most crucial questions. "I don't. But there are some things I need to know." My voice sounds foreign my own ears.

"I won't tell anyone. What do you want to know?"

I creep to a weed patch closer to him. "Do all kids your age go to reform schools?"

"Yeah, anyone over twelve."

"That's where they sent my brother."

"How old's your brother?"

"He'd be sixteen by now."

Eli wriggles a thistle free from the packed soil. "If he's at a reform school, he won't be there much longer."

"And then, do they—do they let them go? I mean, once they're *reformed.*"

He lets out a sarcastic chuckle. "No."

My shoulders go slack. Silas will end up a slave like me. "You turned sixteen, so they sent you here?

"Not exactly. I'm still fifteen."

"Then why—"

He studies the dirt and one corner of his mouth flinches upward. "I was at a reform school up near Dallas, and I tried running away."

My gaze sweeps the yard again.

Eli tosses the weed into the grass beside the garden. "My friend Jesse heard about this guy who hides Resistors. When—"

"What? There are people who hide Resistors?"

"Yeah. Back in October, when we found out that Bank Security was planning to sell Jesse's contract, we decided to go to find the guy. The plan was to set out in different directions once we got out of the school so it would be harder for them to find us. We were going to meet up later. I got caught, but they couldn't find him. For months they tried getting our meeting spot out of me. He made it! He got away!"

"Who is this guy? Where is he?"

He presses his lips into a tight white line. He isn't going to tell me. I can appreciate his silence. I would do the same for anyone who escaped this life. "At that school, did they treat you...kindly?" I ask.

He keeps his head down, concentrates on a stubborn dandelion. "No."

I point to his arm. "Were those bruises from them?"

He covers the bruise with his hand. "Yeah."

"Is that because you tried to run away or do they usually hit kids?"

"Both."

Both. Tears well in my eyes, but I hold them back. My heart aches as though it's being torn in two.

"Do you miss your family?" he asks so quietly that I almost don't hear him over the wind.

"Yes."

"Me too." His eyes turn glassy. He rubs his sleeve over them.

Seeing the emotion in his eyes, I grapple for a more benign subject. "So where are you from?"

"Washington. How 'bout you?"

"Minnesota."

"Cool. That's where my friend Jesse was from."

"Eli, can I ask you a favour?"

He shrugs. "Sure."

"Please don't tell anyone I talked to you. This is important to me."

His eyes lock on mine. "I won't. I promise."

As soon as we finish the work in the garden and part ways, I'm already thinking of more questions, hoping the Banker will give us more duties together. I pass Eli in the halls, sit across from him at dinner, but someone is always watching.

Eight long days pass before the Banker gives us another combined duty. I have to stifle a smile as I climb the stairs to the children's play room to sanitize toys, because I'll finally get Eli to myself again. It isn't just about getting my questions answered. I like the kid. I like that he had the courage to escape and that he's keeping my secret. I like that he doesn't have any hidden agendas like Justin and Nathan. Maybe I'm just looking for another little brother.

He grins when I walk into the room lugging a tub of bleach water, scrub brushes and wash rags. With the Banker at work, the children at school, the wife drugged to the other side of Oz and the other Contracts either downstairs or outside, we're free to chat.

Thinking of my constantly complaining stomach, I launch into my first question. "So tell me more about reform schools. Do they feed you or do they make you go hungry?"

"We ate pretty well. Nothing fancy, but it was decent. Strong looking

Contracts sell for more money."

The word "sell" makes me cringe. "Is it like a regular school, like a boarding school? What do they teach?"

"There's no reading or writing, just practical stuff like how to repair things, change the oil in a car, clean toilets. That type of thing. Jesse said they're just trying to make us into better slaves. They don't care about us."

"Was it—I mean—were you scared when you got there?"

"Yeah. I was pretty freaked. You're thrown in with all these people. Some are angry at their parents, at everybody. Some were scared. Like me." He blushes. "The angry ones took it out on people like me."

Eli dips an action figure in the bleach water and wipes it with a cloth. "Why don't you talk?"

I dry my wet hands on my dress and go to the shelf to retrieve another pile of toys. "Because I wanted something that could be mine. Something I could control. And that's all I had."

I set the pile of toys beside the wash basin, wring out a rag and pick up a pink and purple polka dot box. I swipe the rag over the glass front and it lights. Must be a holo for kids. The holographic image of a life-size baby beams before me.

"I'm Baby Kissy Missy. Hello, Mommy," it yells at full volume. I fumble with the holo, trying to find the off button.

"Mommy, I'm hungry." Whiney this time.

"Turn it off. Someone'll hear!" Eli says.

"I'm trying." I run my fingers over the screen and around the edges. And then the baby opens its mouth wide and cries, a deafening, window shattering cry. Eli grabs the device out of my hand, swirls his finger on the screen and the device goes dark.

Eli and I freeze like ice sculptures, listening. Did Roberta hear? She'd undoubtedly tattle on us for activating the holo.

Eli clutches the rag in his fist, white knuckled.

"I don't think anyone heard," I say.

He nods nervously.

I offer a reassuring smile. "So what about your friend Jesse? Did you know him from before?"

He shakes his head, his shoulders relaxing. "No, I met him when I got there. These guys were picking on me and Jesse stopped them. We were friends after that. He was different from the others. He wasn't scared or angry. He was brave. He made me feel brave too. He used to tell me 'Never give in. They can control your body, but dude, don't let them have your soul.'"

I dip my rag in the water. Never give in. Those were the last words Silas said to me before Bank Security took him away. I scrub my rag over a dart gun, shoving aside the image of my brother, hands bound and walking out the door.

Eli scrubs a toy truck for too long, seemingly lost in thought. Jesse means so much to him. Lydia springs to mind. What would I have done without her? I don't think I would've survived my first months here. She kept me going, kept me hopeful.

Eli pauses scrubbing for a moment, then continues. "Jesse was a force of nature." He flashes a wistful grin. "One time I screwed up and the instructors took away my meals for two days. Jesse stole food for me. Jesse knew his way through all the duct work in the school. That's how he'd raid the kitchen."

His eyes glisten with excitement. "Another time they took food away from a kid for three days. He was a big kid, like six-four. Had to be two hundred and fifty pounds. They threw him into solitary. Jesse stole an entire leftover turkey for the guy. The next morning when the guards checked him, all that was left was a big turkey carcass." Eli chuckles. "It was hilarious. They couldn't figure out how it got there. Until somebody squealed. They threw Jesse into solitary too. But Jesse just took it. Didn't act like it bothered him at all."

We manage to get all the toys washed by dinner. No small task since the Banker makes sure his kids have every toy ever made.

Spring break arrives. The Banker takes Lily, Caleb and Inez north for a ski vacation, but leaves Nina behind. Of course she couldn't go, not without her chip inserted.

I envy them. I miss the snow. Though I have to admit, as much as I hate Texas, the hill country is beautiful in the spring. Everything greens up and the temperature turns pleasantly warm.

The Banker leaves Justin in charge again, but he doesn't show up on the first morning. Everyone mills around the kitchen, looking anxious and irritated. "Mondays are usually laundry days. Maybe we should just get started," Lydia says. We each take a laundry basket and go our separate ways to collect bedding and dirty clothes.

I make it back to the laundry room before Lydia and load the sheets into the machine. Boots pad the floor behind me. I glance over my shoulder. Nathan strides into the room, leans against a tower of cabinets and folds his arms.

I nod and smile at him.

He lets out a heavy breath, irritated. We hadn't seen Justin this morning. What could possibly be irritating him? I fill a plastic cup with laundry detergent and pour it into the dispenser.

"You can talk to that boy, but not to me?" he both asks and accuses.

My mouth falls open. I spin around to face him. He saw us? I begin pouring over every conversation Eli and I had, trying to pinpoint where we slipped up.

"Why won't you talk to me? I know you can."

That boy, as he called him, is safe. I understand Eli's motives. Nathan, on the other hand, confuses me with his unpredictable moods. One minute he's worried about me, then angry, then indifferent. I know he must miss Jessica. Maybe that wears on him.

I lift the empty laundry basket onto my hip, glare at him and walk toward the kitchen. He grabs my arm. "Rielle, I need to talk—"

"There you are. I've been looking everywhere," Justin's voice sounds from the doorway.

Nathan's back stiffens and he tightens his grip on my arm.

"Are you ready?" Justin asks.

Ready for what? I lift my eyebrows.

Nathan's jaw tenses until a muscular outline creases his cheek.

"Morris has the horses ready to go." Justin's eyes move between me and Nathan.

I nod, wiggle loose from Nathan's grip and set the laundry basket down.

"So. Uh…what do you guys do on these rides?" Nathan asks.

I shoot daggers at him with my gaze.

Justin shrugs. "Just trail riding. No need to concern yourself."

Eager to escape the tension, I brush past Nathan, then Justin, dash upstairs to my room and change into my jeans, jittery at the prospect of getting out of prison for the day. I haven't left the yard in months.

We walk down to the stables together and bribe the horses with apples. We ride bareback again, meandering down the trail in silence. I listen to the birds chirping and the rhythmic click of horseshoes on gravel. The breeze smells of cut grass today. I draw in a huge breath, savouring the fresh scent and enjoying the radiant warmth from the sun.

"I think you're going to talk to me today," Justin says.

I roll my eyes, shake my head.

He laughs. "Don't be so sure."

I scrutinize his expression. He seems more optimistic than usual, which makes me nervous. There is absolutely nothing he can say or do that will make me break my silence with him. Nothing.

CHAPTER TWENTY-ONE

Justin Undressed

AFTER AN HOUR OF RIDING, JUSTIN TUGS HIS REINS to the right and leaves the trail. My heart surges. I finally get to see some different country. We ride south, cross the river at a shallow spot and continue our ride on the opposite bank.

By the time my stomach begs for lunch, the weather has turned hot and humid. Ahead of me, Justin is already sweating through his T-shirt.

He guides the horses down a steep embankment alongside the river. I nearly lay on the horse's back to keep from falling forward.

"How about we stop for a bit?" Justin says. We tie our horses to a tree near the water. Cherokee walks into the water as far as her tether allows her and bends her neck to drink. I'm clammy with sweat. I envy the horses as they wade into the water.

I climb onto a rounded boulder at the water's edge and scan the river for snakes before slipping off my shoes and sinking my toes into the cool, murky fluid. The water swirls around my ankles, creating little eddies in the current.

"How about we do better than that, Rielle? Let's go for a swim." Justin strips off his T-shirt and pushes off his shoes. I whip my head the opposite direction when he goes for the button on his jeans. A zipper buzzes, fabric rustles and a splash lobs water droplets onto my hair.

"Woo! That's good! Come on in!"

Every cell in my body aches to slide into the water, like I used to during family camping trips when I practically lived in the lake.

Swimming. Another thing I've lost.

I'd love to submerge myself in that world and forget this one, but I don't have a bathing suit. Neither does Justin. Who knows what lurks beneath the murky surface. And didn't he warn me about water snakes the last time we were here? Now he's bathing with them! I shudder and shake my head, eyeing his crumpled heap of clothes on the rocky shore.

"Oh come on! I've got my boxers on. Don't worry."

A relief, but still, two good reasons not to take the plunge remain.

"The snakes aren't active this time of year." Just says, as if he's reading my thoughts. "You can wear your underwear and your shirt. They'll dry quickly in this heat."

I bite my lip, debating. It would be beyond amazing to jump into the water, but stripped down, half-naked doesn't exactly fall under being careful as Nathan demanded.

I curl my legs to my chest. What I want to do and what I should do parted ways a few minutes ago. Why am I following Nathan's orders? Does he own me too?

"Live a little!" Justin calls from the water.

I'm going swimming! I twirl my finger in the air, motioning for him to turn around while I take off my pants. I toss my pants and my shoes over my shoulder and spring off the rock into the water. One moment hot thick air surrounds me and the next, cool water enfolds me. I hover beneath the surface, weightless, before I kick my legs and stretch my arms forward, sending my body gliding through the liquid.

Dad used to say I was part fish.

I swim to the surface. My head breaks through, and I flip onto my back and relax. I close my eyes against the baking sun, allow the current to carry me and drink in every sensation of freedom. It feels like coming home.

Water stirs, then whooshes and drips. Pebbles clank together. I open my eyes. Justin is on the shore. He climbs onto a stump, reaches up into the tangle of cypress limbs and pulls down a frayed rope. Clasping the rope in his fists, he steps back to the edge of the stump. With a running start, he swings out over the water and lets go of the rope. He flies through the air, howling, and disappears into the green murk. His head breaks the surface and laughter rings out.

"You gotta give that a try!"

I've always wanted to try a rope swing. I climb out of the water. Justin throws the rope my way, and I grab hold with both hands. I pause for a moment, peering down at the water. A deep breath for courage, then I take a few steps back and fling myself forward. Curling my legs up, I cling to the rope and sail out over the river, the air chilly on my wet skin.

I miss my chance to let go and swing back to shore. Laughter ripples through me, stealing the strength from my arms. Justin chuckles. I hang on and the pendulum swings out again. Just as I'm high over the water, Justin shouts, "Let go!" I close my eyes and release the rope. Air whizzes past my ears. I hit the water, then bob to the surface, laughing.

"Want to do it again?"

I nod.

We take turns. As soon as Justin hits the water, I scramble onto the stump and swing out to join him.

The sun moves across the sky. I swim until my fingers are wrinkled and every muscle in my body is loose and fantastically exhausted. Justin makes a show of dragging himself out of the water and collapsing on the ground. I follow him onto shore, my rubbery legs barely able to support me, and drop down beside him to dry in the sun.

I close my eyes, and the sun's rays warm me like caressing fingers. Justin's breathing slows. I relax and drift, not into sleep, but into that paradise between sleep and consciousness.

"Happy birthday, Rielle."

I open my eyes. Is today my birthday?

"March 28th, right?"

I nod and smile. He's right. Today I'm 18. If I were free, I'd be celebrating with my friends and family. But celebrating with Justin isn't too shabby.

My smile wilts. How does he know it's my birthday? My real name and now this? There must be a file. On his holo maybe? I rub the back of my neck, water still dripping from my hair. Another question I can never ask.

I untangle the elastic band and pins from my hair and release it from the bun so it can dry. As the breeze swirls the drying strands around me, I grin and stretch my arms over my head, enjoying every sensation—the warm spring air, my loose muscles, and the freedom of being away from the Banker's house. Happy birthday to me.

Stones stir beside me. Justin edges closer and lies on his side, propped up on his elbow.

"I've never seen you smile like that before."

My grin widens. I feel something strange. Could it be happiness? When was the last time I felt happy?

Justin's liquid blue eyes penetrate mine—searching, hoping, embracing, their magnetic pull irresistible. My gaze locks onto his and thoughts scatter like leaves in the wind. No, not thoughts, because what's going through my head is incoherent, irrational. I shiver as his hand grazes my stomach, comes to rest on my waist and curls around my side. He pulls me into his chest.

I slide my hand up to his elbow to draw him closer. He leans in and presses his lips to my forehead, then to my nose, then to my cheek. His mouth finds my neck, raising goose-bumps on my arm. His breath warms my cheek, and his lips touch the corner of my mouth.

My head spins. I should stop. I should push him away. I should care about my situation and who he is and who I am, but for one moment we are a boy and a girl on a river bank. I long for the instant his lips touch mine.

But he pulls away and sighs. "I'm not going to kiss you, Rielle. I won't kiss you until you give me permission."

I close my hand around his arm to urge him closer. He pulls my hand up to his mouth and kisses it before issuing a playful smile. "Your spoken permission."

Unbelievable. He's playing dirty.

He stands, searches out his T-shirt and pulls it over his head. I roll onto my back and thread my fingers through my hair, frustrated. He will never get my spoken permission. If he wants to kiss me, that plane just left the tarmac. I'm not going to run after him begging, "Oh Justin please kiss me." I don't need him to kiss me.

I don't need him to—but I want him to.

I find my pants, wiggle back into them and glower at Justin while I help him untie the horses' leads. He yanks impatiently at the knot. "You don't have anything to say?"

I concentrate on loosening my knot.

"It's everything I can do to leave you alone. I have to watch as you give your secrets away to that boy. I watch and wonder why him and not me?"

I freeze. Nathan and now Justin. I thought we were being so sneaky. Who else knows?

"I know you're not interested in him that way, but you've let him know you. No matter what I do, I can't seem to earn your trust. Will you ever see me as anything but a master, an enemy?"

He waits for me to say something. What can I say? There's no denying the truth. I am a slave—his uncle's slave. He's free. Facts are facts. I wish I could be free to love him, but love is not for Contracts. It's for free people. If I did trust him and let him in as he's requested, I'd be the one to get hurt. How can he ask that of me after all that I've lost?

"Just as I thought. Don't worry. Tomorrow it will be back to business."

Back to business? What does that mean?

He mounts Goliath. I lead Cherokee alongside a boulder for a boost onto her back. We return the way we came, and Justin remains silent the entire ride home. As the barn rises on the horizon, he turns his horse and rides up beside me. "Are you angry?"

I shake my head. More slighted than angry.

"Rielle, when Nathan makes his accusations, it cuts me to the quick. I'm not that kind of guy. I've tried every way I know how to earn your trust, not so I can take advantage of you, but so I can know who you are.

"I understand where Nathan's coming from, but no matter what I do— lighter workloads, treating you all like friends—it's not enough. If I wanted to take advantage of you wouldn't I have done it by now? Haven't I had every opportunity? Then what else could my motive be?"

I look down at my hands. I want to believe him, but I'm still a slave—a slave his uncle refuses to sell and there's nothing Justin can do to change that.

"I wanted to kiss you. I've resisted the urge because I know you would construe it all wrong. I can't unless you know that I'm doing this because... because... I'm... quite taken with you. Not because you're some sort of concubine or sex slave. I'm not like that!"

He reaches over and takes my hand, holding it gently in his. Pain tugging his features downward, he says, "Does that make any sense at all?"

I nod. He lifts my hand to his mouth, kisses the back of it. "You know, I'm not just a leaner version of my uncle."

I press my lips together to stifle a smile.

"Without the triple chins and the bursting buttons." He kisses my hand again.

My smile breaks free.

He takes a theatrical tone. "If you don't want to kiss me, I understand."

I roll my eyes and try to convey how ridiculous he is.

He huffs out a dramatic sigh and his bottom lip slips into a faux pout. "No, you don't want to. If you did, you'd talk to me."

I pull my hand out of his and throw him a glare.

"Ahhh, I finally found your Achilles heel. I know I'm charming. It's amazing you've been able to resist this long."

I scrub away any hint of a smile. He glances back toward the barn and the setting sun. "I guess we better get back. This is your last chance—"

I nudge the horse with my heels to urge her forward.

I lie in bed thinking about Justin and what he said, trying to sort through this turn of events. I've been fooling myself for a long time, living like a robot, suppressing my feelings. I'll have to be honest with myself in order to figure things out. How long have these feelings been there?

I trace back, back, back. The tingling sensation in my stomach the first time he sat at the piano and asked me to join him. I wanted to sit next to him and play my heart out, so he could see who I really am. But the rational part of me wouldn't let me forget that I'm a slave. If I let myself love him, he'll break my heart. How many times can it break? I've already lost my entire family, my home, and my freedom. Can I risk this too?

The right thing to do is to stay away from Justin. To banish my feelings for him. To lock them away. Enslave my emotions. But an irrational hope rises within me. Maybe he'll love me. I try to shove the hope aside with grim reality, but idiotic optimism keeps rearing its head.

When sleep finally collects me, I dream. I'm sitting under the apple tree in my backyard in Minnesota. I rest my back against the rough tree bark, a book in my hands. Spring is brilliant—vibrant green grass, an azure sky. Blooms decorate the tree, fragrant pink flowers. Their sweet aroma churns about me as a cool breeze rustles the branches and swirls my hair around my shoulders.

I look up from my book. Dad approaches, grinning.

"Dad?" I call in disbelief. He's ice cold water on a parched throat.

"Rielle, honey, what are you doing under this tree?"

I finger the book's pages. "Reading."

A frown pulls his lips down and he shakes his head. "You can't stay here forever."

Somehow I know what he's talking about. I glance around at the yard and drink in the sense of peace pervading this place. The season begins to change. Summer arrives. Blossoms disappear, replaced by tiny green apples, and the cool breeze replaced by summer's intense heat. The sun beats down on me, and I squint in the brightness.

My father kneels beside me, his gaze sombre. "I have to apologize, Rielle. I'm so sorry. Your mother and I raised you all wrong."

I cock my head to the side, stunned and confused. Not the type of apology I expected. I never thought they were bad parents. They were always there for us and they taught us the right things. I just didn't agree with most of their choices.

As I ponder his apology, the season changes again. Glistening red apples hang ripe on branches, dipping low under their weight. Wasps buzz around fruit littering the ground, some rotting. Leaves turn yellow and orange and begin to fall, covering the fallen, fermenting apples.

Dad continues. "You never gave us any trouble. Sure you had your spoiled teenage moments, and every now and then copped an attitude. But we raised a very obedient daughter. You always did what we asked of you."

For some reason his words offend me. They feel like a slight. "Why is that so bad? Isn't that right?" I ask.

"I think we should have cultivated some rebellion in you. Look at you, content to just lounge under this tree. Are you going to stay here forever?"

My cheeks burn. "I don't have a choice!"

The last brown leaf falls from the tree and, one by one, snowflakes coat the naked tree branches.

Dad reaches out to catch a snowflake. "See, so obedient." He stands up and turns to walk away, then stops, glances over his shoulder. "Aubrielle Angelique James, it's time to wake up."

CHAPTER TWENTY-TWO

The Outlaw Jesse James

MY EYES SNAP OPEN AND I GASP, HALF expecting to be in my hometown backyard. But I'm still at the Banker's.

Dad's words ring in my ears. They should have cultivated more rebellion in me? Don't parents want obedient kids, not rebellious ones? Kids like me, not like Silas and his constant challenge to authority. And what the hell did he mean by, "Are you still here?" My chest burns. I'd love to get up and go somewhere else, but that's impossible.

Why am I letting it get to me? It was just a dream.

I descend the stairs to the kitchen. My duty slip reads, "Horseback ride."

"Rielle, it'll be just a few minutes before we leave, I have to message my dad," Justin says.

I nod and plop down at the kitchen table as the other Contracts go their separate ways. Nathan eyes me for a moment, then steps outside. I support my head on my hand and trace the wood grain of the table with my fingernail, my neck warming as I think about yesterday—his hands on me, his lips so close to mine.

Roberta strides into the kitchen, and I suddenly want to be anywhere but here. I notice Eli weeding the garden again.

I cross the yard, stoop down and start weeding. Eli smiles and continues digging his fingers into the soil to loosen roots. He hums a familiar tune as he works. I listen, trying to remember the name of the song. A few more bars—I think he's singing it in the wrong key.

My hand wraps around a patch of wild grasses. My arms go limp. A cold sensation slides over me, like a bucket of ice water dumped over my head.

He's humming *my* song. The song I used to play for Mom. The one she always requested. The one *I* wrote.

How can he know that song? I suck in a breath. Flying into hysterics won't help me figure this out. I repeat Justin's words in my head, "Don't freak out."

I glance around. The yard is empty except for Eli and me. "Um Eli." My voice cracks. "Where did you hear that song?"

"You like it? My friend Jesse used to hum it all the time. Kinda catchy isn't it?"

Do I know a Jesse? How would he have heard my song? I only shared it with my family. There has to be a logical explanation. Perhaps it just sounds like my song. Eli's voice isn't exactly pitch perfect.

Eli dislodges a long dandelion root. "He said his sister made it up."

My body begins to shake. "Eli, what was Jesse's last name?"

He sits back on his haunches and furrows his brow. "Why do you want to know?"

"It's just that I've heard that song. Thought maybe I know him or his sister."

His eyes bore into mine, and he casts a wary glance over his shoulder before returning his stare to me. "James."

My pulse climbs. James? "His name is…Jesse James?" I speak the name slowly.

Eli grins, then continues, "Jesse isn't his real name, though. It's just a nickname I gave him. You know, like the outlaw—Jesse James, 'cause he was always stealing stuff and coming up with escape plans."

My jaw hangs slack, so I fix it shut. Breathe. "What's his real name?"

"Some weird name. Silas, I think."

My heart slams against my rib cage. My brother! Eli knows him! Eli's "Jesse" stories flood back, important details surging to the surface. Jesse escaped. That means Silas escaped!

"Ready to go?" Justin's voice fractures my focus on Eli and I jump.

No. I don't want to go anywhere. I want to pump Eli for more information. All this time, I've been working next to my brother's best friend!

I clench my teeth, glancing from Justin to Eli. I have to go. Eli's forehead wrinkles as I rise to my feet, probably wondering why his story upset me.

I'm a frayed wire—undone and unable to hide my shock. Balancing on numb legs, I allow Justin to secure the bracelet to my wrist before following him to the gate, my head swimming.

"Are you okay?" Justin asks as we leave the yard. "You look like you've seen a ghost."

I trail behind him, trying to force the shock and desperation from my face. Justin chats about the warm weather, but I barely hear him. Images of Silas on the run bombard me as we wait for Morris to bring the horses around.

My brother escaped! He may be free right now. But where is he? If I can get Eli to tell me where he went, maybe I can find him. I'll have to escape from here. But how?

We mount our horses and set off down our usual path toward the old house. With nothing but Silas on my mind, the familiar scenery is reduced to passing shadows.

Si found a way out. Maybe I can too. Visions of running down this trail alone in the dark of night ignites a bolt of panic and excitement. Freedom. But which way would I go? How would I find Silas? And what if I got caught?

And then, Dad's words from my dream race to the forefront and arrange themselves like puzzle pieces clicking into place. I've been the picture of obedience to my master, while my brother played the outlaw. He seized an opportunity and found a way to escape. He was never their prisoner. He was always free, just biding his time until he found a way out. I've just been a good slave.

"You're going to talk to me today," Justin hollers, pulling me from my dangerous thoughts.

Want to bet?

I need to calm down and think. I assumed I was stuck here forever, but maybe I can escape. Would a life on the run be better than this? Without a doubt. When I'm with Justin this place is tolerable, but the Banker will return. This isn't Justin's home. He won't stay forever and then what? The Banker made it clear he's not interested in parting with my contract. I know too many of his secrets.

After a quiet ride, we arrive at the old house and dismount. Again. Why does he keep bringing me here?

"You seem distracted," Justin says as we walk toward the house. "Something on your mind?"

I shrug, try to look casual, disinterested even though I'm on edge, every nerve in my body on high alert.

He opens the door for me. "I want to show you something." He smiles, but there's another emotion, heavy with apprehension, playing beneath his grin—the way his eyes dart into the kitchen and then back at me, his jaw muscles as taut as bridge cables.

I follow him into the dusty kitchen, hoping to get our little adventure over with so I can go back to the Banker's and interrogate Eli. I'm sure he'll tell me where Silas ran to once he knows I'm his sister.

Focus. Breathe. I can't let Justin know what's going on in my head.

Justin leads me across the kitchen to a panelled door. He swings it open, revealing stairs that descend into the basement. I glance from the stairs to Justin's wide eyes and flushed face.

An uneasy feeling settles in the pit of my stomach. Why does he want to show me the basement of an abandoned old house? If he wanted to hurt me, surely he had plenty of opportunity in the past. One minute I yearn for him to kiss me, the next moment I'm afraid of him. This duality bothers me.

He runs his fingers through his hair. "After you." He waves his hand, motioning for me to go downstairs.

I throw him a wary glance and take the first step, then another. His boots thud on the stairs behind me, hinges screech, and the basement door clicks closed, cutting off the light that poured down from the kitchen windows. I stop and press myself against the wall as my eyes adjust to the darkness. Justin squeezes past me. The dry wooden stairs groan as we descend into the musty basement. I halt on the bottom step. He reaches back and grabs my hand, tucking my arm under his. I try wriggling free as he pulls me off the bottom step. His grip tightens.

Panic squeezes my chest. I'm trapped.

As he leads me across the concrete floor, dust stirs. Thin light trickles through the streaked and foggy shoe-box sized window. Except for a couple of saggy cardboard boxes and some metal shelving littered with old oil cans and dust coated bottles, the basement is empty.

"Stay calm, don't freak out, okay?" Justin says.

My heart pounds. Why would he say that? What's down here? I yank at my hand to free it, but he only strengthens his grip. He tows me toward one of the metal shelves and stops a step before the concrete wall.

He drops my hand. I wiggle my fingers to get the circulation moving again.

"Reach down under the lower right corner."

I hesitate, evaluating the wisdom of following his instructions. I angle myself so that I can keep an eye on him as I stoop down. I tentatively slide my fingers under the shelf, bracing for a sting or bite from the deadly insects that probably nest in the basement's cool darkness.

"You'll feel a pin behind the shelf leg. Press it."

I lean my shoulder against the wall and reach further under, wrap my fingers around the leg. Something thin with a rounded head protrudes from the leg. I press it. A low pop echoes across the basement, followed by a gasp, like opening a new jar of pickles.

The shelf swivels forward, just slightly. Startled, I fall backward, but catch myself. I stand up, dust off my bottom and back away. Justin grabs my hand again, gripping it tighter than before. He heaves the shelving back and it swings open as though on a hinge. A blast of moist air hits my face and blows my hair back, stirring the dust until I cough. I squint, searching through the haze. As the dust settles, a dark, narrow tunnel comes into view. The dirt walls of the tunnel continue so far into the distance that they narrow to a point. A fragment of light shines at the other end.

I swallow hard.

"This is how the family who lived here escaped."

I straighten my back. I was right. They escaped. But why would Justin show me this?

Justin stares at me. "You don't know what's going on in the world right now. People are disappearing, people who have chips. There've been arrests, when the only evidence against them is recordings of conversations they've had in the privacy of their own homes. Somehow, Bank Security is listening."

Justin shakes his head. "One world. One currency. One bright future."

Of course they're listening. Doesn't he know? Those bugs could be anywhere. Even at the Banker's.

While keeping a firm hold of my hand, he swings the secret door closed and sweeps his foot across the scuff the door made on the dusty floor.

"Wouldn't it be ironic if the Contracts are the free ones, and those of us who took commerce chips are the slaves?" he whispers, his eyes focused on some object in the distance. "We aren't living in the world we thought we were. Something bad is happening, Rielle."

Something snaps inside me, like sodium dropped in water. My head spins as all these revelations come together—my brother's escape, this tunnel, Justin's new information. I've spent the last year of my life trying to be invisible, hoping for self-preservation. I died inside the day they took me from my family. I haven't been brave or angry—no, a corpse can't experience those things. I've been asleep all this time, and I'm finally waking up.

Rage and adrenaline surge. All the families that have been torn apart. Kids bought and sold as slaves—and only now Justin realizes it's bad? I'm finished listening to him.

I yank away from his grip and thrust my arms at his chest as hard as I can. Justin, his eyes wide, stumbles backward.

"Now?" I shout. "Now it's bad? I lost my whole family and my life was sold to the highest bidder, and *now* you think it's bad?"

I'm leaving. I don't know where I'm going—anywhere away from here will do.

I run for the stairs, jump over the first three treads and sprint toward the kitchen door.

CHAPTER TWENTY-THREE

A Little Worse for Wear

"RIELLE! STOP!" JUSTIN STOMPS UP THE STAIRS behind me.

I fling the basement door open, snag my foot on the top step and fall face first into the kitchen with a heavy thud. Justin grabs my ankle. I kick his hand away, spring to my feet and dash into the living room, across the carpet, toward the front door. I reach for the doorknob. Justin catches me around the waist and yanks me back. I lose my balance and fall toward him. He hauls me up and tosses me over his shoulder.

I pound my fists on his back. "Put me down!"

He carries me a few steps. "Now!" I shout. I pull his shirt up and grab the waistband of his boxers protruding from his pants. I jerk upward. He curves his back as I give him a wedgy for the record books.

"Damn it, Rielle." He lifts me off his shoulder and drops me onto the sofa. He seizes my arms and holds me down. "You're freaking out. Stop," he growls.

I try wrestling out from under his grip, but he presses me into the cushions. "Let go of meeee!" I scream. I struggle against him, angry tears sliding down my temple. "Let me go! You spoiled jerk! I lost everything and now you notice! Now that it's affecting you? Unbelievable!" I twist and writhe beneath his weight. "Get away from me!"

"I'm not letting you go until you calm down."

I glare at him. "I am calm!"

"No, you're not. Look, Rielle, you're right. What happened to your family and the others is wrong. I thought it was wrong from the beginning. I was just trying to tell you what's happening now. And you're right. I'm a spoiled jerk."

The more I struggle the tighter he holds on. The only way to get away from him is for him to let go. I take a deep breath and stop squirming.

Justin examines my face for a few moments. "If I let go, are you going to run away?"

"No"

"You promise?"

"Yes."

He scrutinizes me and gradually loosens his grip. I keep my face calm, focused. His hands lift off my arms. I throw my legs over the side of the couch and roll to the side, pushing him off me. Justin tumbles backward onto the floor. I spring toward the door. He lunges at me, tackling me to the floor. I throw my elbow and nail him in the stomach.

A blast of air explodes from his mouth and he doubles over, but keeps his hold on me. "You said you weren't going to run away."

"I lied! Let go of me!"

He straddles my hips and secures my arms over my head. His weight presses down on me, holding me to the floor. "Will you just calm down and listen to me?"

I eye him, assessing my chance for another escape. Probably not good. He's caught me twice now. I pull in a deep breath. "Let me go. I won't run, I promise." I'll wait for a more opportune time.

He climbs off, but keeps a firm grip on my wrists. He pulls me from the carpet and leads me to the sofa. I sit down. He lets go and sits across from me on the coffee table.

I smudge my tears away with my sleeves. He plasters a big goofy grin to his face. I want to slap it off, but I restrain myself.

"You spoke."

My shoulders slump. I did, didn't I?

"Your voice is different than I thought it would be. I expected high and chirpy, but it's got depth. You can be loud, too, if you want to be. I think my ears are still ringing." He chuckles.

I expected anger, not this. It disarms me.

"Say something else. Please."

I say the first thing that pops into my head. "You're making me crazy."

Placing his hand on my knee, he peers into my eyes. "Good. You've been making me crazy for a long time."

Though the room is hot and stuffy, a fantastic chill ripples over me. I want to scream and shout at him. I want to vent a year's worth of frustration. I should be angry, indignant, unforgiving, but his words melt every last trace of rage, leaving me a warm gelatinous heap.

He leans forward and places one hand on either side of me. I draw in a trembling breath as his lips graze my neck. There's something I need to say, some reason I was angry. I can't remember. I turn my head toward his lips.

He pulls back. His sky blue eyes peer into mine. "Do I have your permission to kiss you, not because I'm your master or because you're afraid of me, but because you want me to?"

How can I want to kiss him and punch him in the face at the same time? Any relationship with him is doomed before it starts. A seed of hopefulness germinates inside me. Maybe—just maybe—there could be a happy ending.

No. This can't possibly end well. This boy will break my heart. But I can take this one moment and make it mine. I will give the orders this time. "Justin, kiss me," I whisper.

Before the last word is fully out of my mouth, his lips touch mine. Warm. Soft. Gentle. He drops to his knees in front of me and takes me in his arms. The cedar and vanilla smell of his hair fills my senses. I wrap my arms around him and grab handfuls of his t-shirt. His mouth presses against my lips in slow, rhythmic movements. I drink him in—his taste, the tightening muscles of his back beneath my fingertips, his fingers caressing my neck.

He's the first to let go. "You have some questions."

I do? I tug my head out of the upper atmosphere and nod.

"No more nodding, please."

I smile. "Why do you keep bringing me here?"

"I need you to remember everything I've shown you: the horse, the trail, the tunnel. Do you remember how to get here?"

"Yes."

He brushes my hair behind me ear. "Promise me you won't forget."

"Yes, I promise, but why?"

"I'm not sure about the details. I'm sorry, but the less you know the better."

"The less I know about what?"

"I can't tell you that. I need you to trust me."

"You want me to trust you when you're keeping things from me? How can I possibly do that?"

"I know I'm asking a lot, but I have good reasons. You'll see."

I sigh, frustrated. Do I trust him? In some ways yes, but in others, I'm not sure. I long to tell someone about Silas' escape, but I can't risk telling Justin. I can't endanger my brother.

"Give me one good reason why I should trust you," I say.

He releases a heavy sigh, rubs his thumb over the back of my hand. "I don't have one. I mean, if I were in your position, I don't know if I would trust me either. All I can tell you is that I care about you and it would kill me if anything happened to you. I'm asking you to trust me even though I don't deserve it."

I study his face in search of deception. "I don't like this."

His mouth curls into a crooked smile. "I don't expect you to."

He slips his warm hand around mine. My hand seems as small as a child's inside of his. A sense of safety envelopes me, as though his hand could protect me from the hostile world. How many conflicting emotions can I experience today?

"We need to head back," he says.

We walk to the back door. He pulls me into his arms and kisses me again. Leaning his forehead against mine he says, "We can't let anyone know about this, or about the fact that you're talking."

"Definitely."

Justin rides beside me down the trail. "Say something again."

I laugh. "Why?"

"I like hearing your voice." He grins like he's just won the lottery.

"What do you want me to say?"

"I don't know. Anything."

I skim my palm over Cherokee's smooth fur. "Well, I don't know what to say. I'm kind of used to not talking."

"You have brothers and sisters?"

"One of each," I say. "How about you?"

"Nope. Just me. Only child. Which explains why I'm so spoiled." He chuckles. "Were you and your brother close?"

"You know, at the time I didn't think so, but now I think we were. I miss him and my sister, if that's what you're asking."

An emotion I can't read flashes in his eyes for just a moment and one corner of his mouth curls up before he presses his lips together. He finds me missing my brother amusing? No. I must be reading him wrong.

The clomping of horse hooves replaces the conversation for a couple minutes.

"Why did your father try to buy me?" I ask.

Justin's mouth falls open, but he snaps it shut. "How do you know about that?"

"Does it matter how? I just know."

"Well, isn't it obvious?"

I shake my head. "No. The two of you want me scrubbing your floors instead of the Banker's?"

His eyes narrow to angry slits.

"I didn't mean—"

He cuts me off. "Take a look at yourself, Rielle." He waves his hand up and down in my direction.

"What does that mean?"

"You're a little worse for wear. My uncle doesn't feed you right. You're overworked and that scar on your face—I know where that came from. I want you out of there. Do you really think I'd have you scrubbing my floors and washing my windows? Is that what you think of me?"

"No. I—I don't think so."

"You don't *think* so?" He shakes his head. He tightens his grip on Goliath's reins and, after a few moments of silence, takes a deep breath and continues, "I hope someday you'll see—you'll understand my motivations and that you'll know you can trust me and that I would never do anything to violate that trust. Never!"

The sunset casts warm orange rays over the horse pasture. We arrive at the stables, dismount and tether the horses to the fencepost. Justin approaches me in the dimming light and takes my hand. "I know you've been hurt, and trusting me is difficult for you. I'm going to try to be patient. I'm sorry for getting upset."

I gaze into his lovely blue eyes. "It's okay. Forgiven."

He presses closer and kisses me. "We need to get back," he whispers in my ear, sending a shiver down my spine.

We walk hand in hand under the cover of darkness toward the gate, talking quietly about swimming tomorrow if the weather is warm enough.

We step inside the gate. Dry leaves crunch. Justin stops short. I drop his hand. Someone's in front of us, muddled by the velvety blackness.

CHAPTER TWENTY-FOUR

Suitcases

"SO YOU'RE TALKING TO HIM TOO," NATHAN accuses in the darkness.

How will I explain this?

He steps toward Justin. "Where have you been?"

Justin squares his shoulders and lifts his chin. "That's not really any of your business."

I step between the two of them and place my hand on Justin's arm. "I need to speak with him. Alone."

Justin glares at Nathan as he speaks to me. "Fine. Come see me when you're done so I can remove your bracelet."

Nathan returns Justin's glower. Justin marches across the yard.

Nathan watches Justin disappear into the Banker's house, then turns to me.

He draws in a deep breath like he's about to speak, but I cut him off. "What's this about, Nathan?"

He folds his arms. "I guess, you can finally answer my questions. Is he—" He grinds his teeth, seeming to search for the right words. "Making you do . . . things?"

"No! No, definitely not!"

"Because if he's hurting you, I could help you get away. We could leave here and he wouldn't be able to hurt you anymore."

"He's not hurting me. You don't need to worry. He's—n—nice." Nice doesn't seem to cover it, but I don't want to give away too much detail. Nathan's face hardens to stone as I stumble over my words.

He lowers his voice. "Is there something going on between the two of you?"

I shrug. "I don't know what you mean."

"You were holding his hand. You were talking to him."

"He's right, Nathan, it's none of your business." I try walking past him, but he blocks me. "Let it go!"

"Rielle, please don't do this. You don't know this guy. He's not good for you. If he hasn't hurt you yet, he's going to." His words gush like water through a cracked dam. "He's not like us. He's one of them. You're not a person to him, just a Contract. He's up to something. I've seen him poking around in the Banker's office."

"Nathan, he's not going to hurt me. He's had plenty of chances and he's been the perfect gentlemen."

"Rielle, let's get out of here. I can get us out. I know I can. I heard of this place near Eagle Pass, if we can make it, there are people who will hide us."

Justin drops from my mind like a ripe apple from a tree. The day's earlier revelations flood back to me. Maybe Silas ran to Eagle Pass. The thought of running away on my own terrifies me, but Nathan's strong. Maybe together we could make it. Can I trust Nathan with the information about my brother, the information I can't trust to Justin? I chew on my lip as I debate. I look into his eyes. I'd trust Nathan with my life.

"Nathan, my brother escaped," I whisper.

"How do you know that?"

"You know how Eli is always talking about his friend Jesse and how he escaped from the reform school?"

"No. You're the only one Eli talks to."

"Well, he told me about this friend Jesse who helped him escape. Eli got caught, but Jesse didn't. And Jesse isn't his real name. Today Eli told me his real name—Silas James. My brother! Maybe he went to Eagle Pass. Maybe we could meet up with him."

Nathan strokes his chin. "We'd have to go while the Banker's away. Justin doesn't watch us as closely. We could probably get a good head start before he'd discover we're gone."

I instinctively rub my right hand over my left as though the tracker chip tingles beneath my skin. "We'd have to—" I gulp as visions of Nina's butchered hands strobe in my mind. "Cut our chips out."

"Don't tell me you're stubborn enough to keep your mouth on lock-down for a year, but the will to make a little cut escapes you."

I trace the edge of my bracelet with my fingernails. "I can do it."

"Then we need to start making plans."

The word "plans" punches me in the gut. Plans—like we're really going to do this. Not just talk. Action. What about Justin? How could I betray him like that? And then more reality sets in. What if we get caught? They would send us far from here and perhaps I'd never make it to Silas.

"No, Nathan, we can't do it."

"Yes, we could. We could make it,' he whispers.

"I can't."

"It's because of him." Nathan shakes his head, slowly as though scolding me. "You've fallen for him."

"That's not it." My denial is weak, even I can hear that.

"He can't care about you the way I do. Don't trust him, Rielle."

I have to get away from Nathan—away from this conversation. I push past him again, but this time he lets me go.

"Rielle," he calls after me in a loud whisper.

I throw him a backward glance.

"You need to stop being such a good girl and start doing what's right."

I freeze. The sentiment echoes what Dad said in my dream. "What's that supposed to mean?"

"Figure it out." He brushes past me. "Think about my offer." He hurries toward the men's quarters.

I can't sleep. Nathan asked me to think about it and that's all I can think about. Hours pass to the steady rhythm of Lydia's breathing.

Is there even a remote possibility we could escape? How would we survive on the run without money, without food? We could take some supplies from the kitchen, but we can only carry so much. And how bad will it be for us if we get caught? Eli's purple and yellow bruises flash in my thoughts. I skim my fingers over my cheek where the Banker struck me the first time.

Nathan is right, though. We'll have to do it before the Banker returns. I just don't think I can betray Justin that way. I'd hate myself for it. But do I let him take away my only chance at freedom and my only opportunity to find my brother? Is Justin's attention worth staying enslaved for? And what about Lydia and Eli? How can I leave them behind?

I don't have much time to decide.

In the morning, I force down my oatmeal, exhausted from lack of sleep and still conflicted. Shoes click in the hall. Oh, no. Justin's riding boots don't sound like that.

The kitchen door swings open with too much vigour. The Banker appears in the doorway.

Early. He's early.

We scramble into line.

The Banker buckles his hands behind his back, his shirt buttons mismatched, leaving his collar too high on one side. He scratches his head, causing his thin hair to stand on end.

The Contracts exchange perplexed, uneasy glances.

"Today, you find your own duties. I'm not your babysitter. I don't have time to be coddling you all. Get to work and I better not catch you slacking off. If I don't see you working, there won't be any food. Lydia, the nanny is no longer with us. You are in charge of the children." The Banker storms out, Lydia jogging behind him.

What happened to Inez? The Contracts scatter. I hurry after Nathan. I don't know where he's going or if it's even something I can help with, but I need to talk to him about last night. He slows his pace just enough for me to keep up.

I follow him into the shed where he retrieves a scraper from a plastic bin. He hands it to me, then digs out a paint brush and snags a can of paint. He leads me to the sun scorched south side of the shed.

I scrape, sloughing off flecks of bubbled paint. Nathan follows behind me with a paintbrush, smoothing a fresh layer of colour over the old one. We work in silence. I'm dying to talk to him, but I can't risk the Banker seeing my lips move.

We work our way around to the back of the building, wedged between the wall and fence. I glance around to make sure no one can see us. "We won't be leaving anytime soon, I guess."

"You must be relieved."

"A little. The pressure is off. Don't you find it a little strange? I mean, why would the Banker come back early? And what happened to Inez? I thought giving us our orders was the highlight of his day. Now he tells us to go and find our own work."

Nathan dips his brush in the paint. "More than a little strange."

I have a nagging suspicion that whatever is eating the Banker won't bode well for us. I slide the scraper under another bubble of paint. "Can I ask you a question?"

"Sure. Shoot."

"How is it that you know how to do all these things?"

"My dad taught me before he died."

I pause mid-scrape to look at Nathan. "Oh, I'm sorry."

He issues a weak smile, but sadness lines his features as his brush floats over the siding. "That's okay. He got sick when I was thirteen. They gave him a year to live. So one day he sat me down and told me I was going to be the man of the house."

"That's a big responsibility."

"It felt more like an honour than a responsibility. He really loved my mom and he wanted me to be able to help her around the house. So he showed me how to fix just about everything. The last thing he said to me was 'take care of your mother,' so I did. At least, until they came and took her away." He stops working and drops his gaze, paint dripping from his brush. "If my dad had been there, he would've stopped them. He would have died to protect her."

I stop too, my thoughts turning to Dad and the last time I saw him. When I close my eyes I can still see him lying on the floor. Did they kill him? Did he die trying to protect us?

"You can't beat yourself up like that, Nathan. My dad tried to stop them from taking us, and they bashed him over the head and took us anyway. There's nothing you could've done." I place my hand on his forearm.

"I should've tried. I should've taken the beating. At least then I'd have the peace of mind of knowing I did everything I could. Instead, I just stood and watched them drag her away. And then they came for me. I'm not courageous like my dad was."

So much loss. And then he comes here, falls in love with Jessica and ends up losing her too. I want to ask him about her, but I shouldn't even know about Jessica, and maybe it would cause more pain to bring her up. My heart thumps out a thick, heavy beat for Nathan. Escape for me is about finding my brother. For him it's about finding Jessica.

A bird chirps and rustles a nearby shrub, and then those sounds die away too, as though nature is allowing us a moment of silence to honour those we've lost.

Nathan lifts his paintbrush, pulling his arm away from my touch, and smears more paint onto the wall. "Rielle, are we friends?"

I check again for witnesses, then follow Nathan's lead and start scraping again. I glance at him out of the corner of my eye, suspicious of the question. "Yes."

"This thing you have going with Justin, you need to break it off."

I roll my eyes. "This again? Come on Nathan, could you give it a rest?"

"It's just that he's not—"

"He's not like me. I know. I'm dealing with it."

"Have you thought this through? I mean, how's it going to end?"

Nathan chose the question that plagues me. The one I can't answer—the one I'm afraid to answer.

I dig the scraper too hard into the paint and take a chip out of the siding.

"Do you think he's going to free you and you'll both ride off into the sunset? This isn't going to end well."

It sounds ridiculous when Nathan says it, and yet, if I'm being honest with myself, that's exactly what I hope for. I stare at my shoes.

"I just don't want to see you end up like Jasmine. You're a nice girl," he says.

I jerk my head up. "Like Jasmine? What's been going on with her?"

"Lydia didn't tell you about her…her role here?"

"Lydia said she's the Banker's assistant." Something feels wrong about my words. I scrutinize his face, taking in the lift of his brows and the set of his lips.

He sighs. "I guess that's one way to put it. That's like Lydia to give everything a positive spin."

"She's not his assistant?"

The corners of his mouth curls, but there's no humour there. "Come on, Rielle."

"I don't understand what you're getting at."

"You are so naive. How do I say this nicely?" He thinks for a moment. "She's his mistress."

The scraper drops from my hands. "What! No, that can't be! I don't think Jasmine would—I mean the Banker is so—" I can't finish my sentences. The words jam in my throat.

"She didn't exactly have a choice."

His words hit me with the force of a freight train and my body congeals into a rigid mass. I have been naive. Poor Jasmine. The thought of her with the Banker turns my stomach. "But he—he's—he's married with children and—"

"Not every family is like yours. According to Morris, the Banker and his wife have an agreement. He looks the other way about her affair with Morris and she does the same for him with Jasmine."

"Nina and Morris too?"

"That's why I don't want you hanging around Justin. We are just tools and toys for them. He will use you and throw you away. He wouldn't feel bad about it, but I know it would hurt you. You and I are from families who raised us with morals and values. These people aren't. If they will buy a human being, what else will they do?"

Despite the day's heat, my hands and feet turn cold. I stare straight ahead at nothing in particular. "I see."

Nathan lifts my chin and peers into my eyes. "Do you? Do you finally understand?"

"Yes." I bob my head up and down. "Thank you for telling me." My voice comes out hoarse, strained, barely above a whisper.

Why didn't I see it before? How could I *not* get it—get that our owners would use us that way?

Maybe I didn't want to get it

I've been foolish and reckless. I kissed Justin. Worse, I spoke to him. My silence was mine. Now I've given away the only thing that belonged to me. I'd rather die than become his concubine.

Poor, poor Jasmine. Images of her with the Banker play form a mental horror movie. I shudder and push them away. They're grotesque, twisted, disgusting. I brood over this revelation while we finish painting the shed and then move on to separate chores.

I go through the rest of the day like a zombie, so consumed with regret that I can barely function. I won't spend any more time with Justin. I can't, no matter how much I want to be with him. I'll make up whatever excuses necessary to avoid time alone with him.

I should've listened to Nathan in the first place.

CHAPTER TWENTY-FIVE

Rethinking My Priorities

THE NEXT MORNING, THE BANKER HEAVES the swinging kitchen door open so hard that it crashes against the cabinets. A five o'clock shadow dirties his jaw line. His eyes are wide and darting, and his fevered cheeks shine with sweat. After what Nathan told me yesterday, the sight of him turns my stomach.

He slowly marches down the line of Contracts, nostrils flaring. I tense as he passes me. What did we do? Who's going to get a dose of his spite this time?

He stops and turns toward us. "Which of you worthless thieves has been in my office?"

I glance sideways at Roberta. She's the only one I've ever seen in that room, but I refuse to rat out my fellow Contract no matter how much of a witch she is.

The line of Contracts remains silent.

"I know someone was in there!" he shouts.

More silence.

In one long stride he's in Lydia's face. I steel my legs, ready to step between them, but that would only make him angrier.

Spit flies from his mouth. "Who's been in my office, Lydia?"

Tears form on her lower eyelids and she shakes her head. "I've never seen anyone in your office." Her voice trembles.

He steps back. "I see thieves stick together." He plants his feet and lifts his chin. "A week off to the Contract who answers my question."

Silence.

Movement at the end of the line draws my attention. Roberta steps forward. "I saw someone in your office."

The Banker struts down the line to Roberta, a satisfied sneer wrinkling his face. "I can always count on you Roberta. Name the rat."

"I saw Rielle in there while you were gone."

My breath catches. Liar!

"Thank you, Roberta," the Banker says.

His hands curl into fists as he stares at me. "Of course it was you. Treachery runs in your family." He snorts. "Rielle, stay. The rest of you, get to work."

No one moves for a long moment. First Morris breaks from the line, then Jasmine.

Nathan and Lydia don't budge.

"Lydia, go!" The Banker yells. She scurries out of the kitchen .

Nathan stares ahead, his shoulders thrust back like a soldier. "It was me. I was in your office."

I aim my panicked gaze at him and shake my head.

The Banker saunters up to Nathan and pokes him in the chest. "You're a filthy liar. Now get out of here or I'll arrange to have you sent somewhere far less pleasant than this."

Electric tension zings through the air. Nathan looks at me, his eyes clear, reassuring. He strides past the Banker, through the swinging door. It flaps closed.

I concentrate on my breathing to keep it from turning erratic. What is he going to do to me?

"I should've known it was you. Never trust a James." He grabs my hair and yanks my head back, pulling strands from my scalp. "What were you looking for?"

My eyes water.

His lips pull back, exposing teeth. "You're not really mute—it's all been a ruse hasn't it. Hasn't it?" He slaps my face. "Who are you working for?"

Tears roll down my face. I shake my head.

His fat face jiggles as he quakes with rage. His fist slams into my side. Pain shoots up my back. I double over. His fist connects with my cheek, thundering inside my head. I fall sideways and hit the floor.

"What did you tell them?" he bellows.

I don't answer.

He kicks me in the ribs. Air bursts from my lungs. Can't breathe. I fight to suck in oxygen. Finally it comes—air—but as my lungs fill, pain flashes over me.

"Tell me! What'd you tell Bank Security!" He drops onto his haunches beside me. "Did you tell them about my meeting?" Saliva flies from his mouth.

Each breath brings another shock of pain. I stare at the floor.

"Answer me!"

My shoulders heave with a sob.

The Banker grabs my throat and squeezes until his hand trembles. I try to breathe, but nothing gets through. Darkness blots the edge of my vision. I claw at his hands, pry at his fingers.

"Tell me who you're working for!"

Blackness closes around me. And then a noise. The kitchen door. A voice. "Uncle Arthur, no!"

"This is not your business, Justin." The Banker's eyes bore into mine. Hate. Pleasure. He's enjoying watching me die. His fingernails dig into my neck.

A pin-sized speck of vision remains.

Justin clamps his arms around the Banker's shoulders and wrestles him back. "She wasn't in your office. She wouldn't do that."

The Banker's grip on my neck loosens, enough that I get a breath, a whistling rasping breath.

He fights against Justin. "She's a James!"

"Do you really think a James would help Bank Security?" The Banker's nails scrape my neck as Justin drags him away from me. Another jerk and his hand releases. I flop back onto the floor. Blood rushes to my head.

Nathan rushes past Justin, who is still restraining the Banker, and lifts my head off the floor. "Rielle, are you okay?

Looking up at Nathan, I blink, and hot tears run down my cheeks. My throat aches as I swallow.

The Banker throws off Justin's arms. Hands balled into fists, he looks from Justin to Nathan, then to me. Justin steps between the Banker and me.

"I see." The Banker shakes his head. "Protecting Resistor trash over your own family." He marches from the kitchen.

I grab onto Nathan's shirt. He wraps his arms around me, pulls me upright. I sob into his shoulder.

"Is she okay?" Justin asks.

"I think so." Nathan strokes my hair.

Justin kneels beside us. "Rielle?" He rubs my arm.

"I'll take you upstairs. Can you walk?" Nathan asks.

Justin picks up my hand. "I can take her."

"Don't touch her," Nathan says.

I pull my hand from Justin's, and Nathan helps me to my feet. I try to straighten up and groan. Nathan, his arm around my waist, guides me upstairs and eases me down onto my bed. He begins an inspection, starting with my neck. "That bastard."

I pull Nathan's hand away and whisper, "I'm okay."

Lydia rushes into the room. "Oh my gosh. Rielle, are you okay?"

I nod.

Nathan brushes a tear from my cheek. "Lydia, will you check her over? I'm worried she's got broken ribs."

Lydia shoos him from the room, helps me take my shirt off, then pokes around my rib cage. I can tell she's trying to be gentle, but she may as well have a knife in her hand. When she grazes the spot on my chest where the Banker's pointed shoes connected, I gasp.

"Bruised for sure. Hopefully not broken." She helps me put my shirt back on. Lifting my arms over my head is torture. She leaves the room and returns with a cloth and moves in to wash my face. I stop her, take the cloth from her hand and pry myself off the bed.

I shuffle down the hall to the bathroom, lock the door and stare at the mirror. My lip is split. An imprint of the Banker's hand paints my neck in shades of red and purple. I lift my shirt. More developing bruises.

I lean against the bathroom counter for support and sob. Pain shoots through my ribs. The Banker could've killed me today. He almost did.

I eye the girl in the mirror. Her arm is wrapped protectively around her middle, her shoulders slack, as though she's defeated.

I stand up straight, square my shoulders despite the pain and smudge away my tears with the washcloth. What am I doing? Why would I choose to stay here?

It's like I've been wandering, lost in a forest and someone just handed me a map. Priorities start falling into place.

My first priority should be my family. I faulted my parents for choosing their ideals over their family. I wanted Mom and Dad to fight for Alyssa, Silas and me, to do whatever it took to keep us free. And yet, what have I been doing? I chose Justin over Silas. Silas may be out there alone somewhere. He may need me.

My second priority should be with my fellow slaves. They need help. They deserve my loyalty and friendship. If Nathan and I can escape, maybe we can help others like Lydia and Eli to escape.

Justin. My heart aches. My resolution to stay away from him is thin at best. If he invites me on another horseback ride, will I be able to say no? Would I refuse his warm hand around mine? Or his kiss?

I sigh, the air leaving me in ragged, painful bursts. How will Justin feel when he wakes up one day to find Nathan and I gone—together? He's been kind to me and the others. And he saved me. The Banker would have killed me if Justin hadn't stepped in.

He'll feel so deceived when he realizes Nathan and I are gone. He spent all this time trying to earn my trust and I'll be the one to betray him.

But there is zero chance of a future for us.

I don't think Justin's intentions for me are like the Banker's for Jasmine. Nathan's right about one thing, though. Justin is not like me and he never will be.

Escape is risky. We could get lost or worse—caught. I can only guess how we'd be punished for that. Beatings, prison, maybe an owner that makes the Banker look like an angel. And without commerce chips, we can't go near populated areas or even buy food.

But if we make it to Eagle Pass, we're free!

I probably have a better chance of playing piano for the President than actually making it to Eagle Pass.

Am I going to spend the rest of my life afraid of what *might* happen?

No! I'm finished being ruled by fear. If making it to freedom is a one in a billion chance, then so be it. Silas had the courage to run. I'm not going to be outdone by my little brother. He's out there somewhere and I'm going to find him. My freedom is worth whatever price I have to pay for it.

I pass Roberta in the hall as I walk back to my room. She smirks. I glower back. I won't have to deal with her much longer.

Lydia startles when I march through the door of our bedroom. "How are you doing?" she asks.

I don't answer. Instead, I ignore the pain in my ribs to lean over and breathe on the window. I write, "Escape?" in the cloud. If I leave, I'm taking her with me.

Her eyes widen and her face turns ashen. "No, Rielle!" She jumps to her feet and scrubs the word off the window. "We can't do that. We have to obey our master."

I shake my head.

"If we're good, they'll release us from our contracts once we're rehabilitated." She tries a smile, but it falls flat.

I cock my head to the side. She can't really believe that, can she?

I huff onto the window again and start to write, "Let's run," but she grabs my hand and wipes her palm over my message.

"No! Stop it! We'll get in trouble. We stay and do as we're told." Her voice pitches higher. "Do you know what they'll do to us if we leave? The Banker takes care of us. We have to obey him. I'm not talking about this anymore. What if he hears?"

I stare at her in disbelief.

She stands and smoothes her dress. "The banks know what's best for us."

I look down at my hands as she rushes from the room, back to her chores. She believes all the lies.

I follow her downstairs and do my best to finish my share of the work, despite the pain. I need to get used to suffering. Escape won't be easy. Who knows what we'll encounter on the run.

Sleep drags me under despite the throbbing in my ribs and cheek.

One of those falling dreams startles me awake. I glance at the clock. 3:33. I close my eyes but my mind is already at work, planning an escape with Nathan. We'll spend the next few weeks stealing and hiding food for the journey, cutting our tracker chips out. Maybe Nina's chip, tucked safely in my shoe, will come in handy if we run out of supplies.

We'll be ready to set out at night as soon as the Banker leaves again.

I'm leaving! I'm going to see my brother again. I want to run outside and tell Nathan, but I need to play it cool. For now, I need to sleep or tomorrow will be miserable. I press my eyes closed and take deep, focused breaths to calm my galloping heart. My head clears and muscles relax, and the pain in my ribs mellows to a gentle background buzz. I drift closer and closer to sleep.

Shoes scuff the floor outside my bedroom, shocking away sleep. I sit up and listen. The scuffing stops for a moment. Then stairs creak.

I creep to my door, careful not to wake Lydia. I turn the knob slowly and press my other hand over the knob to muffle the latch click. Then I peek through a sliver-wide opening into the hall. A metal-on-metal whir carries upstairs. The sliding glass door is opening in the kitchen. I ease the bedroom door closed, tiptoe to the window and peer outside.

Moonlight illuminates the yard below. Roberta skulks across the grass toward the shed. She opens the side door and slides inside.

Why does she sneak out to the shed at this time of night? So many things have been going on here under my nose, my imagination flies in every direction. Does she have some sort of clandestine affair going too? Who would it be? Jonah? No, not unless she could force him against his will. Oh, I hope not. I swallow back the bile that creeps up my throat. I wait, wait, barely breathing, for a light to come on or for someone else to slink into the shed to meet her.

A pale, silver-blue light flickers in the shed window. Kind of reminds me of a holo start-up screen. But must be some sort of flashlight.

Ten minutes pass and the light disappears. Moments later, Roberta pokes her head out the door, scans the yard and hurries back to the house. I dash back to bed and yank my blankets over me. The stairs creak, feet shuffle, and then silence.

CHAPTER TWENTY-SIX

Dangerous Plans

AFTER A SHORT SLEEP, A SHARP SMELL wakes me. Ammonia. Glass cleaner. Something squeaks and then sprays. *Fffft. Fffft.* More squeaking. I pry my eyes open and look at the clock. My alarm hasn't even gone off. Lydia is scrubbing the window in tight circles. She turns the rag, sprays more blue fluid on the glass and scrubs again.

Is she nuts?

Pain resurfaces as the residue of sleep lifts. I sit up, every joint and muscle aching. My body feels like—like it was beaten to a pulp by a cruel little fat man. Oh wait, it was. But for the last time.

I touch Lydia's arm and she starts. She clutches the rag to her chest. "You scared me. Did I wake you? I'm sorry."

I make a show of furrowing my brow and glancing from her to the window.

"After what you wrote last night, I was afraid that someone would still be able to see it on the window. If anyone found out…"

She sprays the window again and wipes. I sit on my bed, staring at her. How many times does she think she needs to clean it?

She continues. "I'm sure within a year or two we'll be rehabilitated and they can let us go home. If they found out we were trying to—you know—they'd make us stay longer. And this is a good place. The Banker takes good care of us." She folds her rag and scours a spot so hard I think she might rub a hole in the glass. "You can't bring that up anymore, Rielle. It's wrong. We need to obey our master. That's the right thing to do. It's pleasing to God."

I touch Lydia's arm to still its frenzied motion. A tear rolls down her cheek. "We just need to have faith, Rielle. The Banker will tell them we're rehabilitated and then we can go home to our families."

Sadness settles over me. I see it now. If I try to escape, Lydia can't join me. She's too scared. I remember what Uncle Rex said. "It's nice to see you still have some fight in you. You may need it."

Lydia's lost her fight.

I need to find Nathan so we can start planning. I have to move even though my aching body protests.

I'm in the bathroom before the other girls, brushing my teeth and pinning my hair. I sit on the bed jiggling my knee, waiting for breakfast so I can go downstairs and see Nathan.

Lydia walks into the room and stops, stares at me. "You're ready early."

I shrug. Of course I'm ready early. You were kind enough to wake me with your obsessive scrub-tantrum.

"Are you okay?" she asks.

I nod and put my hand on my knee to stop it from moving. I let my shoulders drop, trying to look as tired as I usually do. I can't look so energized. It might worry Lydia, or the Banker might notice and suspect something's up. I turn my lips down, but my cheeks still burn with excitement.

I've never been so happy to follow Lydia down to breakfast. I swallow my oatmeal without tasting it. We mill around the kitchen, monitoring the clock. Waiting for the Banker is excruciating. Where is he?

Nathan paces and Jonah follows suit. Megavolts of tension sizzle in the air.

Lydia watches Nathan march from one end of the kitchen to the other. "Maybe we're supposed to do like yesterday—just find our own jobs," she says.

Jonah stops. "Yeah. Maybe." A few uncertain glances are thrown around the room and then Roberta hurries off to the pantry. Jonah shoots out the back door.

"I guess I'll vacuum," Lydia says.

Nathan exits through the sliding door and heads for the shed. I march outside through the front door and around the side of the house so it doesn't look like I'm following him. Then I go straight to the shed.

Metal clangs in the back corner where Nathan straps on a tool belt. I pretend to consider which spade to use. He approaches, a roll of screening under his arm and a hammer swinging from his belt.

I glance around the garage to ensure we're alone, then turn to him. "I need to talk to you."

"I'm on my way to the gazebo. Wait a few minutes, then meet me there."

Nathan disappears into the sunlight.

I stare at the spades and wait for time to pass, my heart thumping. I've made my decision. I want to leave immediately.

I wait a few more excruciating minutes, then grab a broom and march through the curtain of weeping willow branches to the gazebo. Nathan is perched on a ladder, prying away old screening from the structure. I go inside and sweep cob-webs from the ceiling. My ribs protest with every swipe.

"You wanted to...talk. Didn't think I'd ever get to say that to you."

He's still on the ladder, so only his legs are visible through the gazebo window. I lean my broom against the wall. "I've been doing a lot of thinking and I've made my decision. I want to take you up on your offer. That is, if you're still offering." Cool relief settles over me as I utter the words.

He steps down a few rungs, enough to look me in the eye. "That's a change. What about your boyfriend?"

The word "boyfriend" irritates me. He probably intended it to. "Let's leave him out of this, okay? I think my priorities have been all screwed up. My loyalties should lie with my family and my fellow Contracts."

His voice playful, yet heavy with sarcasm, he says, "Your priorities were screwed up? Hmmm, you don't say."

I roll my eyes. "Are we going to talk about this or not?"

"I just want to get this straight. You are willing to leave your beloved Justin and run away with me?" He flashes a crooked grin.

"Can you quit with the jokes. I'm serious."

"Okay, Okay." He steps off the ladder, scans the yard, then enters the gazebo. He leans against the wall in front of me.

"Nathan, I need to get out of here. I need to find my brother." Tears sting my eyes and escape onto my cheek. Nathan seems to watch them trail down my face. He frowns.

I rub the moisture away. I want to be strong—strong enough to do this.

He wraps his arms around me. "I'll get you out of here, Rielle. You don't need to worry. Everything is going to be okay."

His embrace wrings out more tears. What is it about him? I'm safe in his arms, like the world could implode around me and he could somehow protect me. When he says everything is going to be okay, I believe him.

I pull back and reach to wipe my tears, but he's there first. His hand cradles my face as his thumb strokes the tears away. His hazel eyes peer into mine. Jessica must have adored those eyes. Who wouldn't? My breath hitches and my heart flutters against my ribs. I steal my gaze away and disentangle myself from his arms.

Nathan is off limits—he's Jessica's, not mine. Why would he be mine? I have a thing for Justin. Don't I? "How are we going to do this? I mean we'll need food and water and places to hide, especially during the day."

"Done and done. Now what do you want to talk about?"

"Nathan, this isn't a joke! This is serious. I mean, what if we get caught? If we don't plan this right we could end up worse off than we are now."

He leans against the cedar framework and folds his arms. "If you calm down, I can explain."

I snap my mouth shut and wait.

"I've been working out an escape plan since they sold me into this hell hole. I've stockpiled food and water inside the old truck the Banker keeps in the shed. I cut out my chip over a year ago. I wasn't shooting from the hip when I suggested we escape. I knew exactly what I would do and how I would do it."

"Oh."

"If you'd have come to your senses earlier it would have made this a lot easier. We could've left before the Banker came back."

Although he's right about it being easier to get away with Justin supervising, I'm relieved this is no longer an option. I don't want him to be blamed for our escape. I don't think I could bear that level of betrayal.

"I don't think we can wait until the next time the Banker leaves. Something is going down. It's going to be bad. I can feel it," Nathan says.

I nod.

"Don't nod."

I form an apologetic smile. "Sorry. I agree. I want to get out of here. The sooner the better."

He peers over his shoulder. "Morris said there's a wicked storm blowing in."

I follow his gaze to the cloudless sky.

"We'd make slow progress traveling through a storm."

My mouth falls open. "You were thinking of tonight already?"

"I thought you said you wanted to go, 'the sooner the better.'" He mimics my voice.

"I do! I just—I thought it would take more planning. I didn't realize you had it all figured out."

"Are you ready to go or not?"

"Yes, I'm ready."

"Are you sure? Once we leave, there's no turning back. You may never see him again."

A stab of guilt roils in my chest. "Yes, I'm sure."

"Okay, then, we leave tomorrow night. Meet me at the back gate at midnight. We won't talk about this again. Can't risk anyone overhearing, okay?"

"Yeah, I'll be there. Don't leave without me."

He holds me in his gaze. "Of course not. I'm not going anywhere without you." Nathan looks out over the yard, then back toward the house. "We better get back to work." He turns to leave.

"Nathan," I call, stopping him in the doorway. He glances back at me. "If you had this planned out for so long, why are you still here? Why didn't you just get out? I mean, I'm only going to slow you down."

"How incredibly selfish would it be to save myself and no one else? No. I promised myself that if I figured a way out, I'd take at least one other person with me."

He pauses and studies his shoes for a moment before returning his hazel eyes to me. "I was going to take Jessica, the girl who was here before you. We planned it together. That was our biggest mistake. The Banker must've seen us sneaking around. One day she was here—the next day she was gone."

He pushes the door open, and returns to his perch on the ladder. Wary of being seen or even suspected of conspiring with Nathan and suffering Jessica's fate, I leave the rest of the cob webs on the ceiling and return to the house. Laundry awaits.

In the laundry room, I pick up an empty basket. Turning, I take one step toward the door and halt. The Banker fills the doorway.

"Rielle, you're needed upstairs." He turns on his heel.

I don't move.

"Come!" He motions with his hand.

What does he want with me upstairs? Cleaning? Or a private place to finish beating me to a pulp? My feet lock to the floor as my pulse climbs. If he's going to beat me, I'd rather him do it here where someone could walk in and stop him or at least find me when it's over.

"Come!" he shouts.

I refuse to move. He marches up to me. Lifts his chin, looks down his nose at me.

I steel myself for the first blow.

"I'm not going to hit you. I'm satisfied you weren't the one in my office." His eyes dart from side to side, as though checking to make sure we're alone. "More than satisfied. I have some work for you to do."

I chew on my cheek, debating. Reluctantly, I set the basket on the washing machine and follow the Banker up the marble steps to Caleb's bedroom. He directs me to two suitcases. "Rielle, I need you to pack for the children. They're visiting some family in Canada. Please pack their warm clothes and try to fit as much as you can in there. It will be an extended visit."

Please? Did hell freeze over? I don't think I've ever heard the "P" word come out of his mouth—especially not in the presence of Contracts. He hurries from the room.

I pluck pants, shirts, dresses from their closets and dressers, fold them and tuck them inside the suitcase. Then I start on pajamas.

The Banker lumbers back into the room, startling me. Two thick manila envelopes are clutched between his fingers. He kneels beside me as I stack his daughter's nightgowns in the suitcase. His arm grazes mine. I bite my lip and edge away from him.

He tucks one envelope into an inner pocket of each of the suitcases. He looks me over, top to bottom. I shudder.

"Rielle, my children haven't done anything wrong. They're innocent." His eyes flutter as though he's nervous. "You won't tell anyone where they're going."

The Banker lifts his hand toward my face. I flinch away, but he's undeterred. I turn my head away from him and hold my breath, bracing. He brushes my cheek and drags his hot fleshy fingers over my neck.

CHAPTER TWENTY-SEVEN

The President of What?

I SWALLOW HARD AND SHIFT AWAY FROM the Banker's touch. He yanks his hand back. "I'm sorry. You'd have every reason to hate me. But please. If—if something happens. If. If. I know I don't deserve it, but keep the secret for my children. Protect them for Nina." He leans in closer and whispers, "Guard *it* with your life." He throws a cagey glance at the door and then up to the ceiling. "They're watching." He stands and rushes out of the room.

My heart pounds and I hold my chest, finally able to breathe. My confusion at what he was talking about is dwarfed by the horror of his touch—alone in a bedroom, upstairs, far from the other Contracts. Not that they could've helped me anyway. And I thought his fists were the worst dangers here. I was wrong.

I want to go someplace where there are witnesses. Frantically, I empty the children's underwear and sock drawers on top of their other clothes. I sit on top of Caleb's luggage and zip it closed.

When I go to close the other suitcase, I eye the manila envelope and stop. I glance at the empty doorway and listen. Silence. I draw out the envelope and listen again, straining for footfalls that might indicate the Banker's approach. After fumbling with its flap, I peel the envelope open.

Proper bills. A dense wad of them. Instead of answering my questions, the envelope only begs more.

The Banker is sending his children away, alone, with piles of money. Strange. He sounded frightened, paranoid. They're watching. Did he mean Bank Security? But why would they watch him? He has a chip, a high position in the bank and more money than my family would've seen in ten lifetimes.

I stuff the envelope back into the pocket and close the suitcase.

Footfalls on carpet. I jump to my feet, spin around. Nathan strides through the doorway. "The Banker told me to load the suitcases into his car."

I sigh with relief. Just Nathan.

He carries the bulging suitcases downstairs. I follow.

The Banker waits in the foyer with Lily and Caleb holding his hands. They each have a backpack on their shoulders. "Hurry up!" the Banker shouts as he tows the children to the garage, Nathan striding behind him.

Within minutes the garage door opener rumbles and the car engine roars.

I snag an empty basket from the laundry room and head to Justin's bedroom. I should be avoiding him but I'll have to do his laundry eventually. I may as well get it over with. I stand outside his door. I sigh. Who am I kidding? I want to see him. I miss him.

I'm pathetic.

I knock. No one answers. The deep screen blares on the other side of the door. I knock louder. Still, no answer. I beat my fist on the door one more time, then ease the door open and step inside. Water rushes in the next room; he couldn't hear me over the shower. I sweep across the room to Justin's laundry hamper, sneaking a glance at the deep screen. CNN is on.

I rifle through the hamper, pluck out the dark clothes, load them into my basket and hoist it to my hip. Applause rise from the deep screen. I sneak one last look. A man—a familiar man—speaks from a podium surrounded by a thick cheering crowd. It takes a split second to recognize him.

I gasp. The laundry basket slips from my fingers, hits the floor and the clothes spill into a denim puddle. Sir Smiles-a-lot, the younger and friendlier of the three men who visited the Banker months ago. When I had to wear that sleazy dress.

"Rielle?" Justin's voice startles me, but the deep screen holds my attention.

I force my eyes to find Justin, though the image of the man at the podium is burned into my vision. Justin stands in the bathroom doorway, clouds of steam behind him and a towel wrapped around his waist.

"Are you okay?" he asks.

The deep screen, like a magnet, pulls my gaze back to it. Justin brushes my arm as he moves to my side. The familiar cedar and vanilla scent surrounds him, but even that can't distract me. It's nothing but a vague side note.

I glance at the door to ensure I closed it when I came in. "Who is that?" I whisper.

He shakes his head. "You seriously don't know who that is?"

"I've seen him before."

Justin chuckles. "Of course you have, Rielle. Everyone has."

I furrow my brow and cock my head to the side.

"You really don't know who that is?"

"No, I'm not allowed to watch the news. Remember?"

"Oh, right, sorry. He's the new President. He just took office a few months ago."

"The president of what?"

Justin coughs out a hearty laugh. "The President of the United States."

"What?" The President, before he was the President, came to the Banker's house. Why? I try to remember what they talked about. They discussed "insurance," "recounts," and a computer program the Banker created. What was it called?

"Is something wrong?" Justin asks.

"No, nothing's wrong. What do you know about him?"

"Well, he used to be the Massachusetts regional bank director. He still sits on their board of directors. I find it a little unsettling that we have a banker in the White House, but the people voted and that's who they chose. It was a come-from-behind victory too, he trailed in the polls all the way up to the election."

I search my memories for the letters they talked about. Was it ECPU? Maybe I'm being paranoid, making a conspiracy out of nothing. "Do you know anything about an ECPU?"

"Yeah, it's the Electoral College Polling Uplink, a new digital voting system. People can vote by logging on with their chip. It's supposed to be more convenient and eliminate human error when counting ballots. It seemed to work well. Voter turnout was higher than it's been in the past."

My throat is paper dry. I swallow hard. Can this be any worse? Justin rubs the back of his hand up and down my arm. I lean away from him, though I want to lean closer.

"Something *is* wrong. You look like you're going to be sick."

When the Banker accused me of entering his office, he demanded to know if I told anyone about his meeting. Now I know why. He wanted to know if I told anyone about him and his friends fixing a Presidential election. I can't tell Justin. This is dangerous information.

I shake my head. "No, Justin. I'm fine. Just tired." He reaches for me, but I step away, scoop the clothes back into the basket and rush from the room.

The Banker returns home without the children as I finish the laundry. I go straight to bed. The world stopped turning this afternoon and now seems to be spinning the wrong way.

Did the Banker really fix an election? If someone found out what he did, it could be bad—not just a little bad, but very, very bad.

A fire smoulders inside me. All this new information—information I don't want.

I can't get past the feeling that I'm running out of time. The urgency to run has me on a jittery high that keeps me awake when I need to sleep.

To settle my mind, I concentrate on all the "lasts" I'm experiencing: My last night in this bed, my last day of chores, my last orders from the Banker. Freedom. I'm almost there. Justin pops into my head, but I force him aside and glance over at Lydia, who's already sleeping. I'll miss her.

I fall into a light sleep, but a familiar hallway noise wakes me. I climb out of bed and peer through the window to see Roberta creeping across the yard again. I'm beginning to doubt her trips to the shed have anything to do with romance—it is Roberta after all. I wouldn't put it past her to be up to no good.

The same dim silver-blue light glows inside the shed. Could it be the glow of a holo screen? With all the weird stuff going on here, I'm starting to believe anything is possible. But what would Roberta be doing with a holo?

Fifteen minutes later, she emerges from the shed, dashes across the lawn and up the stairs. I sit on my bed, staring at the door. What could she be doing out there? Roberta has always kept herself separate from the other Contracts. She's happily played the Banker's informant. My last beating was thanks to her. I'd never even set foot in the Banker's office. Roberta on the other hand—did she accuse me so she wouldn't get caught? Or was she just following through on her threat to tell the Banker I was in his office when I refused to tell her where I was going during my horseback rides with Justin? What if she's spying on the Contracts and reporting it all back to the Banker? Lydia did say Roberta was the one who snitched and got Jessica sent away.

A hot wave of anger rolls over me. Could she sink any lower than to betray her fellow slaves that way? If I wait until she's sleeping, I can sneak out and see what she's been up to. Roberta has snuck out repeatedly without getting caught. What's the worst that could happen—another beating, withholding food? I'm leaving tomorrow night anyway.

Minutes tick by so slowly that I pick up the clock and shake it to see if it's broken, but then the number changes. I watch Lydia sleep. I stare at the moon—at its craters, dark grey spots and bright white spots. I clean all the grit from under my fingernails.

After twenty-six minutes I can't take it anymore. I tiptoe to the door and slowly, methodically twist the doorknob. I open it just enough to slide through and then pull it shut behind me, cringing as the latch clicks. I stop and listen, expecting Roberta to jump out from the shadows at any moment. I pad down the hall and take the stairs one step at a time, easing each bare foot onto the next stair tread, praying it won't squeak.

At the bottom, I pause and listen again. The sliding door stands in front of me. A blind corner hides the rest of the kitchen. I startle when the refrigerator clicks on. Its hum is welcome though. It gives me a degree of sound cover. I place my right foot on the cool tile and then the left. I peer around the corner. The kitchen is dark and empty.

I creep across the floor and roll back the sliding door. The mild grate of its rollers sounds jack-hammer loud. I grind my teeth and ease it far enough open to squeeze through, then close it behind me.

Crickets creak. Wind whispers through tree branches. Distant thunder purrs. Lightening flickers. No other signs of life.

I cross the patio and step onto the coarse lawn, cool and gathering dew. Blades of grass spring up between my toes and I remember Lydia's warning. "Scorpions like cool, moist places." Why didn't I think to slip on a pair of shoes before coming outside? I rise up on tiptoe, as though that might save me from their sting, and scan the darkness for movement. The yard is empty.

After dashing to the shed, I duck under the eaves and check the windows back at the house. All black. No one heard me leave. Hopefully it'll be this easy to sneak out tomorrow night. I twist the knob then silently creep into the shed and close the door behind me, cutting off the comforting drone of wind and crickets.

I lean against the door to catch my breath and slow my pounding heart. I made it. Stagnant, mould-scented air tickles my nose. Moonlight filters through the small windows into the shed, washing its contents in silvery light.

What was Roberta doing in here? I don't know what to look for or where to start. Dusty water-stained cardboard boxes rest against the wall. A rotting wooden motor boat stands in front of me like a beached whale, its aged lacquer dulled by a thick coating of grime. Beyond the boat, an ancient truck hides under a canvas cover—the truck where Nathan stockpiled food.

The dust on the boxes looks undisturbed, so whatever Roberta was doing in here didn't involve them. I drop to my haunches and peer under the boat. Nothing there either. A glint of moonlight on boat's surface catches my eye. There's a wide shiny spot along the rim on the side of the boat. I stand and move closer. Everything else on the rim is dusty, but the dirt has been wiped clean from that section. I stretch up on tiptoes to examine the inside of the boat. Grimy red and white leather seats. Dingy orange life jackets litter the floor. A couple have bright orange footprints, as though someone trampled over them, lifting away the dust.

I heave myself over the side and into the boat, stifling a scream as my injured ribs bump over the boat wall. I lay there for a moment staring at the ceiling, letting the pain subside, straining my ears again.

Thunder growls, closer than it was before, then silence.

I crawl on hands and knees to the back of the boat, searching. Searching for what? Old fishing poles with matted lines lie in a tangled pile beside a pair of wooden oars and a deflated air mattress.

The moonlight filtering in through the narrow windows dims. Clouds slide over the moon like black-out curtains. A hint of sapphire blue breaks through granite black on the eastern horizon, but the clouds are slowly veiling that too. I need to be back in bed before sunrise, before the alarm clock wakes Lydia.

Trying to balance speed with silence, I pick my way through the darkness to the front of the boat, tossing life jackets and a musty beach towel aside as I search. Nothing. Only one spot remains: the cubby hole in the bow of the boat.

Reaching a bare hand into any dark hole in this god-forsaken place is dangerous. Anything could be in there—rats, scorpions, spiders. Goosebumps prick my arms and I shiver, picturing hairy-legged tarantulas. The hole is like an entrance to hell.

I need to hurry—either do this or go back inside.

I bite my lip and thrust my hand into the blackness, patting around the opening. The first few swipes yield nothing, but on the third, my hand falls on rough fabric with a spot of cold metal and the vague outline of something rectangular inside. I pull out a canvas bag with a leather strap and a flap held down with belt-like leather tabs.

I unfasten the clasps, fold the flap over the back and pull a square of cold metal from the bag. It molds to the shape of my hand. A holo. I was right.

But what's Roberta doing with a holo?

CHAPTER TWENTY-EIGHT

Bait

I SWEEP MY THUMB OVER THE HOLO AND the screen glows, but not with the usual start-up screen. A warning box hovers above the device, a yellow triangle spinning at the center. "Device will permanently terminate Unified Intelligence interface in fourteen seconds. Thirteen. Twelve." A green progress cylinder, almost full, slowly creeps higher. "Deleting cache memory. ten, nine, eight." I touch the red spinning orb flashing, "Cancel."

The progress cylinder freezes. "Operation cancelled."

The warning box disappears leaving a silver-blue background dotted with only one document icon and a mail icon suspended mid-air before me. I tap the document and it opens. A spreadsheet full of symbols and numbers appears on the screen. I scroll down, page after page, only to find more of the same.

I shut down the file. The only other icon is a tiny white envelope. I touch it, then tap my fingers nervously on my leg while I wait for it to load. The inbox lists two types of messages: a series with dates as their subject line and another that reads, "RE: BAIT."

I click on the most recent message. "THANKS. CAN ALWAYS COUNT ON YOU, BEAUTIFUL. C.F."

Who is C.F.?

I scroll down to see the original message. It outlines all the Banker's activities for that day: when he left for work, when he returned home, phone calls. I go to the previous message and it's more of the same.

Roberta's spying on the Banker.

I glance out the window. A strip of pink lights the narrow band of horizon still unobscured by clouds. Time is running out, but I'm curious about the emails entitled "BAIT." I click on the most recent.

"BE READY. C.F."

What does that mean? I scroll down.

"ONLY BAIT AND A.H. -R.T."

More initials. A.H. is probably the Banker, Arthur Hays and R.T. is likely Roberta. I never did learn her last name. I run my fingers over the image, scrolling to the previous message.

"WHO KNOWS ABOUT THE BREACH?"

It's like following a trail of bread crumbs to their source, but these crumbs aren't leading me home. More like Hansel and Gretel lured by a house made of candy, every scrumptious morsel devoured leading them closer to their demise. Closer to becoming meat for the witch's pot. I should be scampering back to the house, but curiosity drives me to the next message. What is bait?

I scroll all the way to the bottom, to the first "BAIT" message, sent over a year ago.

RE: BAIT

RIELLE JAMES WILL ARRIVE TOMORROW. KEEP A CLOSE EYE ON HER. WE ARE USING HER TO FLUSH OUT ANGELIQUE JAMES. CONTACT IMMEDIATELY IF YOU NOTICE ANY UNUSU-AL ACTIVITY.

C.F.

My mouth falls open. I'm "BAIT."

I stare at the hologram wide eyed, trembling. I tap on the final message.

BE READY. Sent two hours ago.

Ready for what? What is going on?

What breach are they talking about? What breach do only the Banker and I—? Oh, no! I throw my hand over my mouth. The election. My heart punch-es my rib cage and adrenaline courses in my veins.

Nathan and I are leaving tomorrow, but what if that's too late? I need to tell him. I need to get out of here. Why did I come out here barefoot in my pajamas?

I slide back over the side of the boat onto the concrete floor and dash back to the house under a flash of lightening. After shoving the glass door open, I creep into the kitchen and retrieve a razor sharp paring knife to tackle the task I've been dreading. It's time to remove the tracker chip.

I dash upstairs, straight to the bathroom. After locking the door, I lean over the sink, the knife poised. I really hope my chip is in the same spot as Nina's. I pause, the blade pressed to my skin. I can do this. I have to do this. I haul in a lungful of air and hold it, clamping my teeth together. The knife digs into my skin. Pain shoots up my arm. Blood drips down my hand and into the sink. I stifle a moan as I push the knife deeper. Deeper.

I drop the bloody knife into the sink and tug the skin apart. Something glints beneath the surface. I try to pinch it between my fingernails, but I can't reach it. I fling the vanity doors open and rummage through the first aid kit until I find a pair of tweezers.

A deep breath to combat my dizziness, then I carefully extract the chip. Relief, like a monsoon rain, pours over me. It's out! I hold it up to the light. Hatred for the thing warms the back of my neck. It can't imprison me any longer. I drop it into the drain.

I press adhesive strips and a bandage over the wound, rinse the blood from the sink and sneak back to my room.

Lydia's sleeping. I stare down at her and try to make sense of what's happening, but fear and my do-it-yourself surgery have my head spinning.

Though I know she can't hear me, I whisper, "If I make it, I promise to find a way to get you out too."

The stairs groan. My head snaps up. And then there's another creak and another, higher on the staircase this time. I fall back on my pillow and pull the blanket over me. The latch on my door clicks. The hinges groan.

I close my eyes and control my breathing, trying to match Lydia's slow and shallow sleeping breaths. My heart pounds and my lungs scream for more air. I'm rigid, still as a stone, as footsteps pad toward me. I sense the figure's closeness, as if the air grows thicker, heavier as it approaches. I fight to remain still, wanting nothing more than to open my eyes.

The form leans over me, hovering like a spectre. The scent of cedar and vanilla. Justin? He can't be here. Not now! My eyes pop open. I gasp and a large hand slams down over my mouth. I search the darkness, but I can't make out anything beyond a male silhouette. I sink my teeth into the flesh covering my mouth.

"Ow! Rielle, don't scream," Justin says in a loud whisper.

I tear his hand away from my mouth.

He crosses the room, opens my drawers and throws my clothes at me. "We don't have much time."

I sit up. "What's going on?"

"I'm getting you out of here. Now!"

"No!" I say in the most severe whisper I can muster.

"What?"

I fold my arms. "I'm not going anywhere with you."

"I do not have time to explain. If you don't leave now, you may not get out!"

I set my lips in a rock-solid line.

"Rielle, you're in danger. Bank Security is coming and they're going to level this place."

The words "be ready" echo in my mind. I motion for him to turn around while I pull on my pants, shirt and shoes. He grabs my hand and tows me down the stairs. "What about Lydia?"

He doesn't answer, just keeps dragging me across the lawn toward the back gate. Nathan comes into view, descending the stairs from the men's quarters. He freezes on the bottom step.

"What's he doing out here?" Justin mutters under his breath.

I can guess. Probably preparing something for tomorrow night's escape.

Nathan marches to block our path.

Justin sighs. "Not now."

Nathan takes a firm hold of my upper arm and places himself between Justin and me. "Where are you taking her?"

I want to know too.

"I'm getting her out of here. They're coming for my uncle."

Car engines rev in the distance, growing louder, descending on the estate like a swarm of bees.

"I don't have time for this, Nathan. You're going to have to trust me. In about two minutes all hell is going to break loose and I can save her if you get out of my way."

Conflict erupts on Nathan's face. His eyes crease with worry as he glances from Justin to me. Two gun shots boom inside the house. Shouting. A scream.

Nathan throws his arms around me and whispers in my ear. "Be careful. I'll try to find you." He steps out of the way.

Justin snags my hand and holds out the bracelet I wore on all our horseback rides. "It's gone. I cut it out," I say.

"You what?" He shakes his head, then glances back at Nathan. "Never mind." He leads me through the gate and stops under the cover of a large tree, as a few swollen raindrops splash to the ground. He opens his mouth to speak but a crack of thunder interrupts him. When the rumbling subsides he tries again. "I can't go with you. They can't suspect I helped you. You remember how to get to the stables. Take Cherokee and ride as fast as you can. A mile out from the old house, ditch the horse. Scare her off. Get to the tunnel. I'll come for you. It may take a while, but don't leave the tunnel until I get there. Go!"

He takes off running around the north side of the fence.

I turn the other way and sprint toward the stables as rain begins to pour in sheets. Thrumming helicopter blades draw closer. Circles of light shine on the haze over the house. More gunshots slice the through the downpour. Between the rain and the darkness, I'm running blind. I trip over rocks, falling and bloodying my knees and hands. I get up. Keep running.

I slide to a stop at the stable fence, searching the field. How am going to find that horse? I force out a loud whisper, "Cherokee." Will she hear my call over the pounding rain and thunder? Thumping hooves beat toward me. I lift the latch on the gate and swing it open.

She rounds the gate as I push it closed again and searches me for apples. "None today." I stroke her muzzle, nudge her closer to the fence and use it to boost myself onto her back. I wrap my legs around her, wind my hands in her mane and dig in my heels. She takes off at a full run. I lay my head against her, allowing her do the work. The darkness is too thick for me, but she knows the way.

A churning, grinding sound rumbles from the sky—stones rolling in a barrel. Lightning flickers as steady as a strobe light, bathing the hillside in an eerie green light. I ride for over an hour through the driving rain, following the river as I always had with Justin. I peer backward every couple minutes, my heart racing, expecting to see Bank Security pursuing me.

Deep, chest-pounding explosions echo in the distance. Thunder cracks. The two sounds blend until I can no longer distinguish between them. Rain streams down my forehead into my eyes, blurring my vision. I trust Cherokee to take me where I need to go, so I'm caught off guard when she takes a sharp turn and gallops up the hill. That's the wrong way! I lean to the side, trying to urge her to turn back, but she gallops faster. I pull back on her mane, but she yanks her neck forward and gallops up the incline.

"Cherokee. Stop!" I shout with another jerk of her mane. A jagged bolt of lightning tears the sky in two. A deafening peel of thunder sets my ears ringing. The sound bounces off the hills and resonates in the distance. But the sound isn't growing quieter, it rumbles louder and louder. Closer and closer. Cherokee whinnies, and lunges full speed up the hill, her muscles straining beneath me.

And then it hits me: she's scared. I look up through the rain. What spooked her? I gasp. That sound isn't thunder! A towering wall of water surges toward us. I kick the horse and loosen my grip on her mane, freeing her to charge forward. I tangle my hands in her mane, hoping and praying she can make it to the hilltop before the water reaches us. She leaps up the rocky hill frantically, slipping on the stones, but finds purchase. The pinnacle's in sight. We're almost there. Water licks at her rear hooves like a ravenous animal stalking its prey. A wave hits and nearly knocks her over, but she manages to keep her footing. A second, larger wave hits. The entire world goes sideways.

I tumble into the rushing flow. Holding my breath, I cling to the horse. The raging water topples over me, sucking me under. Thick muck pours over my face. The river transforms sandy debris, leaves and slivers of wood into sandpaper against my skin.

The current drags us downstream. I try kicking my way toward the surface. Something whizzes past me, pulled along by the ripping current. It slices into my right shoulder with a white hot flash of pain. I open my mouth to scream, but it fills with polluted water. My lungs crave air, but if this slurry enters my lungs I'm done for. My muscles burn as I kick and dig with one arm and grip Cherokee's mane with the other. It's not helping! My pulse rushes louder than the current in my ears. Which way is the surface?

The horse jolts forward, yanking my arm. I hold tighter. She pulls me in short, jerky bursts. With the next lunge she drags me further forward. My lungs burn like I've inhaled acid. My legs find her back as wind brushes my hair. Another spurt forward and my face hits the air. I vomit the vile water from my mouth and gasp for breath.

Cherokee runs until we're beyond the raging water. She stops, panting. I slide off her back and collapse on the ground. I lay there, trying to catch my breath. Cherokee's hooves beat the dirt as she dances nervously. She finds a tuft of grass and bites off a mouthful. As my breathing slows and the dizziness passes, the danger I'm in bursts to the forefront of my mind. How far did the river carry us back toward the Banker's house? Are they looking for me? If so, I'll be easy to spot lying atop this hill.

I approach the horse under flashes of lightning and the commotion of rushing water. She deserves a lifetime supply of apples. I rub my hand over her soaked muzzle. "Thank you! You saved us, but we have to go. We can't let them find us." I lean my head against hers for a moment, attempting to communicate the depth of my gratitude. She's reluctant to leave the patch of grass, but I tug her toward a juniper stump to give me a boost. I fling my leg over her back and urge her on.

For the first hour I search the sky and plan what to do if I spot a helicopter or a search party. As I ride, the gash in my shoulder begins to ache. Blood coats my arm and drips from my elbow. I inspect the wound—a deep gash at the top of my bicep. My stomach churns. Having nothing to bandage it with, I slow the horse, remove my shoe, slip off my sock and press the sock over the wound, applying pressure to slow the bleeding. I tie the sock around my arm, but the blood soaks through. I knot it tighter which makes my arm throb with every heartbeat.

I check beneath the sole of my shoe to ensure Nina's chip is still there, then slip my foot back into the shoe and nudge the horse faster.

The clouds thin and rays of sunlight peek between them. I spy the bushy area surrounding the old house and pull back on Cherokee's mane to slow her, then dismount. "Thank you girl. You're free now too." I begin to walk away. Her hooves tap behind me.

"No. You can't come with me. Go." I wave her away and take a few more steps. She follows. Riddled with guilt after all she's done for me, I slap her on the rump and shout "Go!" She darts back the way we came. I jog in the opposite direction. With daylight upon me and helicopters in the area, stealth is more important than speed. I keep my head low, beneath the leafy canopy. I skulk through the scrubby trees and underbrush until the yard comes into view.

Crouching behind a shrub, I survey the yard. Thirty meters stand between me and the safety of the old house. Helicopter blades thump, thump, thump in the distance. I scan the skies. Empty. I break out of the underbrush and sprint across the open field, then duck under the eaves of a small, weathered outbuilding on the edge of the yard. I'm almost there, close enough to see the peeling paint on the back door.

Pressed against worn siding, I scan the yard again. Nothing. I race toward the house, run up the steps and fling myself through the door. Slamming it closed behind me, I twist the deadbolt.

I lean against the door, to catch my breath, then tiptoe across the kitchen toward the basement door. I peel it open and descend the stairs, slowly, carefully, cringing with each squeak of the treads.

I find the metal rack with just one change since the last time I was here: a jug of water. I haul down the jug with my good arm. After depressing the pin under the shelf, I swing the rack back to reveal the hidden doorway. The long, dark tunnel stretches before me. I step into the cool, musty air and close the door. I inch down the tunnel until the door disappears into blackness, hoping the darkness will conceal me if Bank Security somehow discovers the secret door. I lean against the dirt wall and slide to the floor. Relief settles over me. No one can find me here. I'm safe.

My throbbing shoulder begs attention. I untie the sock from my arm, unscrew the cap on the water jug and pour fresh water over the gash, sucking in a hissed breath as water stings the wound. Bits of dirt flow down my arm, but flecks of debris remain imbedded in my flesh. I reach into the wound to remove the dirt, but a sharp wave of pain sparks dizziness and spotty vision. I stop and rest my head against the dirt wall until the dizziness passes, then I retie the blood-encrusted sock onto my arm. All I can do now is settle in and wait for Justin.

CHAPTER TWENTY-NINE

Scorpions Love Cool, Dark Places

EVERY MINUSCULE SOUND TRIGGERS both hope and dread. Is Justin coming for me? Or has Bank Security found me? I curl my legs into my body as closely as I can without my bruised ribs adding their pain to the one in my shoulder. I want to make myself smaller, invisible. The light at the end of the tunnel shifts from one side to the other as the hours pass.

With time on my hands, I sort through the dizzying events of the last twenty-four hours—the Banker's strange behaviour, the election revelation, but most importantly, Justin. All that time, he was planning an escape for me, but something went wrong. The Banker's agitation is beginning to make sense. He must have known they were coming for him. That's why he sent the children away. But why did Bank Security come after him? He was one of them. He rigged the election to put a banker in the White House. Isn't that what OneEarth Bank wanted?

And then the faces of people I left behind flash by like a mental slide show. Each one intensifies a deep ache in my chest. Lydia. Eli. Nathan. There had been gunshots and explosions. What happened to my friends? Are they still alive? What if? What if—

Nathan.

A lead ball drops into the pit of my stomach. Why didn't I insist that Nathan come with me? He was going to help me, but I didn't help him. Selfish, like Nathan said. He wouldn't have left without me. My throat tightens and tears sting my eyes. How could I do that to him? How could I leave him behind? If he's dead, it's my fault. Why didn't I help him?

Streams of tears wash my face. The narrow beam of sunlight at the far end of the tunnel dims, then disappears, plunging me into total darkness. Exhausted, I fall into a restless sleep, haunted by fire and by faces contorted in pain.

I jerk awake. My neck burns! Something moves in my hair. I jump to my feet and smack my head on the ceiling. Another sting pierces the skin behind my ear. I bat at my hair and three small things softly hit the floor. Scorpions? I comb my fingers through my hair to ensure there aren't any more.

By the time I'm done, my shoulder aches. The sock covering my wound is warm and squishy with fresh blood. I must've reopened up the wound. I peel away the soaked make-shift bandage, take off my other sock and press it to the gash to stem the blood flow. The bleeding slows, but I can't sleep now. I move away from the walls to the center of the tunnel, afraid other creatures might nest in my hair.

A thread of light at the end of the tunnel drives away the darkness. Morning. Finally. Justin will come today. My stomach rumbles. I guzzle some water to stave off hunger pangs. Staring at the spot of light, I wait for Justin to appear. I draw in the dirt with my finger—hearts, faces and then names. Silas, Lydia.

Nathan.

I stop drawing and sweep his name away with my fingers, as if removing his name could remove my guilt.

I'm afraid to move or make a noise, but as the day wears on, boredom and curiosity get the better of me. I crawl to the far end of the tunnel. An exit shaft goes straight up. I stand, stretch my legs and peer up through the gaps in the slatted wood hatch above me. It looks like another building—not a house, a shack at best— with greyed wood-framed walls, sagging rafters, sunlight leaking through holes in the roof. I stand there for a few minutes enjoying the dryer air and sunlight before crawling back to my spot.

I entertain myself by imagining new additions to my song, the one Mom loved and Eli learned, but it isn't enough to get my mind off my growling stomach. Could there be something to eat up in the house or in the shack? No, I can't risk leaving to search for food, so I gulp down more water.

The sun shifts from one side of the tunnel to the other, and then the tunnel dims. The scorpion stings are now painful bumps on my scalp. The dull ache in my shoulder transforms into the low, steady throb of a tympani drum. Heat radiates from the skin around my cut. It hurts to move it, yet it hurts to have it hanging at my side. I hug my arm to my chest.

"I'm sure Justin will come soon," I say aloud, attempting to soothe my own anxiety. Light disappears from the tunnel a second time.

Please don't go.

When I first got here, the silent darkness was a warm blanket that protected me from Bank Security. Now it's terrifying. My imagination works overtime, filling my sleep with nightmares. I'm trapped in a pit with snakes and spiders falling on me, crawling down my neck. My family lies dead beneath the undulating mass of creatures. My own screams wake me.

Hazy light filters into the tunnel. I'm drowning again and the light is an outstretched hand, a life preserver. The light stays murky though, except for flashes of lightning. Thunder booms. Then the rain begins. The dirt walls ooze water until a small stream carves its way down the centre of the tunnel, soaking my feet and pants. I start to shiver, the air as frigid as a Minnesota winter.

"Justin will be here soon." The sound of my own voice startles me. I wrap my arms around my legs and rock back and forth, quietly singing to drive away the sound of dripping water and venomous critters scurrying in the tunnel to escape the storm. The temperature drops further. Colder and colder. It can't be this cold. Maybe the tunnel temperature isn't getting colder. Maybe I'm getting warmer.

I touch my hand to my shoulder. It's hot and the bandage is moist again. I untie the sock and peel it back. It's not moist with blood this time. A foul smelling fluid oozes from the wound. My stomach heaves at the putrid smell. I check the incision I made in my hand to remove my tracker chip. At least it doesn't look infected.

There's nothing I can do though. Even if I leave the tunnel, where would I go? I start rocking again. "Please come soon, don't forget about me. Please come soon, don't forget about me. Please come soon, don't forget about me."

Forgotten. Like I forgot Nathan. I convulse with sobs.

As the sun sets on my third day, the night attacks me—a pillow pressed to my face, suffocating. Shivering, I begin to float in the darkness. I claw at the skin on my face, my neck. Scorpions are crawling over my body. They're everywhere. I can't get them off. I scream and gasp for air.

No one will ever come for me.

Two sensations dominate my dark world: the bitter cold and a throbbing ache that radiates from my arm over my entire body. I close my eyes, but when I open them there's no change. Darkness. Am I dreaming or am I awake? I can't tell. Figures float in and out of my vision. My parents are here. They stand at the other side of the tunnel; they don't speak. They watch me, scrutinize me, judge me—probably for leaving Nathan behind.

"You did this to me! You did this to me!" I shout, hoping someone will hear and find me. Put me out of my misery.

I close my eyes against the darkness, not that it makes any difference. An image lights behind my eyelids. My family sitting at our kitchen table together. There's food piled on plates, like it used to be, before....

I'm at the table, but also watching from a distance. Alyssa drinks from her sippy cup. Silas chatters. I watch Mom and Dad chew. They always said they wanted what's best for me. Is this what they had in mind? Being sold as a slave. Buried alive? "Why did you do this to me?" My voice echoes over the kitchen, but they don't look up from their meal. "Why didn't you do whatever it took to save us?" They ignore me. Hot anger washes over me. "Answer me!"

Dad smiles at Mom, puts another bite in his mouth. I stare at his hands, then Mom's. A chip—that's all it would have taken to keep us together. I would have taken it to keep us together. Then, we'd be happy. Safe. Warm.

Alyssa's chubby fingers pick up a pea. My hand feels weird, itchy. I look down. A red dot glows in the soft flesh beside my thumb. It moves. My skin bulges. I scream. The sound hurts my ears. I claw at my hand—I want it out. Hair-thin metallic legs burst through my skin.

The bug drops onto the floor and scrambles toward Alyssa. "No! Stay away from her." I want to stop it, but my feet are locked to the floor. I scream again. They can't hear me.

The thing burrows into her hand.

I don't want that monster inside her.

I don't want it inside any of them.

I just want everything to be like it was before.

I want to go home.

I push my mind to envision something else—our lives if Mom and Dad would have taken the chip. We'd be together. I look past my family, out the window, at the apple tree. We would have been safe, but what about the others? What about everyone else who refused the chip? Another girl like me would be here right now longing for her family. Mom and Dad taking the chip wouldn't have stopped any of this.

It's not them.

They didn't do this.

The banks did this.

A few more hours pass and my mood grows as dark as the tunnel that's become my tomb. I'm going to die here. Alone. I lie down on the wet floor, my hair in the mud and wait for it to happen. I fought as hard as I could. I tried to preserve my life. Now it's ending. Maybe my family is dead too and I can join them at the table.

At my end, I see everything with perfect clarity. I'm proud of my parents;

they did the right thing. They stuck to their convictions. My parents didn't make me a slave. The OneEarth Bank made me a slave.

If I took the chip, would I have had the courage to stand up for Resistors? No. I'd be as guilty as those who sold me, looking the other way while other people suffered. Fear would have been my master.

But I'm not afraid anymore. I will die free. I close my eyes in peace.

CHAPTER THIRTY

Identity

"RIELLE," MY FATHER CALLS. HIS VOICE is distant, but growing closer.

I can't make my voice work to answer him. I smile and a tear rolls down my cheek. He's coming for me. Rapid footfalls move toward me, splashing as they hit the ground. He stops, kneels beside me.

"I missed you so much," I whisper, weeping.

A tall, lean form hovers over me. "Yeah, I missed you too. Rielle, let's go. We don't have much time."

I try to sit up, but I fall backward. Large hands pull me up. The face is familiar, yet strange. I blink to focus, but it's too dark. The figure half carries, half drags me to the end of the tunnel opposite the old house.

He flips open the hatch above the tunnel and blinding sunlight cascades over me. He heaves me up through the hatch into fresh, clean air. I gulp it in. He carries me over a dirt path to a car. Someone else opens the door and helps to haul me inside, and I lay my head on a leather seat. Dad crawls in next to me. The door slams. A gas engine roars and the car speeds away.

"Rielle, look at me"

It's too bright. My eyes refuse to open for more than a second. One glimpse of Dad and they snap shut.

"I think she was down there too long. There's something wrong with her," he says.

"Don't worry, kid, she'll be okay." A deeper voice, the other man.

Dad runs his fingers over my forehead, pushing my hair back. "Oh, no. I think she's sick. She's burning up!"

He touches my make-shift bandage. I wince as he pulls the sock away. He gasps. "Hurry, we need to get her home!"

I lay my head on his thigh and sigh. Dad's here. I'm going home. I relax as the rocking car and the bright light seeping through my eyelids assure me that I'm no longer underground. I shiver. A blanket slides over me. And then I sink into murky oblivion.

I wake as the car slows and stops. I open my eyes long enough to see that it's dark outside. I close them again.

A door opens. "Help me get her out of here," Dad says. It's his voice, but different. Two sets of hands pull me from the car. Thick unfamiliar arms carry me. The other guy. I groan. No. I want Dad to help me. I reach out for him.

"It's okay Rielle, we're almost there," Dad says.

I peel my eyes open for a moment. I'm being carried toward a dilapidated single wide trailer in the middle of a wasteland of scrub brush. This isn't home.

My eyelids are too heavy to keep open. The other guy carries me down, down and then that smell returns. Moist earth. I want to stop them. No more tunnels. "Please," is all I can muster.

A frantic voice shouts from a distance. "What happened to her?"

Justin. "Let me have her."

"She's fine. I've got her."

A frigid hand presses against my forehead. "Oh. My. Get her into the house!"

I'm carried up, up and the earthy smell disappears. A woman's calm voice says, "Lay her down here." Something sharp pokes at my hand. It hurts! I push her hands away. Don't hurt me.

"Honey, it's going to be okay. This will help."

The throbbing begins to subside. I look up at the woman, blinking to focus my vision. I want to thank her, but my eyelids clamp shut again. Everything is dark, peaceful, painless.

Sometimes voices hover. People are near me—some familiar—but I don't have the strength to wake.

Justin's despair-soaked voice surrounds me the most. Did we both die? "Please Rielle. Please wake up."

Another voice answers. "She's stronger than you think. She'll be okay."

No. I'm not okay. I'm too weak. Can't they see that? And then, everything turns quiet and they don't bother me anymore.

Breath flows in and out of my lungs. I need more air. I expand my chest until it hurts. Other sensations join that one—light behind my eyelids, something on top of me—warm and soft. I struggle to wake up. It's as difficult as swimming for the surface in raging flood waters.

I force my eyes open. Brilliant light. I squint to take in the surroundings. I'm in a spacious room, about the size of the Banker's bedroom. White curtains draped over the windows can't dull the sunlight streaming through them. I lie under the canopy of a queen sized bed. Creamy coloured blankets, soft to the touch, cover me. Perhaps I died. Heaven is very comfortable.

I lift my arms to discover silk pajama sleeves in the same creamy colour as the rest of the bedroom. Something tugs at my left hand. An IV protrudes from my skin, held in place with clear medical tape. No, this can't be heaven. I'm pretty sure there won't be IVs in heaven.

A clicking latch startles me. The door opens a crack and steel grey eyes under a mop of chestnut hair peek in. "You're awake!" says a voice that sounds like Dad's, but is too enthusiastic. The door flings wide open.

The person who rescued me from my tomb stands in the doorway. But it's not Dad. The face belongs to Silas.

It can't be Silas—this is a man, not a boy.

"Silas?"

In three longs strides he's at my bedside. He throws his arms around me.

Though it sends a stabbing pain through my shoulder, I pull him close. I bury my face in his neck and breathe deeply—the smell of soap and outdoors and Silas—and I clutch him tighter. Tears fill my eyes. He strokes my back and I shake with sobs. I can't believe he's here, in my arms. For so long I thought I'd never see him again.

He draws away, though I don't want to let him go. "I was so worried." he says. "You had like fifty scorpion stings or something. And a raging infection. It was bleeeeeding and *oooozing*." He seems to enjoy the gruesomeness of it. Same old Silas. "But everything's okay now. You're safe."

"Where am I? How did I get here? How did you get here?"

He holds up his hands. "Whoa, slow down. We'll tell you everything you want to know. But I was told, on pain of death, to let you rest. Are you hungry?"

Am I? "Yeah, I think so."

He jumps to his feet. "Okay, I'll go get you something."

"No, Silas, don't go." I sound desperate.

"Don't worry. I'll be right back." He bounds out of the room.

By the time the door squeaks open again it wakes me from a light snooze. A new face greets me. "Good morning, Rielle. I'm Sarah, the nurse around here." Sarah lights up with a warm, motherly smile, the skin around her eyes wrinkling. The lines framing her mouth remain after her smile fades.

Her bobbed silver hair falls forward as she inspects my IV. "You were a very sick young lady." She lays my hand down and fills a syringe with clear liquid from a glass vial. She takes my temperature with an ear thermometer.

"Your fever's down, but I think we'd better leave this in for one more day. I want to be sure the infection is completely cleared."

She inserts the syringe into the IV tube. "I also want you to stay in bed and rest."

"Okay. I don't think I could get up if I wanted to."

Silas comes back carrying a tray loaded with food.

Sarah chuckles. "How much do you think she's going to eat?"

Silas sets the tray on my nightstand and sits on the edge of my bed.

"I'll be back in a couple hours to check on you." Sarah closes the door behind her.

Silas eases me upright and tucks pillows behind my back. I groan and my head whirls. I drop my head back against the headboard until it stops spinning. He arranges my breakfast in front of me.

I glance down at the loaded tray and grin. "Thanks Si. You must think I have an appetite like yours."

"What? It's not that much."

As I swallow my first few bites of toast and a gulp of orange juice, he watches me, his brow creased.

"You had some questions," Silas says.

"Yeah. More than a few. Where are we?"

"This is Uncle Rex's place. Not bad, huh?"

"Uncle Rex? He's the one helping Contracts escape?"

"Yep. I've been here for a few months. I think they're pretty sick of hearing me nag them about freeing you. That Banker idiot made it soooo difficult. I thought they'd never get you here."

"All this time, Justin knew about you?"

Silas gasps and leaps to his feet. "Justin! I was supposed to tell him as soon as you woke up. I'll be back." He flies from the room. By the time I finish a half a piece of toast and the glass of orange juice, I'm full. I set the tray aside and then a light rap sounds on the door.

Justin pokes his head in. "Is it okay if I come in?" I expect a broad smile and dancing blue eyes, but he looks unsure about entering.

I smile and wave him in. "Of course."

Shoulders slumped, he eases himself onto the bed, his lips turned down at the corners. "How are you doing?"

"I'm tired, achy. My arm is sore."

He touches the tape securing my IV. His eyes turn glassy. "Rielle, I can't tell you how sorry I am."

"For what?"

"For leaving you in that hole for so long."

That all seems distant, like a bad dream. Images rush back to me, though I try to suppress them. How long was I down there? Three days, more maybe? "I thought you forgot about me."

"No. Never! I wanted to come get you, but we couldn't. Bank Security was everywhere. It killed me to leave you there. And then you were so sick—you almost died—I—" His voice breaks. He stops and stares at the window.

I slide my fingers around his hand. "Stop. I forgive you."

"Don't." He shakes his head. "I don't deserve it."

"You did everything you could."

"I wanted to come get you. We finally had to send Silas. He's the only one I knew you'd trust besides me, but that risked his life too. This whole thing was a failure."

I cock my head to the side and peer into his eyes. "I'm out and I'm free because of you. Whatever I had to go through was worth it. I'm not upset at you. Not even a little. Thank you, Justin. Thank you for freeing me."

He wraps his hand around mine.

"Smile Justin, it's a good day."

One side of his mouth lifts into a familiar crooked grin. I squeeze his hand and the other corner lifts.

Silas returns. I grin at my brother, amazed to be with him again. "What happened to you Si? You have to be a foot taller than you were the last time I saw you." The image of Juvenile Division leading him out the front door of our home flashes through my mind. I blink it away. He's here now—with me—that's all that matters.

He smiles and pride beams from his eyes.

"In the tunnel, I thought you were Dad. You sound just like him."

Silas' grin falls just slightly and his eyes dart to Justin for a split second before returning to me.

"Yeah, this kid's eating us out of house and home," Justin says with a tense chuckle. "They probably let him escape from that school, so they wouldn't have to feed him anymore."

"What's wrong? Silas?"

His gaze lifts to the ceiling, then back down again. "Nothing."

He's lying.

"Everything's fine, Rielle," Justin says.

"You're keeping something from me." I glance from one to the other.

Justin gets up and stands next to Silas, both silent as I wait for an answer.

I open my mouth to repeat my question, but Sarah sweeps into my room. "Are you boys keeping her awake? She needs her sleep. Besides, I need to change her bandages."

Justin leans over me and kisses my forehead. "Have a good rest."

I glare at him as he tows Silas out the door.

I can't stand to look when Sarah removes the bandage. I stare at the glowing red digits on the alarm clock instead, to keep from losing my breakfast. Sarah tells me it's looking better, applies a clean bandage and encourages me to get some sleep. That's an easy request. I'm already exhausted.

It's the day Bank Security came for us. I sit on the floor holding my crying sister, except the Banker's there. He's laughing at us. I'm angry. My father's lying on the floor. I look closer. Not my father. Nathan—bleeding, beaten unconscious.

"No! Nathan! No, get away from him," I scream at the Banker.

My sister disappears and I chase after Nathan as Bank Security drags him away. I try to catch up, but no matter how fast I run, he only moves further away. "No!"

"Rielle, wake up! Rielle!"

I wake, disoriented in the darkness and gasping for breath.

Justin pulls me into his arms. "It's okay."

Sobs rock my body. I suck in too much air and I can't exhale.

"Rielle, calm down. Everything's okay. You just had a bad dream."

"No, no, it's real! What happened to him?"

"Who?"

"Nathan. Is he—is he dead?"

Justin looks me in the eye. "Rielle, we're going to discuss all this once you're feeling better."

"Quit putting me off. If he's dead, it's my fault. I should have taken him with me."

"You did everything you could. It just wasn't an option. You didn't have a choice." He brushes a tear off my cheek.

"I should have insisted. He said he would never leave me behind and—" I swallow hard and more tears overflow my eyelids. "He could've left, but he waited for me! And I left him behind."

Justin pushes my hair behind my ear. "It's two in the morning. You need to rest."

"But I need to know—did I leave him there to die?"

Justin's stare drops to his lap. He releases a heavy breath and then finds my eyes again. "No. He's alive."

His words are cool water on a burn. "He is?"

"Yes. Now will you calm down and get some sleep?"

I lie back on my pillow and Justin covers me with the blanket. There's something in Justin's eyes—something strange, but I can't decide what it is before sleep claims me again.

Each day I'm a little stronger. I try to be content with the tidbits of information Justin and Silas allow me. I'm a good patient and follow Sarah's rules. But when the week is up, I come to the end of my patience and demand to know what they're keeping from me and most of all, to get out of this bed.

"Whoa," Silas says. "The freak-out queen is back."

"Silas! Do not call me that!"

"Oh, sorry." His voice drips sarcasm. "I'm revealing all your deep, dark secrets."

"Don't worry, kid, that one's no secret," Justin says.

"Nice. Gang up on the poor, helpless invalid. Have a good laugh, but tomorrow I'm getting out of this bed."

Justin straightens his back. "Fine."

"Fine," I shoot back.

"But for today, you need to rest." Justin kisses my cheek before leaving.

Justin holds the door open for Silas. "Let's go. Did you know she didn't speak for almost a year?"

"No way!" Silas says dramatically. "Wouldn't that be nice."

"True story," Justin says as he closes the door behind them.

Though I'm irritated, I smile to myself. I don't even mind the ribbing. I missed arguing with my brother. It feels good, normal. It's strange, though, seeing the two of them together—my worlds colliding.

CHAPTER THIRTY-ONE

The Legendary Jessica

I WAKE THE NEXT MORNING TO FIND Silas dropping off my breakfast tray. "So you're sure about being up and at 'em today?"

"Yep, today's the day."

"There are some clothes in the dresser for you. I picked them out." Silas flashes a proud smile. "I'll come back to get you in about an hour."

Clothes! I gasp.

Silas freezes in the doorway. "What's wrong?"

"Si, where are my shoes?"

His shoulders drop as he releases his breath. "Whoa, chill. Is that all? You scared me! I told them to throw them away, but Justin said to let you do it when you're ready. All your old clothes, including your shoes, are in the closet."

I sigh with relief.

"Sheesh, you haven't turned weird have you?" He laughs.

I sit up in my bed. "I think maybe I have."

Silas leaves and I lift my breakfast tray onto my lap. Every day my appetite has grown, so I'm ravenous. But a foul item sits on the tray. Oatmeal. Eww. After eating it every day for the past year at the Banker's, I'd rather go hungry than stick that slop in my mouth.

To the left of the bed, an archway leads to the bathroom with a walk-in shower and soaker tub. I fill the tub and ease myself into the hot water. A hot bath. Is there anything more wonderful? A variety of shampoos and conditioners sit on the edge of the tub. I sniff each one of them before choosing the lavender scented one. I take my time washing my hair—with shampoo, real shampoo.

Being careful not to soak my bandages, I use a loufa to scrub every inch of my body. I step out of the tub, dry off and go to work on my hair, starting to twist it into a bun. I stop. I can do whatever I want with my hair, which is nothing at all. So, I comb it and let it fall long down my back.

So Silas chose the clothes in my dresser. A little frightening. That kid used to wear tube socks with shorts and sandals. I rifle through the contents of the drawers, find some jeans and a T-shirt, pull them on and look in the mirror. He actually did a good job. They fit and I look so—so—normal. But the person in the mirror is a stranger. She looks like a regular teenager, like someone about to head off to college or hang out with friends, not a slave.

For the first time since I arrived here, I venture into the hall. I slide my hand down the mahogany railing as I descend the wide staircase. When I reach the tile at the bottom, I stop, having no idea where I'm going. Voices murmur from a set of double doors on my right, so I go the opposite way. This house makes the Banker's look like a quaint little cottage. I pass a music room with a beautiful grand piano. I have to remember where that is. The unmistakable clink and clang of a kitchen carries down the hall. Maybe I can find something decent to eat.

A young woman, blond hair tied back in a ponytail, slathers mayonnaise on slices of bread. When she notices me standing in the doorway, her eyes light up. "You must be Rielle." She sets down her knife and wipes her hands on her apron. She throws her arms around me. Surprised, I stumble backward. She removes her arms before I have a chance to hug her back. "It's so good to meet you. We've been waiting for you!"

I smile, lift my eyebrows, hoping she'll tell me who she is.

"Oh, I'm Jessica."

Jessica? Nathan's Jessica? What are the chances? "Hi, it's nice to meet you."

"Are you hungry? I have some pancakes I can warm up."

"Very. That sounds really good." I sit at a small square table in the corner.

Jessica retrieves an aluminum foil covered casserole dish from the refrigerator. "Justin and Silas seem beside themselves to finally have you here. For a while, we wondered if we'd be able to get you out." She forks a few pancakes onto a dinner plate and places them in the microwave. "The Banker was being so difficult. He must've really liked you. He didn't seem to think twice about selling me. It's kind of a weird thing to be irritated by, I guess."

She places syrup and a cup of milk on the table in front of me before retrieving the pancakes from the microwave. It feels odd to be waited on.

I smear the pancakes with butter, pour syrup over top and breathe in the sweet aroma. I cut off a portion and stuff it in my mouth. The feather light morsel melts on my tongue.

Jessica drops into the chair across the table from me. "They taste amazing after all that oatmeal at the Banker's, don't they?"

I swallow my bite and look at her. "You're that Jessica?"

"Yeah, you were my replacement."

This is Nathan's Jessica! The one that had to be sent away because they fell in love with each other. If only I had a way to tell Nathan. "Nathan would be so happy to know you're okay."

Her eyebrows lift, surprised. I shouldn't have said anything. Maybe she doesn't like talking about him. Perhaps it's a sensitive subject.

"Ah, he knows." She waves her hand in front of her as though batting away a fly. "I mean he doesn't know I'm free, but he knows that Uncle Rex bought me and that he treats his Contracts well."

The way she dismisses him irritates me. Doesn't she miss him at all? "Has he known you were here all along?"

"Yeah."

"Do you miss him?" The question pops out before I have time to consider how nosy it is. Though, I don't want to take it back. After watching Nathan suffer, I deserve an answer.

"Yeah, I wish we could've gotten him out too, but Nathan's a survivor. I know he can make it. Hopefully we'll be able to get him out next time."

I tilt my head to the side as I watch her talk. She says she misses him, but doesn't seem anxious to rescue him, as if waiting is no big deal. It would be a big deal to me. Has she fallen out of love with him this quickly? A surge of anger rolls through me.

"You look confused," she says.

"I am confused. You just sound so—" I wrack my brain for a nice way to say it. "So detached, I guess. I mean the two of you were—together. I thought you would be more worried about him." I try to control my irritation and say all this in the most non-accusing way possible.

Her forehead crinkles. "Oh, that. I see why you're confused. That's just what the Banker thought. Nathan's parents and my parents had been best friends, so we grew up together. He was like a brother to me. When they sold us to the Banker they had no idea we knew each other. You can imagine our surprise and relief to find ourselves sold to the same person.

"We knew that if anyone found out we'd be separated. They don't want Contracts in cahoots. We tried to act like strangers, but watch each other's backs. That's hard to keep up for very long. Eventually, the Banker noticed we were a little too familiar with each other and assumed we were having some sort of affair. So, he sold me to his brother. I love Nathan like a brother, nothing else."

While I struggle to process her revelation, Jessica glances down at her watch. "Ooh, I didn't realize the time. I have to get lunch ready." She jumps up and goes back to work on her sandwiches while I finish my pancakes, though my appetite has taken a nose dive.

I'm confused, not by Jessica, but by my perception of the whole situation. I attributed so many of Nathan's motives to a broken heart over losing Jessica. I was totally wrong. An uneasy feeling tightens my stomach—that feeling that I've forgotten something important, but can't put my finger it.

I wander out of the kitchen, my heart fluttering like hummingbird wings. Maybe everything that's happened over the last couple of weeks is coming down on me. Nathan's face dominates my mind. I pour over my memories—our conversations, his expressions, the time he picked me up off the floor and carried me to the kitchen. A swell of heat blossoms in my chest and spread over my body until it reaches my toes.

After meandering down various halls, too busy thinking about Nathan to watch where I'm going, I realize I'm lost. I'll have to ask Justin to draw me a map of this place. I take a few turns and find myself at the music room again.

Part of me fears touching the piano. But I'm free. I can do what I want. So, I seize upon my freedom, pull out the piano bench and sit down, straight and tall, as free people do. I position my curved fingers over the keys. It's been over a year since I played my song. Will it live up to the beautiful melody in my head?

I lower my fingers onto the cool ivory keys. Notes trickle from my fingers, one flowing into the next, releasing a year's worth of anxiety. The melody sounds even more beautiful echoing through the large music room than it did in my head. I allow it to envelop me. I swim in its calm tones.

When the song ends, a feeling of well-being has penetrated my entire body.

"Beautiful." A voice speaks from behind me.

I whip around to see Justin standing in the archway, awe in his eyes. A blush warms my cheeks. "How long have you been standing there?"

"I heard the whole thing. Sorry I didn't say anything. Not that long ago you refused to play for me. I thought you might stop if you knew I was here."

He crosses the room and sits on the bench beside me. "I've been looking all over for you. Dad's waiting for us in his study. We want to explain everything to you. That is, if you're ready."

"I'm past ready."

Justin stands and offers me his hand. I wrap my fingers around his and he pulls me toward him. He touches his fingers to my cheek, places a kiss on my lips and then searches my eyes. He still seems unsure. "I was thinking about something that is long overdue. You know, when I first met you, I was quite taken with you. Spending time with you was so complicated. I didn't want you to think it was mandatory. It nearly killed me when I had to order you around, even when it was for your own good. Now that you're free and you know that it's not a 'have to' but a 'want to,' would you be interested in going on a date with me?"

"Hmm." I tap my finger on my chin, pretending to be deep in thought, as though mulling over world peace.

"You are free to say 'no.' You're a bright and talented girl, you could probably do better." He picks up a strand of my hair and rubs it between his fingers.

"Yes."

"Rielle." He says my name like it's a song. "Would you join me for a picnic in the atrium this afternoon?"

I soften to warm goo and then melt into a puddle on the floor. "That sounds nice."

"Then I'll pick you up at your room at 2:00."

"Sounds excellent."

He brushes my hair over my shoulder. "Well, let's get this meeting out of the way then."

Justin strokes his thumb over the back of my hand as he leads me to the double doors off the staircase. Uncle Rex's office. Uncle Rex sits behind his desk. Silas lounges on an ox blood leather sofa in front of a fireplace. I smile at the sight of him. Will I ever get tired of looking at his face?

Justin leads me to the sofa and we sit beside Silas.

"You look better, almost human," Silas says.

"Thanks. You did a pretty good job with the clothes."

He shrugs. "I've got excellent fashion sense."

Justin squeezes my hand. "Better than human. Beautiful."

Silas wrinkles his nose. "Dude, that's my sister."

A crooked smile plays on Justin's lips. "I like your sister. A lot."

Silas grimaces. It's still surreal to have my brother right next to me, where I can reach out and touch him. I keep looking back at him, wondering if he'll vanish and I'll be without him again.

Uncle Rex moves from his desk and sits down on the loveseat opposite us. Justin keeps staring at me, but looks away as soon as I turn my head in his direction.

"Welcome to my home, Rielle," Uncle Rex says with an approving nod.

"Thank you."

He continues, "We've kept you in the dark for a long time for you own safety, but I think it's high time you understand what has been going on. Justin, I think you should start."

CHAPTER THIRTY-TWO

Heroes

JUSTIN NODS. "WHERE TO BEGIN? I CAME to live with Uncle Arthur under the guise of attending school. It was really to, well, I hate to use the word spy, but that's what it was. The chips were being used for more than just commerce, so we wanted to figure out their capabilities. My uncle was the head engineer for the chip, so we figured he had information we needed.

"We've also been smuggling Contracts out of the country. We bought Jessica to free her. It arouses less suspicion when these transactions happen between family members. Of course, my uncle had no idea that was our intent. We thought we'd purchase another Contract to free. I had already chosen you when we had an unexpected visitor. We found your brother wandering in the desert, nearly dead."

I slide my arm around my brother and squeeze him. He must have been through hell. I could've lost him.

"From the moment that kid could form coherent thoughts he began nagging about finding you and your sister."

Alyssa. My sweet baby sister. Justin opens his mouth to continue, but I cut him off. "Did you find her—do you know where Alyssa is?"

"We'll get to that." Uncle Rex says. "You don't need to worry. She's safe and doing well."

Relief settles over me. Justin squeezes my hand and continues. "When Silas told us your name, you can imagine our surprise. We thought, what're the chances it's the same girl? When Dad visited at Thanksgiving, he snapped a picture with his holo when you weren't looking. Silas confirmed it was you. It's like it was meant to be.

"Dad tried to purchase your contract soon after, but my uncle adamantly refused. Dad offered him twice what he paid and still he wouldn't part with you. We couldn't figure it out. He's all about money. We figured you must've known or seen something that made him want to hold onto you."

Indeed, I do know more than a few of his precious secrets: the incident with his wife, where he sent his children and that little matter of rigging the presidential election.

He pauses and takes in my expression before starting again. "We also discovered that Uncle Arthur was being watched by Bank Security. There seemed to be some sort of suspicion surrounding him. Since he refused to sell, by Christmas we had to come up with another plan. Do you remember?"

I thought for a moment. "Yeah, that's when you started taking me on those horseback rides."

"Exactly. Dad helped the original owners of that old house to escape. We knew about the tunnel. I planned to get you there, but you couldn't know what I was up to in case something went wrong. I needed you to trust me in order to accomplish what I was planning. That was the hardest part of the whole plan." He laughs and strokes my hand. "I needed you to know the way, and I needed the horse to know the way, and the horse to know you. We'd been planning on getting you out in a couple of weeks, but when we received information about the raid, we had only hours to act.

"I cannot tell you how sorry I am for leaving you in that hole for so long. We wanted to come sooner, but Bank Security…we finally couldn't leave you any longer. Of course, your outlaw brother volunteered for the mission. It was risky, but we were out of time. We thought it was too dangerous, but in the end we relented."

Uncle Rex gazes at me, his brow wrinkled. "Do you have any questions?"

I think for a moment, trying to organize my questions by level of importance. Questions gush like an open fire hydrant. "What about my parents? Are they okay? And what happened at the Banker's house? What happened to the other Contracts? Why would Bank Security come after the Banker? He was one of theirs."

Uncle Rex uncrosses his legs and leans forward. "From what my sources tell me, upper leadership in the regional Texas bank was uneasy with his wife's past. Though Arthur assured them she was not sympathetic to her parents' cause, they saw her as a liability. When she had her breakdown, it confirmed their fears. They couldn't have their head programmer, who knew all the ins and outs of the chip's capabilities, become sympathetic to Resistors. The official story is that there was a natural gas leak causing an explosion; Arthur and Nina were killed in the fire. The house was decimated."

I clutch Justin's hand in a white-knuckled grip. "The others—Lydia, Nathan, Eli?"

Justin lays his other hand over mine. "Jasmine was killed in the explosion."

I know it's wrong, but part of me is happy for Jasmine—happy that she no longer has to live with what the Banker did to her. Perhaps she's finally found rest. Jasmine lost more than any of us.

Justin raises his eyebrows. "You'll be interested to know that you were also killed in the explosion. Morris, Jonah, Lydia and Eli have already been sold. They appeared on E-auction the next day.

"We're not sure about Roberta—"

I cut him off. "Roberta's a spy."

Justin's eyes widen. "What? How do you know that?"

"I found her holo in the shed."

Justin throws an uneasy glance at Uncle Rex who leans against the back of the loveseat and sighs. "Justin, what did she know?"

Justin looks down, deep lines cut between his brows. "I don't think she ever saw anything."

"She saw you two together, though," Uncle Rex says.

"Yeah, but if she was there to spy on Uncle Arthur—"

"And me. She was spying on me too. But it's okay, right? I mean, they think I'm dead."

Uncle Rex folds his hands in his lap. "Rielle, that's the official story, not necessarily what they believe. They couldn't let anyone know if they thought a Contract escaped. Especially not you. There's been no evidence to indicate they are looking for you, but it's too early to tell."

Justin strokes his hand over my back. "Don't worry, it'll be fine. We'll just get you on the next transport out of here. No big deal." He's trying to comfort me, but concern hangs heavy in his eyes.

"Transport?" I ask.

"It's the way we get escaped Contracts out of the country. One leaves in a few months," Uncle Rex says.

Justin flashes a strained smile. "Silas and Jessica will be going. I'll go with you too. You can spend the rest of your days lying on the beach."

He wants me to lie on the beach while my friends are still slaves? And I can't help but notice that when they explained where the other Contracts ended up, they missed someone. "What about Nathan? What happened to him?"

"I told you he survived."

I pull my hand out of his grip. "Yeah, but where is he?"

Uncle Rex opens his mouth to speak, but Justin glares at him.

Uncle Rex shifts in his seat. "Nathan survived the bombing, but—"

"Dad." The muscles of Justin's jaw flex.

"Son." Uncle Rex shakes his head and begins again. "I'm concerned because he never went up for sale on any of the auction sites. He was placed rather than sold. For some reason they wanted to control where he ended up."

"Why would they do that?" I ask. Justin tries taking my hand again, but I fold my arms.

"Who knows why they do the things they do," Justin says.

"Son, she has a right to know."

Justin glowers. "It won't help anything."

I tense. He's keeping something from me. Again. I peer into Uncle Rex's blue eyes. "Why do you think they placed him?"

"I think he knew something—something they want kept quiet. He's at a logging camp up in Montana. The work is dangerous."

His words punch me in the gut, knocking the wind out of me. It's my fault he's there. I have too many "if's" swirling in my head to think clearly. If only he would have come with me—if he would've escaped without me—then he'd be safe now.

"I know this is a lot to take in, but there is more you need to know and we don't want to keep it from you," Uncle Rex says. "Silas, do you want to tell her?"

Colour drains from Silas' cheeks and his mouth turns down. My heart jumps. Oh no, no, no!

"Could you tell her?" Silas asks, his voice barely above a whisper. I wrap my arm around him and hug him to me. What hurts him this deeply will also cause me pain.

Uncle Rex presses his lips together in a sympathetic smile. "Your parents died a few months ago. The prison conditions were harsh. More of a concentration camp."

Every eye in the room fixes on me. Tears blur my eyes. Deep down, I knew, but hearing it confirmed cuts into me like a jagged knife. I spent so much time angry with them, hating them, but I still love them.

"They died valiantly, my dear, you can be proud of them. They were an example to all of us." Awe saturates Uncle Rex's voice.

Does he feel this way about all Resistors? I remember the conversation I had with Justin on one of our rides. He revealed the same profound respect. There's a piece I'm still missing, something they know that I do not.

Justin picks up my hand again. This time I let him. "I know you think they didn't fight for you, but they did. More than you know."

I look over at Silas, tears spill over his cheeks. He throws his hands over his face.

I squeeze my brother again. "Si, what do they mean?"

Silas reaches into his pocket and pulls out a worn, folded envelope. He hands me the small package, the paper feels soft and fragile. I carefully open the envelope and read the address—"SILAS AND AUBRIELLE JAMES C/O REX HAYES.

I fold the flap back and removed the contents of the envelope. The paper inside is as worn as the envelope and firmly creased as though it's been unfolded, then folded many times. My hands begin to tremble as I read.

Dear Silas and Aubrielle,

I wrote this letter in the hope that it will someday make its way to you. I cannot imagine how difficult your lives have become, but I hope that you will find comfort in what I am about to tell you. I want you to know the truth about your parents. It pains me that you might think ill of them, wishing they would have chosen another path, or at least, not been so staunch in their beliefs.

Your father and I were working together to hide families from Bank Security. We'd already managed to get six families out when we learned that they were coming after yours. I pressed your father to get you all out while he still could, but there were other families in danger too. He felt he couldn't live with himself if he just abandoned the others who had come to him for help.

Somehow Bank Security got wind of his involvement in these escapes and came earlier than expected to collect your family. I sometimes wish he hadn't been so altruistic. I'd still have my brother and you'd still have your parents.

Please know that I continue the work we started together. Maybe someday, when this evil has passed, we can meet each other again.

All my love,
Aunt Angelique

The room is still, as though the world stopped spinning. I try to hold the tears back but it's no use. I lean into Silas and we hold each other and cry. All this time, all this wasted time I spent thinking they didn't care. Thinking that my father was a coward, that he didn't fight for us. He fought for us. Not just us, but others like us.

A strange mix of joy and grief, guilt and satisfaction overwhelms me. My heart aches to apologize for every bad thought I've ever had about them. And yet, I feel release. I love them. I can be proud of them. I can be brave like they were.

Silas breaks the silence. "There is some good news, Rielle." He forms the saddest smile I've ever seen. "Alyssa is okay. She's been adopted by a really nice family."

"Her being adopted is good news?"

Uncle Rex says, "There are others like me who disagree with what the banks are doing. The family Alyssa is with is one of these, secretly of course. They will take good care of her and raise her as their own. She is as safe as possible right now."

Silas looks at me encouragingly. "The family lives in Minneapolis. She was in preschool this year."

It comforts me to know she's safe, but I hate that other people are raising her. Will she even remember us?

My tears are exhausted. Over the past year and a half I've cried a lifetime's worth. I stare at my hands, but I don't see them. I see faces—the faces of those I've lost.

"I think that's all for today. Let's give her some time to think this through," Justin says.

"There is one more thing we need to discuss," Uncle Rex says.

Justin clutches my hand tighter. "Later."

"Justin, you know how important this is."

CHAPTER THIRTY-THREE

Locating the Back Door

I GLANCE UP AT UNCLE REX.

Justin sighs. "Only if she wants to."

Uncle Rex looks at me apologetically. "Rielle, there's another matter. Are you up to it?"

"Yeah, I'm okay."

"Are you sure?" Justin asks.

I nod.

Uncle Rex glances at Silas. "I'm sorry Silas, but I'm going to have to ask you to step out of the room."

I let go of Silas. He stands and walks out through the double doors.

Uncle Rex begins, "Rielle, we are hoping you can help us."

"With what?"

"Do you know where the children are?"

My guard goes up. That's the last question I expected. Why does he need to know that? I don't want to tell him. I need to protect them. "I thought the Banker would've told you where he sent them."

"No, my brother was unaware of my political leanings. He assumed I would be like anyone else and report any rebellion to Bank Security."

Rebellion? Sending the children away was an act of rebellion?

Justin angles his body toward me. "Rielle, he let you see more than anyone else in the house because he thought you couldn't tell anyone."

Justin doesn't know how right he is.

Uncle Rex picks up his cup of coffee and takes a sip. "It's imperative that we find them."

"Why?"

"They're my niece and nephew. Of course, I'm concerned."

He breaks eye contact and blinks several times. He's lying. A shock of anger wells inside me. Justin and his father once again have information they're purposely keeping from me. This time I'm not going to be kept in the dark.

"I know where they are."

Uncle Rex's face brightens and he claps his hands together. "That's excellent! Where?"

I don't return his smile, just give him a dead-pan stare. "I'm not telling you."

"Rielle?" Justin says in a surprised tone.

"I'm not a slave anymore and I won't be treated like one. And I'm not stupid either. You may be concerned for your niece and nephew, but there's something else you're not telling me. You can either tell me what's going on or you can find them yourself." I yank my hand from Justin's grasp and stand.

Justin throws his arms up. "Just tell her. Believe me, if she decides she's not going to talk—" He tries pulling me back to the sofa, but I stand my ground. "Maybe it's not with them. Maybe it's somewhere else. She might be able to help us more if she knows what we're after."

Uncle Rex glances from Justin to me, his eyes narrowing. "Fine. This is of the highest intelligence, not to be shared with anyone."

I settle back onto the sofa. "I'm a vault."

Uncle Rex shifts in his seat, then begins, "You may have thought that my brother was the OneEarth Bank's biggest supporter and that he followed them unquestioningly, but that was not the case. Arthur was only loyal to himself. He knew an alliance with the banks was the quickest way to get what he wanted—money and lots of it.

"Arthur was an engineering genius and he sold his genius to the highest bidder. He developed the entire system that runs the OneEarth Bank. The commerce chips, so contested and the cause of all this strife, were designed by my brother."

My mouth falls open. "Really?"

"Yes. Because Arthur was only loyal to himself, he made certain that whatever he created would always belong to him. He once confided in me that everything he ever designed included a way for him to crash the technology and reclaim it. He didn't trust the banks. I suspect he built a back door into the OneEarth system and the commerce chips, so that if the banks ever turned against him he had something to hold over their heads."

I scoot to the edge of my seat, leaning toward Uncle Rex. "A back door?"

Justin breaks in, "It's a way of getting into the system that no one else knows about. It's essentially like having a key to the back door of a house. Whenever you want you can come in, take what you want, even cause damage. Then you can leave and no one knows how you got in or can prove you were there."

My eyes widen. "It could shut down the whole thing?"

"Yes," Justin says.

Uncle Rex straightens his back and lifts his chin. "We've received intelligence that this back door does exist and it's the real reason Bank Security came after him. When his children disappeared, Arthur dropped off the grid for several hours. No building or traffic monitors registered his chip. They tried to figure out where he went and what he did with the children, but there was no record, no electronic trace anywhere. Then, as suddenly as he disappeared, he reappeared right back at home. They were watching him closely already, and this confirmed he was somehow manipulating the system."

"You're wondering what this has to do with the children's whereabouts. Arthur knew his time was short, so I think he would have hid information about this 'back door' somewhere so that the right people could find it. Our theory is that he sent it with the children."

"Did you notice him put anything unusual in the suitcase, a holo, a tera-card—anything?" Justin asks.

I think back to that day, trying to remember everything that happened. "I packed everything. The children's clothing, some toys. I only saw him put one item in each suitcase—envelopes full of Prospers. I didn't see him put anything else in."

Justin rubs his chin. "Did he ever let on about anything he was hiding? Did he try to keep everyone away from a certain area of the house?"

"No, we cleaned everywhere—well, except his office." I pause as I think. "And then there was his bedroom. He didn't want anyone disturbing his wife. Roberta was the only one allowed in. He trusted her. I did see her sneaking out of his office one time."

Justin turns to his father, who looks deep in thought. "Do you think he gave it to Roberta?"

"No, if Roberta was working for Bank Security, then they'd have it already and they wouldn't have gone to the lengths they did with destroying the house. No, my informants tell me that they were hoping the explosions destroyed it. They assumed it was in the house."

"Dad, it could be incredibly small. It could be anywhere."

"How small?" I ask. "What could it have looked like besides what you've already mentioned?"

"Well, it could be just a speck. You could've walked by it ten times a day and still not know it was there."

When he said the word "speck," I knew the answer—Nina's chip. "Could the information be on a chip?"

Uncle Rex tilts his head. "Well, yes, I suppose it could be. It seems unlikely though because it's difficult to get a hold of one without it being attached to a user. They're tightly regulated. It would've been much easier for him to use another medium."

"A chip would've been easy to hide," Justin says.

The Banker's words when I was packing the children's suitcases flood back to me. He said, "Guard *it* with your life." It. I didn't understand what he meant. Could he have been referring to Nina's chip? Did he know I had it? Did Nina tell him she gave it to me?

I stand to leave. "Can you give me some time to think? I'm trying to remember if I saw anything unusual. Everything's cloudy right now. I need some sleep."

"You still haven't told us where the children are," Uncle Rex says.

"I'll think about it. I need to know they'll be safe." I throw him a phony smile and walk out the door.

Justin catches up to me and walks me toward my room. For the first time, I wish he'd go away. I have a lot to think about and I want to be alone.

When we get to my bedroom door, he takes my hand. "Why aren't you telling us?"

I press my lips together and look away. I don't want to lie to him, but I don't want to tell him the truth either.

Justin sighs and hangs his head. "You still don't trust me, do you?"

That's one of the many questions I need to think through. "I just don't know what I should do."

He strokes his thumb over my hand. "Maybe if you told me what's going on in that mysterious mind of yours, I could help."

"I need some time to think, that's all."

"Rielle, I hoped that I would've earned your trust by now."

"I do…trust…you." I struggle to get the words out.

"Not completely."

"It's just that…I feel pressured. I want to figure out what I need to do without being pressured. I'm tired of being told what to do all the time!"

Justin's cheeks flush. "I'm not telling you what to do."

I yank my hand from his. "You are! You sat me down in your father's office and expected me to spill my guts. There were two powerful people sitting there waiting for answers and little, ex-slave me under the gun to give them. It was hardly fair."

"Two?" Justin asks indignantly.

I realize my mistake. I lumped him with his father. "I mean, I trust you more than him."

"Do you? I freed you, Rielle. Doesn't that show you how much I care for you? Doesn't that show you that you can trust me?"

"Yes, and I'm so thankful—grateful. I don't know why this is so hard for me. Maybe all those months of not trusting you, not knowing what you were up to is coloring everything now. I just need some time to think." I swallow to wet my dry throat.

He clenches his fists and clamps his teeth together. "Would you tell your secrets to Nathan?"

"What?" I shake my head. "What are you talking about?"

He stares down at his shoes. "Never mind."

Tears threaten to fall again. I'm hurting him and that's the last thing I want to do.

He peers into my eyes and picks up my hand again. "You've been through a lot. You deserve to have it your way for a while. I will earn your trust, Rielle. Someday." He pauses. "I love you." He kisses me lightly on the lips and walks away.

CHAPTER THIRTY-FOUR

Captain Oblivious—By the Way, That's Me

I STAND THERE FOR A MOMENT, WATCHING Justin descend the stairs, then shuffle into my room and close the door behind me. I go to the walk-in closet. Kneeling on the floor, I pull out my old canvas shoes and peel back the insole. The chip lies on the heel. I dump it onto my palm. It's heavy in my hand again, like the weight of the world's troubles rests on my palm. Could it be the key to undoing all of this?

So many questions need answering. What should I do with the chip? I'm almost positive it contains the back door. If I give it to Uncle Rex, what will he do with it? Will he use it to free the Contracts and their parents, or will he keep it to himself to control the banks?

I close my fingers around the chip. I understand now. I understand why the Banker asked me to protect his children. He must've known about my family's work against the banks. Maybe he knew I had his wife's chip too.

Then there's my relationship with Justin. The thought of telling him about the chip, the children, or even the election ties my stomach in a knot. Shouldn't I trust him by now? Why don't I? He said he loves me. Am I in love with him? I think I am. I do love him. He's a great guy. But something deep inside holds me back. Is it still the slave-master barrier I've struggled with all along, or something else?

Am I damaged goods when it comes to trust? If I can't trust my brother or Justin, maybe I can't trust anyone. But that's not entirely true. There is one person I want to tell. One person I trust with this information.

Nathan.

He'd know what to do. I love Justin, but I trust Nathan with my life. Justin's proven himself trustworthy, so why can't I trust him? I bite my lip. What's wrong with me?

I tuck the chip back into my shoe and then search for a place to hide it. The attic access in the ceiling of my closet is perfect. After sneaking a sheet of aluminum foil from the kitchen, I wrap it around the shoe. I drag a chair from the bedroom into the closet and stack some plastic containers on top of it so I can pop the hatch open and tuck my shoes inside. As I replace the hatch, a knock echoes from my bedroom door.

I glance at the clock. 2:00. Justin. I gasp. I almost forgot. I'm surprised he still wants to do anything with me. "I'll be right there," I call. I strip down and pull a sundress over my head, then dash to the bathroom and run a brush through my hair.

I open the door to find Justin, a blanket draped over his arm and a picnic basket in his hand. "Are you still interested in our date?" He holds his breath as he waits for my answer.

"Of course. Justin, I'm sorry. I'm going to get this all figured out. Everything is crazy right now."

He smiles. "You have nothing to apologize for. You're entitled to a little crazy. So, how do you feel about a picnic?"

"Sounds like an excellent idea." Though I've spent a lot of time with Justin, I suddenly feel jittery. This is a real date. My first date. Don't be silly. Same Justin. Nothing's changed.

My stomach flutters and I bite my lip when he offers me his arm. I thread my arm through his and we make our way to the center of the house where a large wall of windows overlook a gymnasium sized atrium.

We follow a stone path that meanders through shrubs and flower beds. Justin spreads our blanket over a small patch of grass shaded by a towering oak tree. Water trickles past us in a narrow, man-made stream. Colourful koi glide through the water and bring their gaping mouths to the surface in search of food. A bee buzzes from flower to flower, attracted by the sweet scent that hangs in the air.

We eat our lunch and talk about regular things, like our favourite movies and books. Normal conversation like free people have. Inevitably, reality seeps into our conversation. We talk about our time at the Banker's home, what we thought of each other the first time we met and our differing understanding of the other's motives.

"Nathan had been so worried that you were going to hurt me," I say.

"He certainly complicated things."

"I thought for sure that you were going to tell the Banker about him challenging you."

"No, I wouldn't have done that, but I was apprehensive about how far he would go to stop me from being with you. When he caught me trying to sneak you out, I thought he was going to ruin the whole plan." He traces circles on the back of my hand. "And that reminds me. Why were you refusing to go with me that night? It seemed like you were finally trusting me and then suddenly you were hostile."

"Nathan warned me to stay away from you. He didn't think you wanted to spend time with me for my personality." I flash an impish grin. "He said you only wanted me for your own personal entertainment. I didn't want to end up like Jasmine."

A deep red crawls up Justin's neck and over his ears.

Attempting to soothe his anger, I say, "He was just looking out for me. I was pretty naive about these things."

"He's a fine one to talk about ulterior motives."

"What's that supposed to mean?"

"Do you really think he was going to such great lengths to protect you just because he liked your personality?"

"I think he felt sorry for me because I couldn't talk, and he said he wanted to protect me because he thought I was a nice girl." Hearing the words aloud makes them seem ridiculous.

Justin chuckles, then laughs and then laughs hysterically, holding his stomach. I fold my arms and glare at him. "What are you laughing about?"

He gasps for air between fits of laughter. "Lucky for me you are naive. I may have had…competition if you'd had…a hot clue."

"Stop laughing," I say, annoyed. "What do you mean 'a hot clue'?"

He struggles to rein in his laughter, a few more bursts escaping his lips. "You really don't get it?"

Why are people always saying this to me? "Okay, I don't get it. Either explain it or I'm leaving. I'm free to do that, you know." I stand to leave. A stellar first date this is turning out to be.

"I'm sorry. Don't leave." He tugs on my hand to try to get me to sit again. "Nathan had ulterior motives too. He wasn't so much protecting your interests as he was protecting his own."

I furrow my brow. I'm still confused, but opt to reclaim my seat beside him.

He lifts my hand and places a soft kiss on my fingers. "I think I'm going to start calling you Captain Oblivious. Nathan had a major crush on you, couldn't you see that?"

"No—I mean—I don't know. I guess looking back…maybe. But I thought he had a thing for Jessica." I'll tolerate the Captain Oblivious comment because he's probably right.

"Look, Rielle, I didn't want our first date to end up like this. I'm sorry for laughing at you. You really have an innocent way of looking at the world. You assume the best of the people around you. That's one of the things I love about you."

"I really don't assume the best, but I don't assume that every male I encounter is in love with me either. I didn't believe Nathan when we had almost the identical conversation about you."

"You didn't believe him?"

"No, remember, I'm Captain Oblivious. For some reason it's easier to believe you had some evil purpose than to believe you really liked me in that way."

"Let me lay this out for you. I like—no—I love the person you are. I don't just want you for your body, although I do really like that. I rescued you because I'm in love with you and I want you to be free to love me too. Is that clear enough?" He strokes his fingers along my neck. "That and your brother's constant nagging."

Heat radiates everywhere he touches me. I look down and let my hair fall forward. I want to hide how deeply his words affect me, yet I don't want to escape them.

Justin is quiet, deep in thought for a few seconds. He pulls my hand to his chest. "Rielle, we're the same now. You are free. There is no more slave and master, hero and damsel in distress. We are finally on equal footing. You have a choice."

I pull a strand of my hair to my nose and breathe deeply. "Yes," I say, taking in the lovely lavender smell. I know he doesn't get what I'm doing. His wrinkled forehead confirms that, so I explain, "The first time you asked me to play piano, I didn't want to sit by you because you smelled so good and I smelled like ammonia and sweat." I chuckle, though it's a painful memory.

He laughs too as he moves in to smell my hair. He buries his face in it. "Yes, you smell wonderful."

His kiss on my neck sends a chill rippling down my spine. I wrap my arms around him and he draws me against him, planting his lips on mine. He tugs me to the ground. I fall against him. My heart races as his mouth moves from my lips to my cheek, to my neck and then circles my mouth. I wind my fingers in his hair and tug his lips back to where they belong—on mine.

Too soon, he pulls away from me and rolls onto his back. I rest my head on his chest, close my eyes and listen to his heartbeat. He takes my hand and threads his fingers between mine.

I can't imagine a more perfect moment. So many things in my life remain unresolved, but I'll take this moment and savour the excitement that comes with it. I'll drink it in as though he and I are the only people that exist, like we're just a boy and a girl with no other worries.

But tomorrow will be different. There'll be no transports or lying on the beach for me as long as my friends are still slaves. As he holds me, I realize that I was wrong about this beautiful and kind boy, my rescuer—he won't break my heart.

I'll break his.

ACKNOWLEDGEMENTS

First, a big thank you to my husband, Eric. Without his support and patience I couldn't have done this. He spoke the words every writer longs to hear, "Why don't you just stay home and write." Thank you to my children who were so understanding and encouraging through this whole process, and especially to my daughter whose mad piano skills inspired me. She composed the theme song for this book.

A special thank you to my mom, Lois, my first reader. She kept me working at this story long after I was tempted to give up. To my early readers, Ellie and Marlene, thanks for telling me it was good even when it wasn't. I don't know where I'd be without those who encouraged my early efforts.

Many thanks to the Vast Imaginations crew—Christina, Larry, Barbara, MaryLou, and our amazing leader, Suzanne. You accepted me into your group and patiently taught me. Being a part of this group revolutionized my writing. I learned so much from all of you. And I can't forget about the Word Junkies—thank you Mel, Christina, and Gabe for encouraging me that this novel had value and for all your critiques which dramatically improved it.

Thank you to my publisher, Rebelight Publishing Inc., who took a risk on me. Even as I entered into the editing process I figured they were going to change their minds. Thank you to my editor, Deborah Froese for kicking my butt and to the rest of the Rebelight team, Suzanne Leclerc and Melanie Matheson. Working with this team has been fantastic.

And finally, thank you to the Alpha and the Omega, the Beginning and the End, who guided and strengthened me on this journey in too many ways to list.

The author would love to hear from you:
www.melindafriesen.com
Facebook: facebook.com/melindafriesen1
Twitter: @melindafriesen #freeRielleJames
Goodreads: goodreads.com/melindafriesen
LinkedIn: linkedin.com/in/melindafriesen

CPSIA information can be obtained at www.ICGtesting.com
Printed in the USA
LVOW04s1245281114

415908LV00008B/29/P